Temple of Hope

Temple of Hope

A Sophie Kramer Thriller

By

Narendra Simone

...killing softly with his words.

ISBN: 1497343739
ISBN 13: 9781497343733

This is a work of fiction. Names, characters, places, and incidents either are the product of the author's imagination or are used fictitiously, and any resemblance to any actual persons living or dead, events, or locales is entirely coincidental.

Prologue

A heavy-set man wearing dark glasses sat patiently in the driver seat of his parked car. He removed his sunglasses, folded them up and put them in the glove compartment. A vacant look in his eyes and a frown on his face indicated his troubled past and also perhaps a blatant antipathy towards the present. He appeared as a harsh and angry man deeply unhappy and dissatisfied with something, perhaps his own life.

He occasionally glanced up and down an almost empty street. He unfolded a copy of Times of India he had bought in the morning and glanced at the front page. The headlines read, 'The US ambassador to India now missing for 48 hours, no possibilities are ruled out.' He smiled thinly and in an almost inaudible tone said to himself, "Huh, Americans. I'll show them." He read the news about the missing ambassador and then re-folded the newspaper. He tossed it over his shoulder and onto the backseat, where it fell noiselessly.

The wind blew through the streets. It seemed empty, as if its spirit had abandoned the chase. He looked at his watch and then peered out his window. He studied a little girl sitting pensively at the doorsteps of a small house located directly across the street from where his car was parked. Seeing no traffic and no people in the street, he nodded, as if convincing himself of something. Something he came to do. Now was the time. He silently opened the car door and stepped out.

Amy held her teddy bear tightly with her left arm, her chin resting on her knees, while her right hand stroked Frankie, a black, small and fragile-looking cat. Amy was sitting on the front steps of her piano teacher's house waiting for her dad to pick her up. Under her breath she whispered, "Do your parents fight too, Frankie? Is that why you're so sad?" Frankie simply rubbed his head against her legs and purred.

Amy lifted her head and looked down the street. It was a long and empty avenue with a few cars parked on both sides. A breeze continued to blow and autumnal leaves dropped from branches of the old trees as if covering a secret, descending to their resting places on the road or sidewalk. A tiny curled-up red-colored leaf drifted like a snowflake and became enmeshed in the fine strands of Amy's blonde hair. Amy pulled out the leaf and looked at it intently and then held it to her cheek. She giggled. She kissed the leaf softly and then placed it inside her pink coat pocket.

"Are you okay there, dear?" a trembling and muffled voice came from inside the house. Amy turned her head and, looking at the closed door, responded, "I'm fine, Mrs. Chawla. Daddy will be here soon. Thank you." Ashok never made Amy wait for more than ten minutes and she always liked having the time to play with Frankie. Amy looked at her Mickey Mouse watch and saw she had been sitting outside on the steps for only five minutes.

A car came down the street and passed Amy, a riot of leaves flying and settling back again on the sidewalk. Amy held on to both the teddy bear and Frankie as if protecting them against the speeding car. It was quiet again.

It was the sixth of October and the time was about five past six, the sun having just set. A hazy purple cloud across the western sky added a melancholy ambiance to the empty street as if the twilight hid a mystery in its folds.

There were no speeding cars and no people wandering about on the street. She noticed the car parked directly across the street from where she was sitting because a man was stepping out of it. He fidgeted and looked uncomfortable in the ill-fitting suit he was wearing. He crossed the street and came towards Amy to stand a couple of paces away from her. She looked up and smiled. He bent down to look at her closely and, with a thin smile on his face, said in an amiable voice, "Hello, Amy. You're Amy, aren't you?"

The child only stared at him with the sad, bewildered, pained eyes of a child who lives in a troubled family.

"Is this your little teddy bear?" he asked. "He is very nice. What is his name?"

"Teddy," she whispered, tightening her grip on the doll.

"I thought so," he continued to smile, "and what is the name of your cat?"

"Frankie," she answered in an inquisitive tone laced with anxiety, and added, "it's not mine."

"That is a very nice name. How are you, Frankie?" He sat down on the steps next to the cat and patted little Frankie, seeming unhurried and relaxed.

For the few moments that followed they both sat on the steps playing with the cat. Finally he spoke, assuming a sincere tone, "Amy, I work with your daddy. He has sent me to pick you up. He wanted to come but your mommy was in a car accident and your daddy is with her at the hospital. I'm so sorry. Would you like me to take you to your mommy? Your daddy asked me to take you there. Would you like to see your mommy?"

Amy's smile dissolved and with a look half perplexed and half filled with sadness, she stared at the stranger. She did not know what to say.

"It is okay, Amy," said the man without showing alacrity, "your daddy would have come but your mommy needs him. You understand that, don't you? Your mommy needs him. It is only twenty minutes away, the hospital. I think we should rush if you want to see your mommy."

"I," she said hesitantly, "I, I'll let Mrs. Chawla know then I'll come. Okay?"

"Oh, no, don't do that. No, no, you mustn't do that. She is an old lady, isn't she? Old people get upset easily. Does she get upset with you?"

"Sometimes. When I don't play the piano the way she taught me," said Amy, nodding her head.

"See, that is what I am saying. She is an old lady. Look, we don't have much time. I think you should come now; otherwise, I am leaving because I have to go to my home to my girl. I've a little girl just like you. Her name is Geeta. Would you like to meet her one day? You two could be good friends."

She smiled thinly and nodded. She gave one more stroke to Frankie's head and held out her tiny hand for the stranger to take. Together, hand in hand, they walked to his car. The wind had ceased and in the air was a curious stillness, as if the secret held in the falling leaves was out.

Book I

48 Hours after Amy's Kidnapping
New York, USA

On the edge of
a new frontier

One

It was a cool autumn day in New York. Under an unblemished blue sky and the mid-afternoon sun, Central Park was ablaze with fall colors. Maples, oaks and elms carpeted the lawns with myriads pattern of glorious gold and scarlet-red fallen leaves.

The Star Lounge of the Ritz Carlton Hotel located in Central Park South was packed, the room filled with lively chatter. The young businessmen in their expensive-looking suits trying to make an impression, and beautiful businesswomen in their body-hugging business attire, making use of all their seductress powers, were locked in battling out their management skills to strike the business deal of a lifetime for their respective corporations. The place was buzzing with the excitement synonymous with corporate America.

Among these young and vibrant entrepreneurs, sitting at the window overlooking the park, was a rather quiet woman. Casually sipping her Martini cocktail and gazing at the life on the street below her, she may have not paid much attention to the men in the lounge, but she could not help but notice the smiling affirmations of the handsome businessmen. Her shoulder-length, red hair playfully caressing her slender shoulders accentuated her sensual look, and her large, deep-blue eyes had a contemplative look in them. But perhaps her best feature was her shapely body, looking as if carved by Michaelangelo himself. She uncrossed and crossed her long and shapely legs again and a couple of the businessmen swallowed hard and smiled at her.

The jazz in the background played the melodious tunes of Kenny G. A waiter carrying a Martini cocktail approached her and smiled amiably, saying, "The gentlemen on the center table would like to buy you a drink."

She shook her head and responded, "You thank them for me and tell them I already have one." The waiter left with the drink and walked to the center table to convey the message.

She continued to look outside the window and, while sipping her cocktail, pondered the phone call from Andrew Hunt, the Assistant Director of the Counterterrorism Division of the FBI. The call had come through over the weekend. It outlined her first major international assignment. She had yet to learn the details. A flicker of a smile played on her ruby-red lips and she felt a sudden surge of excitement in anticipation of the adventure that lay ahead. She was told that Matt Slater, the man responsible for her new career, was involved in a covert operation in Nairobi. Matt had flown straight out to Nairobi after his Middle East mission where Sophie had plenty of opportunity to get to know him on a personal level. Wouldn't it be exciting to get an opportunity to work with him professionally? she mused. The corners of her lips curled up into a deeper smile. As she remembered the past fond memories, a yearning for play and excitement stirred in her heart.

Her world, she had realized, consisted almost entirely of passing fancies. She was outside the reach of firm commitments. Commitments, as she would often say, were chains on personal freedom. She was free and she knew enough of the world system to be certain that a life free of any encumbrance is what she had always desired. Which, after all, was as it should be, though sometimes she had vague misgivings. With a faint shrug of her shoulders as if showing indifference towards her own feelings, she scanned the lounge. It was time for some fun, provided it was on her terms.

She noticed a man sitting alone in a far corner. Head bowed, he was drinking a beer and engrossed in a fat paperback, the title of which she could not read at that distance. She was becoming intolerant of the probing eyes and cheap smiles of the businessmen scattered about and decided to join the man sitting alone for some company. He was well built, like a professional football player, and looked rather handsome in his casual attire of slacks and open-collar shirt.

It seemed that he did not notice her approaching and was a little startled when she said, "You seem to be alone; would you mind if I join you while I finish my drink?" He looked up and half stood in confusion and then sat right back down and stammered, "Ah, well, you see, I mean if you don't mind, I don't want to sound rude, but I need some quiet time. It is my wife. She was recently diagnosed with terminal cancer. I'm afraid I won't be much company for you." He spoke haltingly as if in that lay his means of escape. But something peculiar betrayed itself in the intonation of his voice.

Sophie, opening her purse, pulled out her business card and placed it in front of him, saying, "I'm a doctor and perhaps I could advise you on a few medical treatments. If you think I could help then give me a call." She turned around and, when walking back to her table, heard, "Please forgive me," said the man abruptly and added, "won't you take a seat?"

He stood up, looking as though lost in thought, and a strange, humiliated, half-senseless smile strayed on his lips. He pulled out the chair adjacent to him and Sophie, placing her drink on the table, took the seat. Gazing directly into his dark-brown eyes she asked, "You don't even have a wife let alone one dying from cancer, do you?"

He played with her business card between his fingers that read, 'Dr. Sophie Kramer, M.D.,' and then smiling shyly, he responded, "It is just that I've recently turned pro, I'm a football player. I play for the Giants and you know, tend to get many offers in bars."

"And you thought that I am...." She let her response trail off and he hurriedly responded, "I'm so sorry."

After a momentary silence he spoke again, "To tell the truth, I have been watching you for the past hour; you are very beautiful. I was thinking of approaching you but thought you might be offended by my forwardness. Could I buy you another drink as a token of my sincere apology?" Soon after he finished his offer, he looked uneasy and at the same time, excited, as if surprised by his own courage.

Sophie was remarkably good looking, tall, strikingly well-proportioned, strong and self-reliant—the latter quality apparent in every gesture, though it did not in the least detract from the grace of her movements. There was a proud gleam in her deep blue eyes and yet, at times a look of extraordinary kindness. She had an ivory complexion, but it often didn't show due to her tanned body; her face was radiant with vigor. Her lips were full and inviting; the full red upper lip curled up a little; it gave her a fun-loving and confident expression that most men found irresistible. The shy and simple-hearted NY Giant's football player had never seen anyone quite like her, and, although not entirely sober at the time, he lost his heart immediately.

His contemplation was broken as Sophie said, "You can buy me a champagne as my flight is not until tomorrow morning." Sophie rather fancied spending a couple of hours with this athlete, preferable to being stared at by a bunch of boring businessmen. She detested snobbery.

The football hero ordered a bottle of Dom Perignon and after the waiter opened the bottle and poured them a drink, they clinked their glasses and said almost in unison, "To good times!" As she placed her scarlet, full lips around the champagne glass and sipped on her libation, her sensual eyes lit up with a sparkle. He crimsoned, ceased speaking and smiled nervously. With time, as the champagne took effect, he seemed to mellow and held Sophie's hands, caressing them. His desire surging and eyes laughing, he invited her to his suite for more champagne. She accepted his offer. The hours melted away and it was very late when she returned to her room.

The next morning she woke up in her bed fresh and excited, with a smile on her face. When she looked at her watch she tossed her bed sheet aside and rushed to take a shower and dress. She hurried down to the reception and luckily the check-out was quick. With the promise of an extra tip she enticed the cab driver to hurry to the airport. She could not afford to miss her flight to Washington D.C., as she was quite aware of the importance of her meeting with Andrew Hunt. What she did not know was that it would change her life, perhaps forever.

Two

It was Monday, the eighth of October, 2012, and slipping out of a yellow cab on Pennsylvania Avenue, Sophie was all-business. Dressed in a smart black suit with black open collar shirt and her hair combed back and tied in a ponytail, she bore an urgent look on her face as she rushed inside the FBI headquarters for her appointment with Andrew. She could not escape the importance of the position Andrew held in the office. Andrew as the Deputy Director of the Federal Bureau of Investigation was second in command to the Director of the FBI. He often took over the Director's responsibilities if and when he was absent from the office, and remained responsible for leading many prominent investigations. Andrew's was the highest position attainable within the FBI without being appointed by the President of the United States.

Although President Obama did not have to appoint Andrew Hunt as the Deputy Director, he often requested that he accompany the Director. The Obama administration respected Andrew and his achievements and relied upon him to lead the various new initiatives that President Obama was keen on.

Andrew's secretary smiled at Sophie and immediately buzzed Andrew, announcing, "Agent Kramer is here."

"Send her in." The voice on the intercom, low and serious, was unmistakably that of Andrew.

Sophie in a very short time had become popular at the FBI. People knew she could never be fixed and static as pylons driven into the earth. She wanted to be in the great flux of life, in the midst of all possibilities. She was cool as ice on the outside but in her soul she was in a state of constant flux due to her desire to set things right in the world. Her world. Yet her mind had awakened to the value of fairness. She knew she could fight anything and anyone in the name of fairness. She realized that victims in this world didn't much care for the legal system, what they wanted was expedient justice. This, and the abuse she suffered as a child at the hand of her domineering father, was the reason she gave up her lucrative emergency physician career and became an FBI Special Agent. She ruled her life according to her own set of values.

Sophie's mind craved the thrills and tumultuous storms of fighting felonious gangs, terrorist organizations, and murderers. Seeking adventure in the danger zone often penalizes most by falsely offering a sense of invincibility. Sophie, however, was blessed with clear vision and in such perilous situations she knew that neither mind nor spirit was the right place to search for courage, as strength lies within the heart where instinct governs over prudence.

Sophie knocked at and entered through the heavy door and then shut it behind her. Andrew was sitting behind his large and neatly kept desk reading a file. Without lifting his head, he said, "Grab a coffee and take a seat on the sofa. I'll be with you in a minute."

Sophie poured coffee into two mugs and on her way towards the sofa, placed one of the coffee mugs on Andrew's table. He looked up and smiled, offering a "Thanks."

A moment later, still holding the file in one hand and the coffee mug in the other, he walked over to where Sophie was sitting.

"Had a pleasant weekend?" he asked.

"Yes, thanks," said Sophie with a smile. "New York in autumn is my favorite place, and you?"

"I want you," said Andrew, ignoring her comments and pulling the diamond-studded cuffs of his shirt out from under the jacket sleeves, "to meet with someone that will have a direct bearing on your next assignment."

Before Sophie could respond there was a knock at the door and two smartly dressed gentlemen walked in. The only marked difference between the two was that one was rather tall and the other relatively short.

"Good afternoon," they uttered in unison and came to where Andrew and Sophie were sitting.

"Gentlemen," said Andrew, raising his brows slightly as if contemplating the agenda of the meeting. "Why don't you two grab some coffee so we can begin?"

Once they were all settled in with steaming coffees in their hands, the tall visitor began. "My name is Ken Kilmer. I'm the head of the Special Assignment-Asia Branch of the International Operations Division, and my associate here is Mr. James Kerr, from the US Agency for International Development. We're here to aid you in an initiative of the President that brings new measures in the war against terrorism. Under this initiative we are opening war on all fronts to dismantle the financial infrastructure that supports either directly or indirectly global terrorism. The issue we'd like to address today is trafficking in women."

Ken spoke with a calm and level tone. He was wearing a slate-colored suit, a white shirt with a dark maroon tie, and looked more like an international sales executive than a government official. Ken paused for a second, glanced at his audience and then continued. "Trafficking is now considered the third largest source of profit for organized crime, only behind drugs and guns, generating billions of dollars annually. Trafficking women for prostitution is one of the fastest growing areas of international activity and one that is of increasing concern to the U.S. Administration, Congress, and the international community."

The phone on Andrew's desk rang and he, making a gesture of apology with his hand held up, got up and walked back to desk and picked up his phone. "I had said no phone calls and no interruptions."

But he remained on the line and whoever it was on the other end had Andrew listening to him without saying a word. After about five minutes he quietly put the phone down. He remained standing by his desk in a contemplative mood until Ken asked, "Is everything okay, Deputy Director?"

"My drycleaner has lost my suit," responded Andrew in a serious tone, walking back to the sofa where everyone was sitting. It was his way of saying it was none of their business. Sophie suppressed a smile.

Three

K en made a face as if he had just swallowed something unpleasant. He looked at James who sat there with his head bowed so Ken couldn't tell if he was ignoring Andrew's remark or laughing.

The file Andrew was holding in his hand, he tossed on the coffee table and in a voice that carried authority, he said, "Let's get back to business. I've looked into the details sent to me. We're up against the Chinese and Vietnam Triads, the Japanese Yakuza, South American drug cartels, the Italian Mafia, and the Russian gangs. These groups increasingly interact with local networks to provide transportation, safe houses, local contacts, and documentation. Unlike with the drug business, trafficking is highly fragmented. While we can monitor and control to a certain extent these large groups, it is the local network made up of unknown entities that is extremely difficult to trace or monitor. If we are going to be successful in fighting the trafficking of women then we're going to need to get to the local network level and work our way up. This is going to be a slow and lengthy process, but in the end, should pay handsome dividends."

Ken sat up now and it seemed he was looking for an opening to assert his authority. He tried, "I'll leave the implementation part of the initiative with you, Deputy Director, but will need to communicate to the President the key strategic measures that you intend to employ." Ken had spoken in a tone that indicated he had finished his task by passing the responsibility over to Andrew. He also emphasized the word President to make the point that he shouldn't be trifled with, as he had the President's ear.

Andrew frowned, displaying his displeasure, and in a tone that carried the weight of authority, he said, "Key strategic measures? I don't think you understand what we are up against. Trafficking affects virtually every country in the world; it has become a global issue. Over two million women are trafficked each year worldwide for sexual exploitation. The largest number of victims, almost a half a million, trafficked internationally, comes from Asia. The trouble goes a lot deeper. While we've got some understanding on the national level, we do not have much knowledge of trafficked women within other countries, especially densely populated, large countries, such as India. If we could understand and monitor local networks and help the local law enforcement agencies to control their internal problems with trafficking, then maybe we could have more control on the problem at the international level."

A thin smile appeared on Ken's face as he seemed to mistake Andrew's argument as his inability to cope. He persisted but without conviction. "I appreciate the extent of the challenge you have, but I still need to convey to the President's Administration just how we will be handling this initiative. The responsibility resides with me to monitor and measure its success."

Andrew leaned forward, looked straight into Ken's eyes and responded, "I'm trying to help you out here. India is one of our major concerns. Let me share with you what we already know about trafficking in India. India along with Thailand and the Philippines has over one million women in the sex-trade and the Middle East is keen to finance any such activity that will eventually help in their cause. You want to report back to the President that I'm putting together a special squad and starting our activities in India first."

Ken pondered this for a moment and then looked at his associate with questioning eyes; the man simply shrugged his shoulders. They had no clue as to when such a special squad was initiated.

"Deputy Director," said Ken hesitantly, "I can tell you this much. The U.S. Administration and Congress are now addressing this problem as a priority. We need to be informed well in advance of your strategic measures like this special squad—"

Suddenly Andrew put his hand up and interrupted Ken with, "I've already heard what you need. Let me ask my associate what she thinks of all this. What is your take on it?" he asked, looking at Sophie.

"A whole lot of political bull," Sophie said, calmly sipping her coffee. She added, "Or, if you gentlemen prefer polite words, then it seems to me you'll go a long way around to get nowhere." Sophie spoke in a challenging tone laced with a certain incredulity. She was not the one to mince words.

"Care to explain?" asked Andrew, suppressing a smile.

Sophie nodded for she knew that Andrew had invited her answer for Ken's benefit. For a moment she did not speak, but stared straight into Ken's eyes, as she once did in her previous profession as an emergency physician with difficult patients, exuding a strange, silent authority. "I'm not one to dwell on the 'prevention, protection and prosecution' policy of various governments, including ours," she said slowly to impart gravity. She continued, "It is there for a good purpose, I'm sure, and doing its job as well as it can. I'm not going to stand in judgment on this policy's effectiveness but if we are to succeed in this initiative then I agree, we need a special task force that is placed not here in Langley but in countries like India, tackling the problem head on."

Andrew leaned back on his sofa and uttered, "Well said. Now you can report that to the President." There was a flicker of a smile on his face as if he was impressed with the outspoken ability of Sophie and her direct approach in getting to the point.

"Excuse me," blurted Ken, almost spilling his coffee, "who are you? I don't believe we were formally introduced. I assumed you were here to take notes on the meeting, not give opinions."

"Meet the member of this special squad, Special Agent Kramer," announced Andrew with his smile widening.

"Her? She is the special agent for such an important and critical initiative? How many agents have you assigned to this special squad?" Ken looked at her and then at Andrew, and back at Sophie again, the expression on his face a cocktail of bewilderment, disbelief and shock.

Andrew gave a little chuckle and then with smiling eyes retorted, "Special Agent Kramer is it. Right now she is the squad. I've every confidence in her ability to make a good start while we put together a support team for her."

Sophie smiled but beneath her smile there was puzzlement. She was expecting an important assignment but had no idea that Andrew was about to give her such a major task. She was overjoyed. Her reverie was broken by Andrew's next comment as he stood up. "Gentlemen," he said in a firm voice, "I have good news and bad news.

The bad news is that you will have to develop your own strategic measures to convince the President that you're up to the task, and the good news is that this meeting is over. If you'll excuse us, we have work to do. We'll be in touch when we have something further to share."

To avoid further embarrassment, the tall and the short duo left hurriedly and Sophie followed Andrew back to his desk. Her task had begun.

Four

A ndrew Hunt had a reputation. He was known worldwide in various intelligence agencies for his envious record of solving some of the most complex murder and kidnapping cases and discovering and breaking up various terrorist cells. Andrew overtly appeared as a textbook man that followed policies and procedures as strictly as one could. But covertly he made exceptions, especially when it came to supporting his special agents. He gained his agents' trust by giving them the freedom to exercise their own judgment and in return they produced spectacular results. That was the key to Andrew's success.

When it came to Matt Slater, Andrew always governed his assignments with flexibility. He admired Matt's talents and his dedication to his profession. So when Matt brought Sophie into the Bureau, and Sophie produced some spectacular results in a very short time, Andrew treated her with the same respect as he did Matt.

"It is not going to be a walk in the park," said Andrew, pulling out a file from his drawer. He added, "I have been communicating with the Commissioner of Police of New Delhi who has a new mandate to develop and implement an effective initiative to eliminate the local and relatively unknown networks that feed the large and systematically developed and operated crime organizations in India. They don't seem to have much intelligence on the crime groups behind the trafficking of women and I am sure our files are not quite up to date. You'll have to start from the ground up," Andrew explained in a flat tone.

"I see a flaw," Sophie challenged Andrew. Andrew smiled and nodded at her to show his respect for her sharp mind.

"Oh, and what would that be?" Andrew asked.

"All this sounds like a desk job. You did not hire me for a desk job. I'm a field operative and that is where my skills lie."

"Right. Actually, I'm sending you out there on a specific case that will be your assignment as well as a front to accomplish bigger results by making the local law enforcement agencies effective in dismantling the crime organizations behind women trafficking in India."

"That is what I was hoping. What exactly is the case?" Sophie said with a determined look on her face.

"Last Friday a little American girl called Amy Kumar was kidnapped in New Delhi. As the name suggests, her father is Indian and her mother is an American. The parents did not waste any time and have filed a complaint with the local police as well as with the US embassy. The report was filed on Friday night a few hours after the girl went missing."

"How old is the girl? Are we suspecting kidnapping for ransom or something more sinister?" asked Sophie, sounding a little disappointed with the simple nature of the case.

"She is four years old, hence the urgency in filing the police report," said Andrew, rubbing his chin with his thumb. "No ransom demand has been made yet but the girl's father has a well-known and well-established family business in New Delhi that is worth several million dollars.

One could safely assume that a demand for a hefty ransom could be forthcoming."

Sophie considered this for a moment. The case certainly sounded like a kidnapping for ransom. How could she take advantage of it while unearthing the trafficking underworld of India? Then a faint smile appeared on her face. She had known Andrew for a short time but long enough to detect that something was bothering him. "There is more, isn't there?"

"Very perceptive of you," said Andrew. Leaning forward over his desk he explained, "This has been a hell of a weekend. It could be unrelated but the US ambassador in New Delhi was reported missing that Friday morning by the local papers. We were informed on Wednesday when the ambassador did not show up at the embassy for his meetings. We did not disclose this information and went immediately into action but someone leaked the information to the local press. Anyway, it is not important how the information got out. What is important is that the ambassador turned up unharmed over the weekend and even though it was the weekend, he had managed to contact the Indian Home Office to do something to find the missing girl. It didn't stop there. He has been hammering the State Department to get the FBI involved through his connections with a couple of senior senators, putting increasing pressure on us. The phone has been ringing all morning."

Sophie's spirits rose momentarily when she learned of the ambassador's disappearance, but then when she heard that he had returned unharmed, she felt rather deflated, for it sounded irrelevant to her case. She wondered why Andrew had brought it up. "Do you think that the two incidents are related? There seems to be some connection for the ambassador to get so deeply involved in the little girl's disappearance."

"That is for you to find out," Andrew's voice was filled with urgency. "These senators want one of our best on this case. But keep in mind that the real pressure is coming from our ambassador in New Delhi who is raising all kinds of stink to bring the FBI in. This may sound corny but a woman's touch may mollify some of these male egos. Besides, you are my first choice for this case."

"You won't be disappointed. And if you had doubted my abilities, you wouldn't have appointed me to this case. I guess it won't be the first time that the FBI has faced pressure from politicians and diplomats."

"I do detest their interference," said Andrew in an irritated voice. "But I like to stay one step ahead of such mysteries so they won't boomerang and hit us in the face when we least expect it."

"Are we being officially invited by the Indian authorities or will they see our participation as interference?" asked Sophie.

"Today is Monday, and I have been told that the formalities of a formal invitation for our help and participation will be in place in a couple of days. There seems to be some hitch. India is a highly bureaucratic country, so don't expect anything to come in an urgent and expedient manner."

"Do I wait then or shall I leave now and wait it out in New Delhi? Three days have already elapsed and any further delay could prove fatal for this case."

"I'm aware of that and you can leave immediately, but you will not be of much use for a couple of more days to the New Delhi police authorities. Protocols and procedures must be adhered to. There will be a couple of days delay before you can sink your teeth into this case. So I have another task for you, kind of a warm-up exercise. Matt has called me and asked for you to be there in Nairobi to assist him for a couple of days. I know your capabilities; you're one hell of a player when using your instinct. I think Matt knows that too. So, you can leave now, but swing by Nairobi on your way to India. I'll arrange for all your clearances and paperwork. It should be ready by the time you get to New Delhi."

"You got it, chief," she said, and shook his hand, picked up the file and left his office. What she did not know was that the visit to Nairobi might put her life in jeopardy.

Book II

Seven Years Ago
Spring 2005

An Indian in America

Five

Ashok bowed his head and let out a sigh. At dusk the gradually descending darkness like a darkening ocean under an overcast sky began to drain the residual light of day. All that remained visible at that hour was the fading hue in the western sky like the healing scars of a well-fought day.

The streetlamps flickered as if waking up from a spell. Tomorrow he was leaving. Ashok's flight was scheduled to leave at 9 a.m. He looked out his bedroom window in his parents' house in New Delhi and wondered why his parents were unhappy with his decision to go to the States for higher studies. He had worked hard all through his academic life and now, having graduated from the elite Indian Institute of Technology-Roorkee with an honors degree in Electrical Engineering, he was keen to go to Stanford University where he was offered a scholarship to attend a Master's degree program in Electrical Engineering with a specialization in Dynamic Systems & Optimization. He thought that his father, himself an electrical engineer and owning a small software development company, would have been pleased with his son's decision to secure a higher education from a leading university in the States and then return home to help him grow the family-owned business.

He looked at the waiting luggage that he had meticulously packed that day. As far as he was concerned there was no turning back now. An hour later he heard his mother asking him to come down for dinner. They ate dinner in an awkward silence. After dinner he went out for a stroll to get some fresh air and to clear his head. He walked aimlessly for over an hour and upon return went straight to bed for an early start the next morning.

After a fitful sleep filled with nightmares, he woke up with a start and quickly showered and changed then came downstairs where his parents were already waiting. On their drive to the airport, his mother gave him abundant advice on how he must write weekly and take care of his diet, while his father remained silent. It was with a heavy heart that he waved goodbye to his parents at the Indira Gandhi International Airport before boarding a Lufthansa flight to San Francisco via Germany. He was pleased that it was a long flight for he needed time to gather his thoughts. He had been to Europe many times before but this was the first time that he was going to the USA.

As the hours evaporated, his anxieties subsided and were replaced by the excitement of a new adventure. The plane finally landed at the San Francisco International Airport. It took Ashok about an hour to get through the immigration formalities. He was nervous as he'd heard many stories from his friends of unfriendly and tough US customs authorities. But he experienced none of that per-haps because all his paperwork was in order, and thus the process of entering the US went smoothly. He relaxed. The university had organized his transportation to bring him to the campus. Upon arrival he was overwhelmed with the friendly attitude of the Stanford administration and there-after, easily settled into campus life.

Weeks melted into months and his professors acknowledged his hard work and thorough knowledge of the subjects by letting him develop the business development aspects of his course. Ashok was good at academics but loved and excelled at the commercial development portion of his research. During the course of his studies he was given an opportunity to meet with many commercial companies in the Bay area to learn their business needs and develop guidelines to translate them into research programs.

Months flew by and the business of Silicon Valley grew on him like moss in a fern forest. At the end of the first academic year he dispensed with his summer vacation and spent the time making several business contacts with the help of his professors. His academic interest was strong but he always kept an eye on the business side of his education. Then one day he came up with an idea to expand his father's software development business by acting as his local representative to entice businesses to outsource their work to India.

India was already recognized as a low-cost center with a large talent pool for the US companies who chose to outsource their work. When Ashok contacted some of these companies in the Bay area he found they all tended to have a common complaint—lack of logistic control. All these companies needed was a local person to take care of logistics, especially the side of financial arrangements.

For Ashok, being physically present in the Bay area was ideal, allowing him to oversee both business and financial logistics. Ashok's background was an added asset as he spoke the technical jargon often necessary to develop an effective work execution plan. In the beginning, only a few companies showed interest, but Ashok was not disheartened. He asked his father to borrow money to expand his business to dilute the company's overhead by bringing down the unit cost. With low cost incentives, Ashok was confident of generating substantial business. Ashok's father acted on his son's advice and doubled the output of his business. Ashok aggressively marketed one of the lowest cost solutions with a local logistic services office acting in tandem with the regional software development companies, and the word of his cost- and time-effective services spread quickly through the Valley.

Orders started to pour in and businesses started to grow at a significant rate. Ashok would often sit with his clients and ask them what technical improvements were necessary for them to have an edge over their competition. Soon a trend began to emerge. Ashok realized that the US was the world's largest business economy involving hundreds of thousands of small, medium and large businesses all over the country. These businesses and their customers and suppliers alike needed a low-cost and robust telecommunication network for data transfer known as the Wide Area Network. Such technology already existed; large corporations that charged hefty license fees for its use controlled them. A quality, robust and low cost solution was needed.

Ashok mentioned this to his professor at an impromptu meeting at a coffee shop, and asked how the university could help in the development of such an industrial application. The professor responded, "I'm glad you asked, because the university being innovation-driven is the right place to start for any such industrial and commercial applications." Draining his Starbucks cup, he added, "The US government liberally supports university research financially for such projects, provided that the concept is good. You may not know this but it was the United States National Science Foundation (NSF) that constructed a university network backbone that later became the NSFNet. Once the universities proved the network, and only then, it was offered to commercial interests in the mid nineties. What you're proposing could have tremendous value."

They agreed to work together to develop a lost-cost solution to WAN.

Six

Ashok and his professor got down to work to come up with a business plan for their new venture. Once it was completed to their satisfaction they approached the university and through it various research foundations. It took some convincing but eventually grants and necessary funding, as well as a facility, were secured for Ashok, under the ministration of his supervisor, to undertake the development of a low-cost and healthy WAN technology. Ashok and his professor set out to develop a system from the ground up and believed that the sophistication of such a next generation technology lay in its simplicity.

After a prototype was developed Ashok came up with an idea to apply the system on a selective basis between his father's business in India and to some target clients in the US. After some teething problems, the pilot program proved successful. Other clients of Ashok's father's business showed interest and were included in expanding the use of the newly developed WAN system.

Over a short period of time invested in testing, Ashok and his professor's invention proved to be a highly reliable yet very low-cost WAN. With Ashok and his professor as co-inventors, the university patented the invention. The new WAN was now offered nationwide to a large and growing market. The word spread quickly through the Silicon Valley and then throughout the country and their new invention over a short period of time gained immense acclaim and became an industry standard.

A fast-growing medium-sized software house in the Bay area contacted the University and offered $50 million to acquire the invention. The University engaged an intellectual property law firm, Kirkpatrick & Townsend, to act on their behalf during negotiations and legal representation. The firm asked for the inventor to work with their team. Since Ashok was the real brains behind the invention, he was assigned by the University to work with the legal firm. Ashok was excited to take his invention to new heights and to receive suitable rewards for his hard work.

At the law firm he met with Jenifer, a junior partner with eight years' experience in the firm.

"Mr. Kumar," she said, "I've researched your product and the offer you have received. My company has come up with a proposal and I'm sure you'll like it." Jenifer was in her early thirties but looked more like she was in her mid-twenties, with a small face that seemed to have a permanent and pleasant smile. Her long, flowy blonde hair and clear green eyes with a curvaceous body made her look like a Hollywood star. Dressed in an expensive-looking blue suit with open-collar red blouse, she showed her wit and breasts equally well.

"I'm listening," said Ashok, swallowing nervously, "provided the University doesn't have to fork out a huge fee to your office."

"That is the best part of the deal," she said, coming around the desk and putting down a open folder on the desk in front of him, leaning over his left shoulder while her soft cheek brushed his face. "There would be no fee and we would guarantee you $60 million; that is twenty percent over and above the offer you already have on the table."

"I'm sure that the University would be delighted with your offer. But I don't understand," said Ashok in a perplexed tone, "what is in it for your company?"

She laughed and her pearly-white, perfectly set teeth shined under the bright luminous light of the office. "The deal is that any money we negotiate over and above the $60 million would be considered as our fee."

Ashok pondered the offer for a minute and then said, "Let me make a call."

"Sure," said Jenifer, "I'll give you some privacy and be back in ten minutes."

Ten minutes later they shook hands and a day later the University signed the contract. Ashok met with Jenifer almost daily for meetings and after a few days suggested that perhaps they should meet for dinner. Jenifer agreed and after the first dinner meeting it became a regular occurrence.

Jenifer began to pay more than usual attention to Ashok. She found him attractive. With the long, clean lines of his cheeks; the strong chin; and the slightly arched, full nose; the beautiful almond-shaped eyes with dark long lashes; and naturally shaped brows, he was what she told her friends, an exotic blend. In his romantic moments when he seemed most himself, his face was pure poetry, with black eyebrows raised and brown eyes holding a quixotic twinkle. His good looks were set off by his smooth and tanned skin. That was Ashok at his best, at least in the opinion of Jenifer. In the opinion of her woman friends, he was a fascinating man with a deeper understanding of life and its values and the patience and will to make a woman feel like a princess, which of course was to make a woman realize her true worth.

Over the days the meetings gradually moved from the office conference room to a restaurant table and eventually to bed. Jenifer found Ash, as she fondly called him, a sincere man with charming manners. She felt he catered to her senses, and soothed her soul, while giving her what she had been waiting for all her life—a soul mate.

It took less than three weeks before a suitable offer was made and the deal was concluded. After tax the University received $39 million, out of which they retained $21 million, and from the remainder the professor received $10 million, Ashok $5 million and $3 million was distributed amongst the rest of the project research team. No one knew what the total offer was as that was specified in the contract. It seemed that Ashok won a great deal out of the transaction but in the process lost his heart.

Ashok promptly sent almost all his after-tax money to his father to pay all outstanding business debts and for the further expansion of the business. A couple of months later he wrote to his father saying that his studies were successfully concluded and although he was receiving great employment offers from many major US corporations, he was soon coming back to India to run the family software business with him. He wanted to keep the promise his parents asked for prior to his coming to the States. As a son and the only child, he knew what was expected of him as dictated by Indian family tradition.

Seven

While in the States, Ashok was constantly made aware of his obligations to his parents. Every letter they wrote to him reminded Ashok of his responsibilities at home. And they wrote such letters every two weeks. His first and foremost duty was to obey his parents. He may be grown up and better educated than his parents but that did not give him the right to show any disrespect towards them by questioning their decisions. These centuries-old and unwavering traditions were the key for Indians to claim themselves as perhaps the only race in the world with a continuing and coherent civilization.

Ashok knew that Jenifer would be upset if he were now to return to India to fulfill his promise to his parents. He had several uneasy nights wondering how to disclose his intentions to Jenifer. He realized that he had never loved anyone in his life as he loved her and felt that there was a certain connection between them that brought them together in the first place. She was older, about eight years older than him, but the age gap didn't seem to bother him. He had a choice to make, a difficult choice, and though he knew what his heart wanted, he wasn't sure he could convince his mind to accept it. In his head were images of his parents and all his own thoughts were corrupted by the expectations they had for him.

One Saturday night he invited Jenifer out for dinner and throughout the dinner he was very quiet, preoccupied with the dilemma of how to tell the truth and yet keep

Jenifer happy. It was Jenifer who finally broke the silence. Perhaps to give him the confidence that he often lacked, she opened her heart and spoke in a tone as if asking for assurance, "I love you so much. If I could be assured of your love then all the confidence I need to heal my wounds from lack of parental love would follow."

Ashok simply stared at her as if he hadn't heard what she just said.

She asked, "What's wrong? You're not saying much tonight."

Ashok realized that it was now or never. He put down his knife and fork on his half-eaten dinner. "Jenifer," he hesitated, "I don't know how to say it so I'm just going to come out with it. I'm leaving the US and going back to India." He further hesitated and then added, "For good." He exhaled loudly and felt as if his whole body was suspended in mid air.

Jenifer looked uneasily at him. There was something peculiar in this statement, which seemed under its bluntness approaching something in a strange and roundabout way.

She took a sip of her wine and looked at him with a deadpan face as if she did not hear him. There was an uneasy silence between them. She put her glass down and looked straight into his eyes and said, "I felt that you were going to say something like that. So you chose a public place to announce this hoping that I won't make a scene, is that it?" she asked, looking inquisitively at him.

Ashok's hand trembled as he picked up his glass of wine and before his glass could reach his lips he put the glass down back on the table. He looked as if he was about to say something but then perhaps the repercussions he may arouse in Jenifer stopped him. He tried to smile to lighten the moment, but his pale face suggested something helpless and incomplete.

"When?" Jenifer broke the silence and continued to stare at him.

"Soon," he finally spoke and stretched his right hand out on the table hoping she would offer hers for him to hold, "maybe in a couple of weeks, maybe more. I know what it may look like to you, but I hope you believe me when I tell you that I didn't want us to end up this way."

"What way is that?" she asked in a sharp voice. "Could it be that you had your fun while you were here and now you would like to run back and marry an Indian girl picked by your parents, is that it? I thought you were better that that. I'm disappointed in you."

"Actually," he began to say, but then hesitated, "what I meant to say—"

"Oh, for god's sake, spit it out," she cried.

"Nothing," he said meekly. "I'm so sorry, I truly am."

And suddenly a strange, surprising sort of bitter hatred for the man passed through her heart. Frightened by this sensation, she raised her head and looked intently at him, her uneasy and painfully anxious eyes fixed on him; there was love in them, and her hatred vanished like a morning fog. It was not the real feeling she had; she had mistaken the one feeling for the other. How could she be so wrong in substituting her relationship with him for true love? She felt confused.

Jenifer's face suddenly softened as if a shadow of a thought crossed her mind. She inhaled deeply and let it

out slowly. With moistened eyes she said in a contemplative voice, "The Bay area is full of friends, I've got a lot
of friends. But I wanted more. In you I saw a soul mate, a
lover, a special someone who cared. I wanted you, Ashok,
and I thought you wanted me. I wanted us to be a family. But you proved me wrong. I was used to being alone
and I guess I'll go back to being alone." Her face wore an
expression that was equally sad and suicidal. She sank into
thought.

"You've got your parents," said Ashok, "you can never
be lonely when you have them. You'll always have their
love. I was hoping that as a family person you'd understand
that I owe everything to my parents for they always put
me first, ahead of all their priorities. How could I let them
down when they ask me to come back and take care of the
family business and them? I'm all they have."

Tiny tears formed in the corners of her eyes. "You're
so lucky," she said in a trembling voice. "I don't really know
who my biological father is. After my mom died when I
was still a baby, my stepfather put me up for adoption. Yet
another stepfather adopted me. My new stepfather always
wanted a baby so he adored me when I was little. He gave
me love, kindness and care. But then I grew up and he
didn't want an adult demanding to have her own life. So, he
adopted another little baby. He didn't want me; he wanted
a baby to play with. I have been surviving most of my life
on my own." She wiped her eyes with the napkin and cried,
"Oh, what is the use of telling you all this. You'll soon be
back with your parents. In time you'll have a wife and a
couple of children and a happy life. You'll forget about me,
us. Have a great life."

"But what about your mom, she must care for and love you?" asked Ashok.

"She died a long time ago, as I said, of a broken heart," said Jenifer reflectively.

"I'm so sorry, Jenifer," said Ashok, offering both his hands to hold hers.

"I bet you are." She quickly withdrew her hands, threw her napkin on the table, pushed her chair back violently and rushed out of the restaurant.

Eight

The Lufthansa flight began its descent into the capitol of India and finally touched down at the Indira Gandhi International Airport where Ashok's parents eagerly waited to receive him. Coming through the busy arrival hall he saw them with their welcoming smiles, each holding a marigold garland and waving enthusiastically. As he approached them he touched their feet out of respect and they lifted him up by holding his shoulders, put garlands around his neck and hugged him.

"Welcome back, my son," said Ashok's father in a proud voice, "you look so great. You have done us proud. What a big businessman you have become. Welcome."

"Thanks, Dad, and it is so good of both of you to come to the airport to receive me." Ashok took off the garlands and draped them over his folded arm. He felt exhilarated being back in his own country.

"And why wouldn't we come to the airport to receive our own son?" chirped his mother, holding her head high as if wanting the whole world to see how proud she was. "I haven't seen you for over two years. Do you know how hard that is for a mother, not to see her only son for two years? I am so proud of you."

"I am so pleased to see you both looking happy and healthy. Oh my god, I totally forgot. Talking about happiness, I've happy news for you." He half turned around and continued, "Dad, Mom, meet my wife, Jenifer."

Jenifer folded her hands as taught by Ashok and said in a soft and amiable voice, *"Namaste."*

The smiles on the faces of Ashok's parents dissolved like butter on a hot pan. They stared at her and then at Ashok, their eyes demanding an explanation. More than an explanation, perhaps an apology! Ashok's father, overtly displaying his displeasure with a frown on his face, spoke first, scolding, "Son, this is not proper. You can't marry without our blessings. This cannot be true. Whatever mistake you made in the west we have to put right and soon, before any damage can be done to our family's name."

"You should've said something, son," Ashok's mother piped up. "This is quite a shock, you understand?"

"Mom, Dad," said Ashok, looking embarrassed, "please. This is no way to welcome your *bahu*, your daughter-in-law. I told Jenifer so many wonderful things about you two, and how she would be welcome in our house."

"For us to welcome someone in our house, that someone first must know the rules of the house," boomed Ashok's father and persisted, "was there a proper Indian wedding? No. You know why? It is because we were not there. This is not acceptable to us. You will have to send her back to her parents."

"But Dad," said Ashok, looking around nervously, and then continued in a low voice, "I'm married and Jenifer is my wife. We were married legally and that is the truth."

"Is she pregnant," asked his mother in a whisper.

"No, she is not pregnant," said Ashok, rolling his eyes. "Mom, please. We are married because we wanted to be married. We love each other."

"Huh, love," growled Ashok's father. "Love has destroyed so many families. It is not love but respect for our traditions that induces people to marry."

"Let's not make a scene here in public," said Ashok's mother agitatedly. "We can't just stand here and fight. What would people say? Someone might recognize us."

With his lips contorted in anger, Ashok's father looked at Jenifer and then at Ashok and turned his back on them. His wife grabbed his arm and whispered something in his ear that visibly brought more wrath to his face and he jerked his arm away from her. A few moments elapsed and then he turned around to face Ashok again and said, "She can come home but we will have to talk about it. What you've done is not right. Did you not think of our reputation when you married a white girl?" His voice was stern and turning his back to Ashok again, he walked straight to his parked Mercedes.

Once they reached home, Ashok's father's fury took an ugly turn. Everyone stood in the drawing room with Ashok and Jenifer's luggage still outside in the parked car, as Ashok's father shouted, "Our son would never marry without our consent and would never degrade our honor and destroy our name in society by bringing a foreigner to our home. Did you stop to think what people would say?"

Ashok knew his father's temper and looked at his mother with pleading eyes. She stood in a corner crying. His father continued, "Have you forgotten who you are? You owe everything to us. We saved every penny to provide for you. Sent you to the USA to make you happy and to fulfill your dreams. And this is how you repay us? Did you not think of your poor mother who is already suffering from a weak heart? What if something were to happen to her?

How would you then live with yourself? You have been led astray by the western ways. We will not accept any of this, not in this house, not now, not ever."

That was it. The message was delivered with such finality that it warranted no response. Ashok looked at Jenifer, who it seemed was stunned by Ashok's parents' reaction. Silence like a death knell descended and the room assumed the ambiance of a funeral home.

Nine

Ashok had heard before and on several occasions the story of his mother's weak heart. She had never suffered a heart attack; in fact, she was never even diagnosed with such a condition, but his father believed in it because it served as a convenient tool for him to make Ashok feel guilty. It was a common threat used by aging Indian parents as a final move to end all arguments. A curious sensation started to rise from the pit of Ashok's stomach. He felt humiliated in front of Jenifer and, at the same time, felt sorry for her.

Ashok felt like retaliating by saying that he had paid for whatever his parents spent on him several times over by sending them over two million dollars. How many sons can claim that? But he said nothing because he knew it would only add fuel to the fire. He continued to stare at his mother, hoping she would intervene.

Taking his silence perhaps as weakness, Ashok's father shouted, "What do you see in her? She has strange-colored eyes and hair, not normal for our people. No, no, she will never be accepted by our society."

And when Ashok's mother demanded to know her age and learned that Jenifer was eight years older than Ashok, that was the last straw and she cried out, "I can see now. This old woman has stolen my baby. How could you have chosen an older and strange-looking woman as your wife? This is against all our traditions. Your father is right, she cannot be a part of our family."

When the wave of abusive remarks based on traditional values started to turn into a personal attack, Jenifer decided that she'd had just about enough of it. This was not the behavior of civilized people. She could see that Ashok's parents were quite upset and wondered why Ashok after all this time had insisted on surprising them? He should have written to them first. But now that they started attacking her personally she determined that they were being ludicrous. "I think you are being unreasonable," said Jenifer in a slow and calm voice. "Ashok and I love each other and we are happy together. Ashok knew how old I was when we first met and it made no difference for us. We are both adults and know what we are doing. Mixed marriages are quite common nowadays and actually, if you ask me, more successful than most same-race marriages. Ashok loves you both very much and you need to cut him some slack."

"Now she is telling us that her marriage is better than ours," wailed Ashok's mother, "listen to her! We barely know her and she is criticizing us in our own house." She threw her hands up in disgust and then dropped down in a chair, weeping loudly.

Ashok had never known his father to use physical force but somehow recognized that, if warranted, he was quite capable of it. He wondered if his father would slap Jenifer or throw her out of the house. No one had ever spoken to his father in such a direct and challenging way. But to his utter amazement he saw his father taking a deep breath and walking a couple of steps closer to Jenifer, saying to her, "You are not to concern yourself with our family matters. It is quite obvious that you know nothing about our ways. You're different from us. We are Indians and must continue what we have been doing for generations."

"In what way are we different?" asked Jenifer, agitated by being patronized. "Because I am white? An American? Ashok did not notice those differences. I'm not that different." With clenched fists, frustration showed both in her face and in her voice. She took a couple of deep breaths as if contemplating her next remark. Suddenly her face mellowed and in a soft voice she said, "Please give us a chance and perhaps we all can be a happy family?"

Ashok's father rubbed his head and after glaring at Jenifer, he shouted at her, "As long as you are here we will never be a happy family. You are not a part of our family. This will never work. You cannot stay with us. If you love him then you must leave him. Get this into your head: You can never be a part of this family!"

Hitting the open palm of his left hand with the balled-up fist of his right hand, he solidified his last statement and then stormed out, opened the trunk of his car and literally threw out their luggage from the car on the driveway and moved the car inside the garage. Ashok looked at his mother and said, "Mom, aren't you going to be happy with my choice? Jenifer is my wife and if you're going to ask her to leave this house then you're going to lose me for I will leave with her. I'm your only child. Say something, Mom."

But Ashok's mother said nothing in response and continued to cry. Ashok's pleadings turned into a suffocating rage. He found it hard to breathe. He held Jenifer's hand and they left the house. Jenifer tried to talk with him to stop him from leaving. But he went out on the road and hailed a passing taxi, put their luggage in its trunk and asked the taxi driver to take them to the Hyatt Hotel.

During the taxi ride there was an awkward silence and Jenifer let Ashok have time to calm down. He looked outraged and he was blinking involuntarily as if seething with a suppressed fury. Once they arrived and checked into the hotel, and then were in the privacy of their room, before even opening up any luggage, a sudden feeling of loneliness descended upon them.

They sat on the bed side by side, both mournful and dejected, as though they had been cast up by a tempest alone on some deserted shore. He looked at Jenifer and reflected on how great was her love for him, and strange to say, he felt it suddenly burdensome and painful to be so loved. Yes, it was a strange and awful sensation. On his way to see his parents he had wondered if perhaps he was a trifle hasty in marrying Jenifer; he expected his parents to understand his situation, and now, when he was caught in an impossible choice between his parents or his wife, he was immeasurably unhappier than before.

Ashok held Jenifer's hands and said, "I'm so sorry about what happened at the airport and then at my parents' place. They were rude to you. I apologize on their behalf. Once they have absorbed the shock they will settle down. They are not bad people." He saw sadness in Jenifer's eyes and added, "I'm so glad you are here. You're the only thing in my life that is real and makes me happy."

Jenifer said, "I'm sorry, too, Ashok, about what happened back there. But why didn't you say something to your father? You cannot let him bully you like that. You must stand up to him."

Ashok let go of her hands and his face stiffened. "I'm not—I have not been in a situation like this before. You don't understand," said Ashok. "A son must never answer back to his father, he must respect his father no matter what. Those are our ways. This is who we are. Those are the ways my father knows and expects me to follow unconditionally."

"Come on," she said, challenging him, "you don't believe in that anymore than I do. You're an educated and intelligent grown-up man, stand up for yourself. I know you can do it."

"Please, not now," said Ashok in an exasperated tone, "let's give it a rest. Okay? I am just as surprised as you are by my parents' behavior. Things might be different tomorrow. Let's not talk about it anymore."

Jenifer looked at Ashok and at his pleading eyes. Although she was disappointed by his meek behavior she decided not to escalate the argument. "Would you like to go downstairs for a bite to eat or perhaps a drink? We both need a drink; at least I know I do," said Jenifer trying to soothe Ashok's irritation.

"You go," was the short and abrupt reply he gave. He then locked himself in the bathroom and after five minutes when he came out he found the room empty. Jenifer had gone down to get a drink. Without bothering to have dinner, he slipped into bed and had a fitful sleep all night. His nightmares had returned.

Ten

D
ays melted into weeks and weeks into months and Ashok's parents finally came around to accepting Ashok's marriage and they tolerated Jenifer like one assents to a dull backache. They never fully accepted her as their *Bahu*. Ashok bought a house far away from his parents' house, to put some distance between them and Jenifer. Ashok's parents continued to put demands on Ashok's time and wanted him to come to their house on every weekend dinner. Jenifer always accompanied Ashok but his parents refused to talk with her. She was treated as a stranger and with the minimal courtesy one shows to a stranger.

Jenifer often scolded Ashok for not standing up for himself and giving into every demand his parents made. Ashok wanted to live the western way of life and build his future with Jenifer but his circumstances drove him deeper into the traditional way of living. His mother insisted he come around often to eat Indian food with them and his father, now getting old, demanded more and more of his son's time for the family business.

One day when Ashok returned from work he found Jenifer waiting for him dressed up in a designer dress and wearing her favorite pearl necklace that he had bought her on their wedding day. For a moment his heart sank, wondering if he had forgotten her birthday. Jenifer held his hands in hers and asked Ashok if he would take her out somewhere special for dinner. When he asked the reason, she said she had good news for him that she would disclose at the restaurant.

During dinner Ashok looked at her expectantly, waiting for her news, but she toyed with him by saying she would talk about it after dinner and over dessert and coffee. Ashok had not seen Jenifer in such a good mood for a long time and remained curious as to what it could be. After dinner was finished and the aforementioned dessert and coffee were served, he could wait no longer and asked, "So, what is the good news? God knows I could do with some good news. We haven't had such a pleasant dinner for a long time. At least, not since we left the States."

"Well," said Jenifer stretching time to savor every moment, "I hope you will be pleased with my news. I'm pregnant."

Ashok sat completely still and looked at her in amazement as if he had never heard of any woman ever getting pregnant. "Say something," said Jenifer, "say you're happy."

"I'm ecstatic," said Ashok, "this will change our lives. When did you find out? I mean, when is the baby due?"

When Jenifer told Ashok that the baby was due in five months, he quickly did some mental math and in a tone filled with surprise said, "So you were pregnant when we had that dreadful evening in the restaurant in the States? Why didn't you tell me then?"

"Why? Would that have made any difference? Anyway, that is in the past. What we've got to consider now is the future of our baby. Our baby, yours and mine, yes? We're going to build our own family, our own lives from now on."

Ashok did not quite know how to deal with the fact that Jenifer kept such important news hidden from him.

He felt betrayed by not being a part of it for five months. His enthusiasm waned. "Well, they will be the grandparents and have every right to enjoy their grandchild," said Ashok, in a perplexed tone tinged with irritation.

"I really wish you'd grow up," said Jenifer in an exasperated voice. "They've got their lives and we have ours. This is our baby. I think we ought to return to the States where our baby can have a better future. Being an American, our child would never be accepted here. I don't want our child to go through what I have experienced. I don't think India is the place for people like us." Suddenly she appeared to be very tired. She'd apparently had high hopes that the news of a baby would bring the old Ashok back. But she was wrong.

"Oh, no," interjected Ashok hurriedly, "we had agreed that we would make our home here in India. I can't just leave my parents and run away. This is my country, my birthplace. My parents and our family business need me here. Besides, our child would be an Indian, it will have my name."

"When I married you," she said in a bitter voice, "I didn't know that I was marrying the whole goddamn family. You talk about their lives, what about my life, our lives? Don't I deserve some happiness? In your mother and father I was hoping to find the love of parents that I never had, but their hearts are filled with resentment and even hatred towards me. They don't even bother to hide their feelings. Nothing is going to change that, don't you see?"

She wanted to have children to celebrate her love for him for she believed that a creation from them might restore their wavering commitment to each other. But she was mistaken about that. Such arguments remained a part of their life, gaining nothing and never reaching any conclusions. Slowly the environment surrounding them was corroding their relationship. She realized now the challenges of being married to a romantic, a born charmer, an exotic man, and an entrepreneur, and somehow also this other person, this boring traditionalist, this workaholic businessman, this subtle manipulator of truth. She never could have believed that their marriage hinged on a matter of race as thrust upon her by Ashok's parents. Beyond all races is the problem of man and woman, and how for centuries men have oppressed women, and this she firmly believed. Rather than fight it, more often than not she sat by herself with the horror of her low self esteem reconfirmed, wanting only to escape.

The next few weeks were more confusing than difficult for Jenifer. Ashok had become very moody. He would get excited talking about the baby and their future but would easily become depressed whenever Jenifer brought up the subject of moving to the States. To further confound the situation, Ashok's mother started calling on Jenifer to ensure that she and her pregnancy were all right. Once Ashok's father came with his wife and brought her flowers. But apart from perfunctory hello he did not say much and sat quietly in the drawing room drinking tea. Ashok's mother was full of advice, none of which made any sense to Jenifer. She wished her own mother were alive. She felt lonely during the day and exhausted at night.

The day came when she was rushed to the hospital to give birth. With congestion on the road Jenifer thought she was going to deliver in the back of Ashok's car. He drove like a maniac making constant use of the horn and often shouting out his window at the traffic ahead of him to get to the hospital in time. Everything fell into place and little Amy was born in the late hours of that evening. The following morning Ashok's parents came to see the baby. They were horrified. Amy had light-colored, blond hair and she looked very white with pale blue eyes. Nobody would have believed that Amy had an Indian father. She was the spitting image of Jenifer.

Ashok's mother whispered to her husband something about the baby being a witch and Ashok's father refused to believe that Amy was Ashok's child, so they resorted once again to stone-faced stares and a cold-hearted attitude towards Jenifer. Ashok's mother cursed the day she agreed to send her baby to America and she was vocal about it in the presence of Jenifer. When Jenifer brought Amy home she cried. She cried tears of joy for she held in her arms an extension of her own life, and at the same time, tears of sorrow, for Amy would never have the love of her grandparents.

Eleven

Jenifer poured her life into her baby and continued to work on Ashok to convince him to return to the States with her and Amy. Despite her best efforts, Ashok always found a way to change or avoid the subject. From sunrise to sundown, day after day, Jenifer wrapped her life around Amy.

Ashok's business had truly gone international and he began to travel to Southeast Asia and the Middle East. He was often gone for a week at a time. Jenifer did not mind his absence for she found a curious solace in the quiet of the house. Her life was now centered on Amy. She often wondered if she could find a way to return to the States with Amy and restart her life. She was once a successful lawyer and she remained confident that she could easily get back into her old business.

She found it hard to fix her mind on anything. She longed to forget herself altogether, to forget everything, and then to wake up and begin life anew. She often thought of contacting her previous employer to see if they would rehire her. But she was afraid because the answer could be negative. She somehow preferred not knowing for it gave her hope. But then as time passed it began to nag at her. She needed to be more assertive if she were going to take charge of her life. She had a responsibility to provide for Amy and offer her a better life than she'd had.

One day when Ashok was away she gathered the courage to call her old business partner and inquired how the firm was doing. "Oh, boy," her old partner cried, "where have you been hiding? The married life must suit you well since we haven't heard a word from you since you left us." Her partner was full of compliments for what she had done in the past for the firm and when she opened her heart and told him about her situation in India he responded, "I'm so sorry to hear that. But let me assure you that whenever you decide to return, there will always be a place for you in the firm." After she finished the telephone conversation she let out a silent cry. All was not lost.

That day a new chapter started in Jenifer's life. She made a promise to herself that she would stay in India until Amy's fifth birthday, when she would be ready to start school. She did not want Amy to leave India too early for she did not want her one day to resent Jenifer for not giving her a chance to get to know her father and grandparents.

From that day on Jenifer's world changed and the ever-present gloom began to evaporate from her heart like the morning sun dissolves the mist. She found new energy and felt that she had better control over her life. Her mood was upbeat as she now had direction and was determined to build a new life for herself and her baby with or without Ashok. Only occasionally would she chastise herself for earlier giving into the expectations in Ashok's world. It was now up to Ashok to live with his young and growing family or die with his aging parents. She no longer felt a responsibility towards him. Love does not mean the submission of one's will; it is the liberation of one's heart. Contrary to popular belief, its object is not to give and take, but rather to let and let live. That is what Jenifer now believed, and she felt the better for it.

Although Jenifer remained hopeful that Amy would not lose her father, the optimism of moving back to States made her live with Ashok with a strange, debilitating reluctance. As Jenifer had almost stopped bringing up the subject of moving back to the States, it seemed that Ashok began to operate in a false sense of security, thinking that with the arrival of baby Amy, Jenifer had finally settled down and accepted family life in India. His mother had told him that she would. To show his appreciation, whenever he was not away on business he would take Amy out in her pram for walks, and often played with her. Jenifer wondered if Amy would grow on Ashok to the point that he might consider moving with them to the US. She would like to have Amy grow up with her father around.

As Ashok continued to move upward in expanding the family business, his father bestowed increased responsibilities on him. Ashok was made an equal partner in his father's business. As a part of his increased responsibilities, Ashok looked after product development and international business and often was away, anywhere from an overnight trip to a week at a time. His father devoted all his time to the day-to-day operation of the firm, allowing free time for Ashok to travel on business. There were never any financial issues between the father and the son and Ashok often commented on that to Jenifer, saying that he was lucky to have his father as his mentor and business partner.

She had her reasons to love, be responsible and loyal to him and he had his to follow tradition, be obsequious and place his relationship with his parents above her needs. They were doomed by their curiously twisted relationship, but neither wanted to face the eventuality of those dictates. So they gave each other space. Under the same roof, they became invisible to each other. As they drifted apart silence became prevalent in their diminishing relationship. It was an awkward silence that often made her want to scream. But she was incapable of any such outburst. Her life had a curious darkness as if living in a perpetual shadow of ominous times. But it was not always like this, she often reminded herself.

Jenifer was never driven by money, but motivated by quality of life based on values that promoted happiness. And that meant relationships. She was now in a blissful heaven of her own making, especially when Ashok was away on business and after Amy had gone to sleep. She would sit by the window overlooking the garden with a glass of Shiraz wine and listen to the talk in her head about the wonderful life that lay ahead for her and Amy in the US.

Her all-time favorite singer was Carole King and she loved her album, 'Tapestry,' that she had downloaded on her iPhone. In that album her favorite song was, 'You've Got a Friend.' She would play that song over and over again while sipping on her wine. *'When you're down and troubled and you need a helping hand and nothing, whoa, nothing is going right.'* An image of Amy would drift behind her closed eyelids, as the song would continue to drift on the air. *'Close your eyes and think of me and soon I will be there, to brighten up even your darkest nights.'*

She would pretend that the song was about her and then a smile would play over her lips. Periodically she would get up and check on Amy and give her gentle kisses on her cheek and whisper, "You and I, we're made for each other. I'll never abandon you, my precious. You're my life now."

Jenifer of course never expected Amy to respond. There was no need for words for they spoke the language of hearts. Sometimes she felt that her love for Amy was an illusion. She would then withdraw into her reveries for salvation. She would romanticize that one day her biological father would appear and save her. Worst were the days when her panic-love, her needs for a mother's salvation and a father's love, were recognized as all an illusion. What was left then? The grey shadows of despair and loneliness? Jenifer hated those moments.

She enjoyed watching Amy grow up, but she also began to long for her new career that awaited her in California. Jenifer never brought up her plans for discussion with Ashok or any of their friends.

Fate had other plans for her and little Amy. One day just before Amy's fifth birthday, she was taken from Jenifer. Amy was kidnapped. Jenifer's world came crushing down. Her life became curiously vacant, sad again. She realized how quickly she descended into a pervasive sadness, the intensity of which she had never before encountered. Ashok, timid and hollow, would trudge stumbling and reeling beside her, which she found ludicrous. He was a different man in India compared to what she saw in him back in California. He was a man who would never falter, never give in to weakness. Now he looked crushed. She wished her real father were there to take control and guide her. She was desperately lonely.

Book III

A month before Amy's kidnapping

Dubai, United Arab Emirates

September 2012

Sinner's Symphony

Twelve

Ali Khan was travelling first class on the Emirates Airline. As the plane made its final approach to the glitzy Dubai International Airport, it flew low over the glittering, sprawling city spread out on the both sides of the Dubai Creek. It was the morning rush hour and the Dubai highways were packed with thousands of cars moving at a slow pace like a slithering snake. This was Ali's first visit to Dubai City, the jewel of Arabia. He had heard so much about its wealth and was excited to experience some of its luxury.

It was a short flight, less than four hours, and the noon hour was approaching fast. Outside, the sky was an unblemished blue and the day was filled with the pleasant and warm sunshine that was synonymous with the Arabian Peninsula's climate. Ali said a cheery goodbye to the Ukrainian airhostess that had looked after the passengers in the first class cabin as he stepped off the plane and entered the swanky airport.

A pretty Filipina lady in a tightly wrapped bright red dress was waiting at the immigration desk of the 'Meet & Greet' service to receive him. She held a sign with his name on it. Ali approached her and she shook his hand and asked him to follow her. She speedily assisted him with visa formalities and brought him out to a chauffeur-driven, white Rolls Royce. Once he made himself comfortable in the back seat of the car, it glided towards the Burj Al Arab, reported to be the world's most luxurious hotel.

Standing on an artificial island that was located a thousand feet out in the ocean, the thousand-feet tall hotel was connected to the mainland by a curving bridge. The shape of the structure was designed to mimic the sail of a ship, and Burj Al Arab had earned a reputation as the world's only seven-star hotel. The building, an iconic statement for Dubai, was constructed for the same purpose as the Opera House for Sydney, the Eifel Tower for Paris and Big Ben for London.

The Rolls elegantly sashayed into the hotel's drive and came to a halt smoothly. A guest manager, dressed in an expensive-looking silk suit, received him and greeted him by his name. The manager signaled the bellboy to take care of Ali's luggage, and while smiling broadly, he requested that Ali follow him. The manager, bypassing the reception desk, accompanied Ali straight to his suite where, after offering him a cocktail, he helped him complete the check-in formalities. The manager returned Ali's credit card without taking its imprint and said, "This is the Royal Suite, about $20,000 a night, but your host has taken care of all your expenses. So please, enjoy, and no need to worry about any charges during your stay. Everything has been covered. Here is my card and please call me at any time if you need assistance. Your luggage will be here shortly."

Two minutes after the manager left Ali's luggage arrived. Ali tipped the bellboy generously. After he unpacked, he had a hot shower and changed into a light-colored silk suit with an open-collar black satin shirt. He was expected at a meeting in about an hour and he wanted to look his best. A few minutes later he was once again in the back of the Rolls Royce and driven to the private palace of Abdullah Al Salem, a highly influential and wealthy businessman who was well connected in the elite circle of Saudi aristocrats.

An expansive white palace with its own private white-sand beach, located on the Dubai Palm Island in the shimmering blue waters of the Persian Gulf, it looked like something straight out of a fairytale book. Ali was awestruck by its beauty. He wondered if one day he could afford such a place and live in this heavenly manner. He was sick and tired of the pollution of New Delhi. The Rolls entered through an automatic iron gate monitored by electronic surveillance, and slowed on the cobblestone circular driveway, finally coming to a complete stop at a driveway adorned by large white pillars with Wedgewood crown molding.

A uniformed guard smartly dressed in a crisp khaki uniform opened the car door, stepped back a pace and briskly saluted Ali. Ali stepped out and nodded at the guard as he entered the front door of the palace foyer. Here a French butler greeted him, offering the Arabic traditional cardamom tea accompanied by a single piece of Turkish delight on a silver platter, and said, *"Bonjour. S'il vous plaît, suivez-moi."*

Ali didn't quite comprehend his words but understood his intent and followed him into a large and lavishly decorated drawing room. After gesturing with his white-gloved hand to take a seat the butler disappeared. Ali put the delicious Turkish delight in his mouth and sipped on the hot cardamom tea. The taste was exquisite and he wetted his lips to feel the sheer pleasure of the sweetness of the drink.

A large and high-domed ceiling allowed filtered light through its highly decorated, stained-glass skylights.

Hanging from the center of the dome ceiling was a huge crystal chandelier that shimmered in the filtered and multicolored sunlight coming through the skylights. Gold-plated curtain rods held heavy, crushed velvet drapes that only partially covered large windows, through which simmering blue waters and white sand beaches appeared. Heavily cushioned, French Louis XV-style furniture carved in shallow relief with fanciful patterns of tortoiseshell and ivory inlaid on layers of veneer, accented by gold leaf-painted wood, filled the drawing room. Bronze mounts decorated this high-style furniture. It seemed as if the curved lines and asymmetry were the rule adopted by the interior designer of this palace as it was expressed in the elaborate ornamentation. Semiprecious rocks like amethyst and shells with foliage and flowers dominated the theme of the ornamental with blossoms, sprays and tendrils, reeds, and branches of palm and laurel.

Ali was surrounded by a lavish lifestyle and felt a curious sensation as if this was his destiny. He was meant to be in Dubai to witness this wealth and the extravagant lifestyle of Sheikhs as a sign for his own future. Could this be all his one day? he wondered. He took a deep breath and savored the moment by closing his eyes.

Thirteen

Ali gingerly put down his empty tea cup on an ornate table and sat on the edge of a chair that had bronze legs and large armrests covered in an expensive-looking fabric. Ali was used to a lavish life but such surroundings of immense wealth were way out of his league. He had heard stories from his friends of the enormous wealth of Dubai and its rich sheikhs, but this was his first experience of seeing it with his own eyes. He wondered if the Sheikh he was about to meet would like him.

He stood up, walked over to a large window and gazed outside. Moored to a private jetty he noticed a large yacht and a few men dressed in white busily tending to it. He wondered if he would ever get the chance to sail such a yacht. He smiled and chastised himself for being greedy and said silently, "One thing at a time, let us get the first business deal done."

He said a silent prayer and asked God to bless him with success on this trip. He wondered how happy his wife and two children would be if he could afford to live in a beautiful house on a beach in Dubai. He had high hopes of carving out a big piece of business in the Middle East, his first venture outside India. He went back to the chair and settled in, closing his eyes in another quiet prayer.

It seemed that his god was listening.

"*Assalamu alaykum,*" said a tall man entering the drawing room. He was dressed in snow-white, traditional

Arabic dress and holding a rosary in his left hand. He extended his right hand to greet Ali.

Ali, caught by surprise by his silent entrance, quickly got up and grabbed the hand warmly with both of his hands, shook it nervously and then responded, *"Wa alaikum Assalaam."* The Arab laughed and gestured towards a sofa, "Please, no formalities, have a seat."

"It is my honor to meet with you, sir," said Ali, bowing slightly as if curtseying to royalty, and then sat in the corner of a large sofa next to a highly ornate single-seat sofa chair where the Arab sat.

The butler reappeared and brought in a silver tray holding two crystal-cut glasses half filled with whiskies and two Cohiba Behike cigars; after offering them to the two men, he again disappeared.

After the Arab ceremoniously cut, licked and lit his cigar and took a large sip of his whisky, he said, "You're welcome." Looking at his diamond-studded, gold Rolex he continued, "You're built strong, like an army man. I like strong men for they possess power. I've invited you here because someone has recommended you as a potential business partner. In my business trust is everything. As a result I must tell you that you'll get one chance and if in any way I find you to be dishonest then you will never do business with me again, or, for that matter, anywhere in the Middle East. I will personally see to it. No offense but business is business, you understand?"

Ali felt a faint pain in the back of his neck. His hand involuntarily started to rub it. He always felt neck pain whenever there was a sense of threat or he faced a potentially difficult situation. Ali swallowed nervously, shoved the unlit cigar in his jacket pocket, and responded,

"Sheikh, you'll never have any complaints with me. I've built my business by myself and, thank God, today I've become one of the largest businesses in India. Nobody in India messes with me; I take care of myself. I do appreciate the opportunity that you have given me. I will not disappoint you."

Abdullah while listening rotated his large diamond ring around his finger and then with a casual gesture of his hand stopped Ali from saying anything further, as he said, "Well then, I suppose we have nothing to worry about. Now what we've to discuss is highly confidential. I know all about your business and understand that you run one of the most sophisticated and well-protected businesses of young girls in India. That is good. Men here like girls young, really young." He was referring to one of the fastest growing prostitution businesses owned and operated by Ali that was based on children and he had established it in the heart of the Indian capitol by gaining favor and support from Indian politicians and the local police force.

"With God's blessing we've grown it internationally," said Ali in a humble voice.

"That is why I've asked you to come here and see me," said Abdullah, leaning back into his deep-cushioned sofa. "As long as you understand that this is my territory and I want you to be my supplier. I'll give you a fair cut but you will not support any of my competition or try to come in on your own. Is that understood?"

Ali simply nodded his consent. After a pause he said, "My business is miniscule compared to your empire, Sheikh Salem. I'll do everything you ask and request that you help me grow not just here but also in India. I am ready to support all your businesses."

The Arab puffed on his cigar for a moment and after breathing in the deep aroma of his whisky, closed his eyes and took another sip. After an ephemeral silence he said, "Listen, I'm going to give you one chance to show what you can do for me and if it pleases my partners, then we will do business on a scale that you never could even dream of having."

"Anything you say, Sheikh," said Ali, nodding his head in the affirmative.

"During the religious months it is the duty of our people to give alms to the poor. It is our belief that God's blessings are directly proportional to the extent of alms people give during the religious month so they give generously. I need a couple of hundred children but nothing more than ten years old. Also, I don't want dirty older kids off your filthy streets in India. They've got to look cute so they better be from good families. One more thing: These children cannot be perfect; you know what I mean? Perhaps a leg missing or an arm missing, you get my meaning? It is good for business. The generosity of people heightens with the increased misery of the child. You must get this right because this means money."

Suddenly Ali had a flashback of his childhood when he had seen such kids around his locality. As a boy he had always wondered how so many kids had lost their limbs. Growing up he had no inkling that one day not only would he find the answer to his query but he would be a big part of the answer.

Fourteen

A stream of swirling blue smoke rose towards the ceiling as the Sheikh puffed on his cigar. He studied Ali, who seemed lost in thought. The Sheikh asked, "Is that too much for you? Just let me know what you can and cannot do."

"I think I can manage that," said Ali, appearing a little startled, as he started to scratch his chin with his index finger. It appeared that the wheels in his head had begun to turn.

"Now if you think you can manage this satisfactorily then I would also offer you another business. I need kidneys and corneas so find a clinic and agreeable surgeon in India who could assist us in getting those items. These organs have to be from healthy and living people, not from dead people. A very lucrative business indeed, you'll find. But I again warn you that all organs must come from living people. Our beliefs do not permit the use of organs from the dead."

"This would be a new line of business but I'm sure I could manage it. My specialty as you may know is supplying beautiful girls—"

"Yes, yes," interrupted Abdullah, taking a sip of his whisky. "I was coming to that. My business is built on not just beautiful but young girls, nothing above the age of fourteen. Exactly how many girls, I'll tell you after I talk with my partners. I've many partners and many operations in several cities all over the Middle East."

"Thank you, sir," he said, excited. "I can't wait to get started."

"Oh, there is something else, but perhaps it is not for you...."

Abdullah let his thought linger for a while, which made Ali anxious and he interjected, "Sir, just let me know what it is you need and I'll try my best."

"Well, my cousin is married to an American lady and they have a little girl that needs a cornea transplant. But we need the corneas of an American girl because my cousin believes that otherwise the transplant would not work well. You wouldn't be able to find the corneas of an American girl in India, would you?"

"Give me a few days and let me see what I can do," said Ali eagerly, as if nothing was impossible for him. "There are many American families in New Delhi."

"Okay, you let me know," concluded Abdullah. "Now drink your whiskey and you can take the return flight home tomorrow. Enjoy yourself tonight; I've arranged a little gift for you back at your hotel room. Goodbye and good luck to you, Mr. Khan. God willing, we will build this business bigger than ever."

Ali sprang to his feet and shook hands spiritedly. "Thank you for taking care of my flight and hotel, I appreciate that. I will work very hard to make our business successful." They said goodbye and Ali left the palace to enjoy a client-paid evening at the Burj Arab Hotel. On his way to the hotel he felt as if he was levitating. Every molecule in his body was singing with joy. When he arrived back at the hotel two beautiful young Russian girls were waiting for him. He loved the life of luxury and dreamed of building his empire. He was on his way. He said a silent prayer and thanked God for his kindness.

To take chances is to tempt fate. Ali believed in a secure business even if it meant less profits. Paying off the police and politicians was a part of the cost of doing business. The police had been good to him, because for a little extra payment, he could use their special services to eliminate his competition—permanently. For the seemingly unmotivated murders, they'd throw some innocent beggar in prison, and he had a swift and simple solution to get rid of the otherwise tough competition.

Upon his return from Dubai, Ali was charged with new vigor, ready to embark upon the launch of these new and bigger businesses. Abducting children for prostitution was a business he could grow at a manageable pace for there was no time pressure. But now to become a contract supplier for hundreds of children and arrange for them to be maimed, and have some of their organs removed, presented a challenge. And there was no time to waste. He was pondering this as he sat in his office at the Gandhi Memorial Center, the headquarters of his nationwide operation, known all over New Delhi as simply GMC.

GMC was an old compound located on the edge of the city and surrounded by a high, whitewashed perimeter wall. Embedded on the top of the wall were broken pieces of sharp glass to deter any intruder. The wall surrounded the entire compound and a single-entrance, guarded gate was the only entry and exit point. It was an eight-foot high, heavy wooden gate with an inbuilt smaller gate through which only one person at a time could enter or exit. The larger gate was open only when cars went in and out of the compound; otherwise, the small gate was used for day-to-day purposes. A small security hut sat just outside the gates and sentries were posted on an eight-hour shift basis to provide a 'round the clock watch.

Inside the compound was an administration office building and only through this office could one gain entry to the inside structure with several rooms and a large court-yard. Ali had acquired this compound almost ten years ago. It used to be a private school that, after selling the compound, had moved to a larger facility. After Ali acquired the facility he refurbished it and in a few years managed to build a decent-size business. He had invited the Minister of Trade to inaugurate his facility and the minister had named it the Gandhi Memorial Centre. In the community the GMC was known as a facility that was used as a shelter for children that had run away from home and other, similarly destitute children.

With strong political support in the right places and protection bought from the police, Ali expanded his business and under the non-profit GMC front, operated one of the largest and most lucrative prostitution businesses in the nation, and it was about to get bigger. He thought of calling his associate Javed.

Fifteen

Ali looked at his watch and then dialed a number on his cell phone. After two rings when the phone connected he said, "Javed, I'm back in the office. We need to talk. I've an urgent matter for you. Could I see you here in my office in half an hour?"

Ali listened to the response and clicked off his phone. He had thirty minutes to catch up with his emails. Instead he poured himself a cup of coffee and for some curious reason thought of his childhood, a memory he often preferred to suppress. Growing up in a large family of six and living in a two-bedroom apartment, life was harsh. His father was severely injured in the Indo-Pakistani War of 1971, and after being discharged from the army due to his injuries, he could not find work. The Indian army and the government simply wrote him off. He worked as a baker but could not earn enough to look after the family. So he borrowed money from the loan sharks. Over the years the loans mounted up and when Ali's father could not make the payments, the loan sharks would come to the apartment and humiliate Ali's father by beating him in front of his family. One fateful day Ali's father committed suicide.

Being the eldest, Ali was charged with the responsibility of paying his father's debt. He was ten years old and worked as a shoeshine boy on the street. His youngest brother caught and died of pneumonia, and one night his two sisters were kidnapped. No one knew what happened to them; the police did not even register a case. His mother was heartbroken and took the same way out as his father did. Ali was alone now and often beaten by the loan sharks. Ali lived several years on the periphery of life in this miserable existence. He wished and prayed for death every night he went to bed. Then one day the same man who used to beat him up made him an offer. He asked Ali to burgle homes and that way whatever he stole would go towards paying his father's loan. Ali had no choice but to accept. The man would choose the homes and act as the lookout, while Ali, being small and able, would easily slip in and out of the window bars.

After few months Ali was trained to become a courier for transporting drugs within the city. But one rainy day Ali's luck ran out when a policeman arrested him, but instead of taking him to prison, he took him to a place where there were many beautiful young girls. The policeman told him that he would not arrest him on drug charges provided that he worked at the brothel by bringing in new business. Drug addicts liked girls and Ali's job was to bring those clients to the brothel.

Ali over the years learned everything about running and managing a brothel. He liked this business but hated working for others. He wanted to break out on his own. He had learned that the policeman who had arrested him all those years ago was paid by the brothel owners to provide protection. One day Ali, who was growing up as a tall, strong man, offered a deal to the policeman, who was now a senior officer. "Sir," he said politely, "what these guys pay you is nothing to what you can earn if you and I enter into a partnership. I need your help to put these guys away and you need me to make you rich."

The police officer understood the offer and agreed to the terms. One night an incident was reported to the police that an unknown gang had gunned down a few men suspected of running a brothel and operating a drug business. Gang wars were common in the drug and prostitution business and no arrests were made, and after a few days the case was forgotten. Ali took over the operation and was now the owner of the brothel, with a silent partner. With friends in the right places Ali rose in power as a new boss and he was a natural, taking the operation to new heights. With time the competition was removed and Ali emerged as the undisputed boss of the city, running the largest prostitution trade.

But Ali was a progressive man and wanted to give his business a new image. He bought an old school building, which he used as a holding pen for the fresh recruits and as his headquarters for managing his nationwide dealings in prostitution. This place was GMC.

There was a knock at the door and Javed stood there with a smile on his face. Addressing Ali as an elder brother, in respect he said, "*Salaam* Ali *Bhai*."

"*Salaam* Javed. Come in, come in," said Ali, cheerfully extending his large hand.

Javed was about five years older than Ali and an old friend who over the years had helped Ali build his empire. Javed came from a rough upbringing, evident in a deep scar he carried on his right cheek, perhaps a knife wound that left the nasty scar. But Javed was proud of his scar for he received it in a gang fight defending Ali, and from then on Ali was grateful to Javed and financially looked after him by cutting him in on all his dealings. His face was further disfigured by pock marks caused by the smallpox he contracted when a little boy.

"How was your trip to Dubai? You look refreshed, did you meet the Sheikh?" Javed was always happy to see Ali and shook his hand lovingly.

"Everything went well," responded Ali and then in a low voice said, "We've a huge opportunity being offered to us. From now on you'll have to procure a large number of girls and boys. But I think the Sheikh wants to test us first. He has demanded the corneas of a young healthy girl, a white American. We don't have much time; do you think you could find me a young American girl in New Delhi?"

"Leave it to me, Ali *Bhai*," assured Javed in a relaxed and casual tone. "I'll start on it immediately. But tell me all about your visit to Dubai."

They talked for an hour and spent quite a bit of time on strategizing how to procure a qualified surgeon who would be willing to remove the corneas and kidneys from healthy young children. "This could double our profits," said Javed excitedly, "our customers won't know that children have lost their kidneys so we could make money on selling their kidneys as well as by using them as prostitutes. But what would we do with blind children?"

"Well, I've a solution for that," answered Ali, smiling. "We could use them as invalid beggars for the religious month in Saudi Arabia. Problem solved. Sheikh wants hundreds of young maimed children for begging." Ali spoke in a businesslike manner.

After reflecting on what Ali said for a moment, Javed responded, "I like the way you think, but all this business talk is making me hungry. Why don't we go out for lunch?"

Together they left to continue their discussion over a shared meal.

Book IV

Seven days after Amy's kidnapping

New Delhi, India

October 2012

The Danger Zone

Sixteen

Sophie escaped Nairobi where a knife placed at her neck by a serial killer had almost decapitated her. She survived the ordeal, and felt certain that, after having been baptized by fire, she'd find the case in India to be smooth sailing.

Matt Slater, being half Indian, gave considerable background information on India to Sophie and advised her to watch her step. He had explained that the gift given by the British Raj to India was bureaucracy. The world's largest democracy was infested with the deep-rooted bureaucracy that had led to widespread corruption. In India, to get your foot in the door meant that you must put your hand in your pocket. Offering a little incentive, otherwise known as bribery, was a way of life. But there was humor to be found in all this. Dark humor that would seldom make one laugh, but might at times enrage one enough to kill.

When Sophie had asked him, based on his several years of collective experience, what would be the best word of advice on how to operate there, he, without hesitation, said, "If you're left with no options then try changing the state of play."

Sophie understood what he meant and told him she appreciated the wisdom when he came to the Nairobi airport to see her off and wish her luck.

Upon arrival at the Indira Gandhi International Airport, as she stepped into the arrival hall, she looked for the car from the U.S. Embassy that would pick her up. In a packed crowd, with hardly any breathing space, she wondered how she would find her host. Men and women speaking in a variety of languages in weird accents scurried around like ants. She came out of the terminal and the acrid air hit her full in her face. Before she knew it an onslaught of taxi drivers surrounded her, shouting and jostling for a fare. Amongst them she saw her name placard that read Dr. Kramer held up high by a tall Sikh and his eyes were anxiously searching through the arriving passengers to find his guest.

She waved to him and he, with a broad grin on his face, forced his way through the crowd, poking a few with the placard to make way, and as he approached closer he exclaimed, "You're a woman?"

"Dr. Sophie Kramer," she said, smiling, "and yes, I'm a woman."

With a sheepish look, at once awkward and embarrassed, he quickly grabbed her suitcase then started leading the way to the car parked a little farther down by the roadside. The Sikh was smartly dressed in a white Nehru jacket suit with shiny brass buttons and a matching, blinding-white turban. His beard was waxed and combed and neatly encased in a black netting that was mercilessly stretched and tucked away at the sides under his tightly wound turban, giving him a facelift with stretched, slanting eyes. His moustache, waxed and curled up, gave him an aura of self-importance.

"*Mem Sahib Ji*," he said, politely peering at her through the rearview mirror as he deftly maneuvered, with the constant use of his horn, the car through the crowded streets of the city, where people, animals and all modes of conventional and not-so-conventional transportation were mingling in a mad cacophony. She raised her eyebrows, encouraging him to continue. *"Mem Sahib Ji* is very white. Some hot curry would bring color to your skin. Curries are good, world famous and very healthy. You like curries, *Mem Sahib Ji?"*

She remembered Matt saying that the directness of Indians was something she would have to get used to, for they don't beat about the curry bushes. The words come out of their mouths before even their brains can conceive them. But, she was told, they mean no disrespect, they are simply inquisitive by nature. So she smiled and nodded and said, "Yeah, I like curries."

Upon arrival at the embassy, Sophie was asked to wait a few minutes as the ambassador was on the phone. It was considered rather unusual protocol for the ambassador to personally meet with a FBI agent, but Andrew had mentioned to Sophie that the ambassador had requested to meet with her immediately upon her arrival and before she spoke with anyone else.

Andrew had briefed Sophie that Ian Grunfeld assumed the position of ambassador about three years ago and was almost at the end of his term in India. He was well aware of the importance of Indo-American relationships, in particular those related to trade and commerce as well as military strategic importance, for he had contributed significantly to their development. Over some time now India had proven to be a great ally to the US in order for it to maintain a strong position in the Asian subcontinent. Now at the end of his term, he wanted to leave India with a clean slate and have Amy's case resolved before his departure, or so he had told Andrew.

A few minutes later Sophie was asked to join the ambassador in his office. As she entered, she saw a muscled and rather tall man in his mid to late fifties with hair graying around the temples, and a square face with a strong chin. His light-colored eyes showed no depth of compassion; to the contrary, they had a continual glint of sorrow.

In a gravely and business-like tone, he greeted Sophie, asking, "You are Dr. Kramer, the Special Agent?"

"Yes," said Sophie, with a faint smile on her face, "and I am a woman, I know."

Seventeen

The ambassador made some incomprehensible gruff growl that emerged deep from his throat and his face reflected utter disappointment. Without further conversation, he instead asked his secretary on intercom to connect him with Andrew Hunt. A minute later Andrew was on line.

The ambassador put him on the speakerphone. "Deputy Director," said ambassador Grunfeld, "I've agent Kramer here, isn't she a little young for blood and gore? India can be a very nasty place and no one plays by the rules here."

Sophie heard laughter on the speaker as Andrew responded, "I don't want to sound corny but here her colleagues call her the killer." Using a dramatic tone, Andrew continued, "She's the best instinctive killer when it comes to eliminating bad elements. You're lucky to have her."

"You'd better be sure about that," said Ian in a reluctant tone, "the life of a little American girl is at stake here."

"I'm well aware of that," said Andrew, in an unwavering voice. "And for that reason I've sent Special Agent Kramer. She is one of our most outstanding agents."

The ambassador paused for a moment and then signed off with Andrew. Sophie, sitting with her legs crossed and leaning to one side in her chair, appeared undisturbed by the discussion and said, "Shall we start? The issue is pressing and time-sensitive, but then you know that."

The ambassador stood up and walked around his desk to stand a couple of feet from where Sophie was sitting and, leaning against his desk with arms folded, he said, "Agent Kramer, I'll be honest with you, I'd have preferred male agents from the FBI. India is not a place for women agents. Anyway, since we are already a week late in our investigation, I will do whatever I can to help expedite your work here. Let me know personally what we can do to assist you. You will find that it is not easy to enlist support from the local law enforcement agencies. Ask for my help and trust me, I'll bring in political pressure. The authorities here respect and respond to political pressure. God damn it, this country owes us a lot."

"Thank you, ambassador," Sophie responded in an equally businesslike manner. "I know how to handle myself in politically sensitive countries. It'd be best if you let me handle the case from now on and if required, I'll ask for help. Political pressure is not conducive to a kidnapping case as such tactics give unnecessary attention to the kidnappers and they may increase their demands."

"But I want results and I want them fast," countered the ambassador. "I've built the Indo-American relationship to a level that my predecessors failed to achieve. I'm not going to let crime against Americans in this country, great or small, go unpunished, especially when I am coming to the end of my term here." There was a smile on his lips, and a hint of irritable impatience was apparent in that smile.

Sophie stared intently at him, uncertain of his intent. Isn't he a little overbearing? she thought. "With all due respect, Ambassador," she said calmly, "this case is not about you. It is the little girl I'm more concerned about, more so than the Indo-American relationship or your career. If you want results, then let's not confuse the priorities." Sophie yawned and added, "I'm a little tired and would like to resume our talk at a later time, is that okay with you?"

"Yes, yes," the ambassador said hurriedly, "there aren't many suitable independent accommodations in the city so we have booked you at the Sheraton Hotel. We've given you an office here at the embassy that is fully furnished with computer and Internet and you'll have a security pass to easily go in and out of the facility. And, oh yes, if you like the driver that picked you up at the airport, you may keep him for the duration of your assignment here. He is not embassy staff but an independent contractor. I thought that may suit you better, considering the nature of your work. Anything else, just ask me. You'll keep me apprised?"

"Thank you." Sophie stood up, shook his hand firmly, and responded, "Yes, I'll ask for help if I need it, but through proper protocol. You'll have to clear everything through the Deputy Director; obviously, you know him."

As Sophie readied to leave, she put an index figure up as she was struck by a sudden thought. "By the way, what is the mystery behind your disappearance from the office two days prior to Amy's disappearance?"

"That has nothing to do with the case," he answered in a gruff voice, "it was a private matter and shouldn't concern you."

Behind the Ambassador's abrupt reply she felt the concentration of almost cold anger and an unchanging will. In Ian's stern face she could see the tightening of his jaw, as if he was bottling up an explosive undercurrent of emotion. She decided to explore this reaction further. "It's just that I don't want any surprises later. The two incidents seem to be close in timing and nothing has been explained to me as to why you were absent from duty." Sophie, studying him, saw a shadow pass across his face.

"Why don't you follow protocol," his voice was laced with sarcasm, "and ask your superiors? Just stay focused on the case and help us find the missing girl unharmed." He picked up his phone, indicating the meeting was over.

She walked out of the office and decided to spend part of her time here doing whatever was necessary to get to the bottom of this double mystery. Right now she wanted a hot shower.

Eighteen

The hotel had many vacancies and she chose to be on the top floor, a corner suite on the executive floor. After unpacking and taking a long, hot shower, she ordered coffee. Once the waiter left, she locked her door and pulled out the case file. After studying it, she picked up the desktop phone and then, after a momentary hesitation, replaced the receiver. She pulled out her cell phone and dialed.

She got a response on the first ring. "Hello." It was a trembling female voice.

"To whom am I speaking?" Sophie's voice was cold and leveled. This was a business call with no room for getting sentimental.

"Jenifer Kumar, who is this?" Her voice steadied.

"You don't know me; I'm Dr. Sophie Kramer and I would like to come see you this evening."

Jenifer fell silent. She'd been warned by the police to expect a lot of crank calls from fraudulent people who would claim to know something about Amy's disappearance to collect money.

"Are you still there?" asked Sophie.

"You've an American accent," said Jenifer, and after a momentary pause, asked, "Are you calling from a hospital, Dr. Kramer? Do you have any news about my Amy?"

"I'm not calling from a hospital and yes, I'm an American. I'll tell you the rest when we meet. Don't worry, and don't invite the family and in-laws to this meeting. Just you and your husband, you understand? I'll find your house and see you there at seven this evening."

Sophie clicked off and looked at her watch. It was two in the afternoon. She had a few hours and decided to go over the information Andrew gave her on the case. Her cell phone rang; she looked at the caller name and answered. "You still in Nairobi?"

"No, back in Washington. Just thought to give you a call to thank you for your help in Nairobi. Sorry I had to put you through such a rough ordeal but you've become quite a force to reckon with, Agent Kramer."

"Well, thank you, Agent Slater," she said in a theatrical voice and then, resuming her natural voice, added, "I've just arrived in New Delhi so wish me luck."

"Good luck and stay in touch." Hearing from Matt Slater reminded her of the adventure in Nairobi and she wondered if the Indian case would prove just as dangerous. A thrill went through her and a smile played on her lips. They continued with small talk and then Sophie said goodbye and returned her attention to the case file.

At six-thirty she came down and asked the concierge to call Sher Singh and ask him to bring her car around. Within minutes her Indian-made Ambassador car was outside the lobby.

"Good evening, *Mem Sahib ji*. Where would you be wanting to go this evening?" Sher Singh always stood erect as a soldier waiting for instructions.

Sophie gave him the house address of Jenifer and slid into the back seat. She started to go over the case details in her head. She wondered why someone would kidnap the five-year-old Amy, a child of a wealthy family, and then make no ransom demand. Could it be that the kidnappers were taking their time to let things cool down before announcing their intent? In the beginning of such a case there is always a tremendous amount of attention paid to the individuals involved by both the media and the police. As the case gets older, it isn't news anymore. Maybe the kidnappers were wary of the media. Sophie was in her own world of analysis and evaluation as her car crawled through the thickly populated streets of New Delhi. She leaned back in her seat and allowed her thoughts to race through her head.

On the other hand, if the motive was not money and the kidnapping had to do with an act of revenge, then what is it exactly that the kidnappers wanted? she pondered. Could it be that the husband had pissed somebody off at work and the kidnapping was an act of revenge? Maybe they wanted to keep Amy alive to prolong the suffering of her parents and loved ones, in which case the kidnappers were taking a big chance, as they would remain vulnerable as long as Amy was alive.

What if Amy was already dead? That could explain why no one had bothered to contact the parents of the missing girl. Sophie considered that possibility for a moment and then hoped that would not be the case.

"*Mem Sahib ji*, we are at the correct address," Sher Singh said, with his head moving from side to side, as if quite satisfied with his success at finding the house. Sophie looked at the house through her window. It was a nice enough house, but it seemed to have gone through many restorations, like an old lady surviving only by her charm.

An evening haze had engulfed it like a disease slowly smothering the life of a forest. It stood suspended, calm and cold-hearted. Sophie wondered how an American lawyer, a career woman, could give up her California lifestyle to live here.

Nineteen

As soon as the car arrived at Ashok and Jenifer's home, the front door opened. They were expecting her.

Sher Singh stepped out of the car and opened the back door for Sophie. She stepped out and saw a young man hurriedly coming out of the house. Seeing the concern and anguish in his face, she assumed he must be the father of the missing girl.

"You must be Dr. Kramer? Do you have some news of Amy? Is she hurt? Where is Amy, is she in a hospital?"

Sophie was trained to think that every question has a latent intent. She could sense that behind the concern was a hidden irritation in his voice, as if annoyed by this intrusion by an unknown person. Sophie maintained control by saying, "You must be Ashok. Let's go inside where we can talk. Is your wife at home?"

"She is very upset," he said in a vexed voice and hurriedly added, "I'd much rather you tell me first what you know and why you're here." He stood in front of her as if purposely blocking her way. Sophie's expression changed from an amiable look to a hardened stare. "Turn around," she said in a cold tone and as Ashok flinched, she added, "lead the way. We'll talk inside the house."

He reluctantly stepped aside and simply stood there as if stunned by her stern rebuke. She made her way into the house and he followed her. Inside the drawing room, she found Jenifer, who looked at Sophie inquisitively.

Sophie started, "My name, as you know by now, is Dr. Sophie Kramer, and I'm a special FBI agent assigned to your case by Washington. Let's sit down because I'm sure we all have a lot of questions."

Silence fell over them as if the family was shocked and even perhaps disappointed. Nobody spoke for a few moments. Sophie suggested again, "Shall we all sit down?"

Jenifer gestured with her hand for Sophie to take a seat and as Sophie sat facing Jenifer, Ashok remained standing and said, "Why the FBI? Did the New Delhi police ask for your help? We've been advised by the police not to talk to anybody. How do we know you're FBI?"

Sophie pulled out her identification card and let him examine it. This time Jenifer spoke in a voice that betrayed her exhaustion, "We need help. I'm happy that the FBI has decided to step in. I know my stepfather had promised such help. The local police are very busy, as well as corrupt and useless. We get nothing out of them. It has been a week now and we've heard no word from the police. I'm happy you're here, Dr. Kramer." She looked at her husband and said dryly, "Sit down, Ashok." Sophie observed Jenifer and felt that there was something strange, a light in her eyes as though of intense feeling—perhaps high intelligence, but at the same time there was a gleam of something like anger and frustration.

Ashok, frowning, remained standing. He evidently was not pleased with the presence of Sophie and for some inexplicable reason seemed concerned about the involvement of the FBI.

Sophie looked at Ashok and then at Jenifer, and after a momentary pause said, "A week is too long not to take action and obviously we've no more time to waste—"

"And who wasted this time?" Ashok interrupted, his voice mirroring his contorted face, expressing his anger. "Why did it take a week for the FBI to get involved? I'm not sure if we should be talking to you at all. My father is influential and knows senior police officers and I'll need his advice first before we talk with you. Leave us your card and we'll contact you," he said to Sophie, with a gaze something like a child's, but belligerent.

Sophie put both hands on her knees and stood up. Letting out an exasperated sigh, in a deliberate fashion, she approached Ashok. Standing just a foot away from his face, she looked straight into his eyes. When she spoke, her intent was clear. "You seem to be more concerned about the FBI's involvement than the welfare of your daughter. In most mixed marriages like yours, and especially when an American wife is relocated to her husband's country of origin and her child goes missing, it's often the case that the husband is the culprit." Sophie turned her back to him and looked at Jenifer.

Sophie knew that her aggressive move would result in a retaliatory reaction from him but before he could respond she turned back to face him and said, "And you know why? Because their marriage is not working out exactly as they had expected and he doesn't want his wife to take his child away from him and back to America. Is this the case here? Hmm? Is that what you would like me to believe? Now if you like, we can all sit down and focus on the details of what really happened to Amy, or would you prefer that I focus my investigation on you first? Your call."

Sophie walked back and sat, once again facing Jenifer. Ashok mumbled something under his breath and stood shaking with suppressed anger. Jenifer with annoyed eyes looked at him and in a raised voice said, "Why don't you give Dr. Kramer a chance to explain how the FBI can help us? Stop being so difficult. Come and sit down."

He walked grudgingly and perched on a chair a little distance away from both of them. Sophie began, "I need to hear everything you know. But before we begin, let me explain how I work. I believe in establishing first why someone would kidnap a little girl and then will explore who that could be. It is all about establishing the motive first. I'll explore everything that is obvious and perhaps not so obvious to the case, and I'd like to go over every detail regardless of its relevance to the case. I'll be asking a lot of questions, tough questions, but remember, they are to jog your memories, to determine if you have overlooked something. Everyone's objective here is to find Amy and find her fast. Do I make myself clear?"

Sophie paused for a second and found that both were listening with intense concentration and her question went unanswered. She continued, "There is something else. In cases where there is no obvious motive like this one, where no ransom demand has been made for a week, I'd like to go over all the possibilities and with time or evolving evidence, I'll focus on likely scenarios. I believe in the process of elimination to focus on the real possibilities. What I'm trying to say is that once I start with any one possibility, it does not mean that I have found the answer or that it will be the most likely scenario. It simply means that I am considering a possibility, to either accept it or reject it. Are there any questions?"

This time the face that was filled with a million questions was that of Jenifer.

Twenty

Jenifer looked at Sophie as if seeing the first ray of sunshine entering the room through a pane of a closed window.

"Will you find her?" she blurted out. "What you're saying sounds like it would take time and we don't have time. Will this lead you to her?" She asked this in an anxious voice. It seemed that she saw a glimmer of hope in the FBI's involvement and liked the idea of a woman agent's involvement.

Sophie realized that her question was more of an appeal than an inquiry.

"Keep your hopes up and I'll do what it takes to find Amy. We'll find her." Sophie had spoken with a calm assurance. She did not know how else to console a mother whose only child, her little daughter, had disappeared in a foreign country without a clue.

Sophie let the silence follow in order for her assurances take effect and then said, "Before we talk further, I'll have to begin at the crime scene."

"Okay," said Jenifer. She asked Ashok, "Why don't you take Dr. Kramer over to Mrs. Chawla's?"

Before Ashok could respond Sophie replied, "No, that won't be necessary. I'll find my own way. I'll do this on my own and ask for help when I need it. Don't worry, you'll hear from me very soon."

Both parents looked out the drawing room's window as Sophie stepped out in the street. She told Sher Singh to wait for her where he was parked.

Sophie walked over to Mrs. Chawla's house and counted the number of houses between Mrs. Chawla's and Ashok and Jenifer's. There were eighteen houses altogether on both sides of the street, and fortunately, no tall apartment buildings. She let out a sigh of relief for she did not want to interview hundreds of people, which would have been the case if there were several high-rise apartments. Walking down the cobblestone street she noticed that only four houses down from the Ashok's house was an old iron gate that led to a small park.

She took a detour and entered the park. In one corner were a set of double swings, a see-saw and a small sand pit. The rest of the park was a grass-covered lot, visible from the road. She closed the iron gate behind her as she stepped back into the street and continued on to Mrs. Chawla's house, wondering if someone had happened see Amy on that dreadful evening of her disappearance.

She arrived at Mrs. Chawla's, rang the bell and waited for an answer. A few moments passed and there was no response. She rang the bell again. This time she heard stirring inside the house and a few moments later an old Indian lady wearing thick glasses and a printed cotton dress appeared. "Oh, I've never seen you here before, how can I help you, dear?" she asked.

Sophie smiled and answered, "I'm an FBI special agent, a special kind of police from America." Sophie wasn't sure if the older lady knew who the FBI was so had explained it in simple terms. "Oh, I see, dear," she responded contemplatively, "you're like a lady James Bond then? I've seen James Bond, you know."

Sophie pursed her lips in amusement—she had never been called Lady James Bond. The FBI would be the equivalent of Scotland Yard, rather than the Secret Intelligence Service, otherwise known as MI6, but she decided not to confuse the elderly woman and ignored her rather amusing deduction. "I'm working on the disappearance of Amy. You know Amy, don't you? Would you mind if I came in to ask you a few questions? I'd rather not talk out here in the street."

She invited Sophie in and they sat in the front room where she taught piano. It was a small room with two windows on either side of the front door and these windows overlooked the street. In a corner was an old but well-cared-for piano. Its wood was highly polished and it was partially covered with a white lace, cotton tablecloth. A tarnished silver vase with a few bright-colored, plastic roses sitting on the piano gave color to the place.

She explained to Sophie, "Well, the police have been here once and asked me about Amy, about the evening she mysteriously disappeared." She paused as if recollecting her thoughts and continued, "I'll tell you what I told those nice policemen, that Amy had finished her lesson just a few minutes before six and then like she always did, she sat out on the steps and played with my cat while waiting for either Jenifer or Ashok to come and pick her up."

"Mrs. Chawla, how long would she have to wait normally before one of her parents would turn up? Could you see her sitting outside from your window? Did she say goodbye to you before she left? I'm sorry to ask you so many questions but what exactly do you remember of that evening? It is important because you were the last person to have seen her."

"Oh, dear," she sighed, "you seem to have a lot more questions than the local policemen did. Would you like a cup of tea, dear? It is Darjeeling. I think better when I've had my tea." Mrs. Chawla smiled and after Sophie nodded, she with some effort got up from her chair to make tea.

There was no urgency in her demeanor as if she had all the time in the world. She made a full pot of tea and placed it and two cups and saucers on a silver tray. From a drawer she took out a colorful cat-shaped teacozy that she put on the teapot and then she extracted five digestive biscuits from an old tin box that had a fading picture of the Taj Mahal printed on it. She stared at the biscuits for a moment and then, pointing her index finger, counted them and then put one biscuit back in the tin box. She set the tray on a side table by her chair and said, "It is better when you allow it to steep for a while. Now what was it that you wanted to know, dear?"

Sophie smiled and repeated her questions. "Yes. Well, whenever Ashok or Jenifer came to pick Amy up they would always knock on my window and wave good-bye before they would leave. That way I wouldn't worry about Amy being out there for too long on her own. If I am not giving a piano lesson to another child then sometimes Jenifer would come in and we would have tea. Poor Amy, I hope you find her," she concluded with a shadow of sadness passing over her face. She had that grandmotherly kindness on her face that showed concern.

Twenty-One

Sophie had an amazing memory and could absorb and recall every detail of her conversation without taking any notes. She leaned forward, looking closely at Mrs. Chawla's face. "What happened on the evening Amy disappeared?" Sophie quizzed. Mrs. Chawla paused for a minute as if making sure that she remembered correctly.

"Nothing unusual, really," she said contemplatively. "Ashok was a few minutes late, maybe five, maybe ten minutes but no more. I remember asking the child if she was okay out there and she said she was. Amy was only alone for a few minutes and then she was gone." She rested her chin on the back of her hand and looked at Sophie as if indicating she was ready for her next question. But then suddenly she cupped her face in her hands as if a thought struck her, announcing, "My goodness, the tea should be perfect now."

She removed the tea-cozy and poured tea for herself and a cup for Sophie. She offered biscuits to Sophie, which Sophie politely declined. Mrs. Chawla picked up a biscuit, dunked it in her tea and then sucked on it.

After Mrs. Chawla finished her biscuit and put her cup back on the side table, she looked at Sophie again with smiling eyes as if showing her readiness.

Sophie was not fully convinced; her experience was that busy people tend to overlook details. She probed a little more. "Mrs. Chawla, something unusual did happen that evening, otherwise Amy would not have gone missing. I'm sorry if I sound a little harsh, but I'd like you to try to remember. Earlier that evening, did you see any suspicious-looking person in the neighborhood?" she persisted.

Mrs. Chawla's eyebrows narrowed into a little steeple as she tried to recollect the events. She rubbed the side of her head as if to shake-up some of those gray cells asleep in her head.

She started to think aloud. "Well, let me see, dear." She readjusted her glasses and gazed upward, as if looking for an answer from heaven. "I went to the local market by bus. Came back a few minutes before five o'clock and then made myself a cup of tea. I like my cup of tea, you see. I called Frankie, my little cat, to come inside the house and have his food and then I waited for Amy. Jenifer had dropped her here exactly at five o'clock and told me that Ashok would be picking her up as she was expecting a call from America about six that evening. I would say at about five minutes to six or very close to six o'clock Amy went out and sat down on steps to play with the cat." She faced Sophie expectantly with an expression on her face as if she wanted to know if she had passed the test.

"That is very good, Mrs. Chawla," encouraged Sophie. "You have a sharp mind and I'm wondering if you could try to remember what you saw on the street, closer to your house when you got off the bus. For example, was there any strange-looking person wandering around or maybe a strange car you had not seen before?"

"Yes! Yes!" Mrs. Chawla replied in an excited voice. She half raised her hand like a little schoolgirl trying to attract her teacher's attention. As Sophie nodded, she added, "There indeed was a car parked only a few feet from my house that looked a little different to me." She went quiet for a while and then added, "Heavens, my memory isn't what it used to be. You'll have to forgive me, my dear."

Sophie gave her another nod of encouragement and said, "You're doing well. Now think again. What was different about the car? Was it one of those fancy foreign cars? Was it an unusual color? Were people waiting in this car? Was it a big car? Anything you can remember. Take your time."

"No, nothing like that, but I did notice that it looked different. Yes. I looked at it but not because it looked suspicious. No, no, it was more because of admiration. Yes, I know now that car was shiny. Shiny like a new car and it was snowy white." She remained in a contemplative mood as if she was going to say more, but remained silent.

"Was it a big car?" Sophie persisted.

"No, dear. It certainly was not a big car. Huh, I don't know much about cars. But it was a small car like you see everywhere in New Delhi," she said as she stirred the air with her hand, as if thinking of names of some Indian-made cars, but none came to her head.

"And when did you notice that car was gone?" Sophie continued to probe.

"Well, I don't know. You see, when Ashok came and told me that Amy was missing, I was not thinking of cars," Mrs. Chawla said, presenting her thought with perfect logic.

Sophie was convinced that she had done enough for now, having asked Mrs. Chawla to ponder that fateful evening, and perhaps it was time to give her a break.

"Wouldn't you like some biscuit, my dear? They are very good. I could make a fresh cup of tea. Did I tell you it is Darjeeling?" It seemed that Mrs. Chawla was enjoying herself and wanted Sophie to stay a little longer.

Twenty-Two

Sophie covertly looked at her wristwatch. She must get back and resume her conversation with Jenifer.

"Maybe next time, Mrs. Chawla. Once again, you have been a great help. But before I go, one more question: What did people think of little Amy?"

"People? Like who?" Mrs. Chawla looked perplexed by this question.

"You, for instance," Sophie asked, trying to get Mrs. Chawla to give her as much unbiased information as she could about Amy.

"Me? Oh, I though she was delightful little girl. You know kind, well mannered and so sweet," chirped Mrs. Chawla.

"If you were to describe Amy in one word, what would that word be?" Sophie was good at putting people at ease and leading them to focus on important issues as well as make them trust her to openly discuss their feelings.

"Hmm," Mrs. Chawla's eyes narrowed in concentration and, looking for a single word to describe Amy, she in a contemplative voice said, "Unhappy. Yes, definitely unhappy."

This was the small breakthrough Sophie was hoping for and, sitting back in her seat, she said, "Perhaps I will have another cup of your delightful Darjeeling tea, and a biscuit too."

Mrs. Chawla's eyes lit up with flattery and she poured another cup for Sophie and offered her a biscuit. Sophie, taking the cup and biscuit, asked, "So, what do you think made her unhappy?"

"Well, you know, it isn't my place to gossip, but poor Amy would often talk to me about Ashok and Jenifer having arguments about living in India. It seems that Jenifer wanted to return to the US for a better education and future for Amy, but Ashok liked living near his family and friends. Poor Amy."

A motive worth pursuing, thought Sophie.

"Goodbye, Mrs. Chawla, and thank you *very* much for your help and thank you for the wonderful cup of tea." Sophie rose to her feet and held the older woman's hands to thank her and show her appreciation.

She wanted to make sure that she would be welcome here again as Mrs. Chawla's house was of critical importance to this case and she was the last person to see Amy. After all, the crime was committed right outside her house.

Sophie stepped out and started walking back to Ashok's home. Not a bad day of work, she thought. It was her first day on the case and she had already interviewed a vital witness and may even have found her first clue to a potential motive. Not bad at all.

Sophie wondered if a small white, new-looking car could be a clue to solving Amy's mysterious disappearance. In a city of four million cars, most of them small and quite a few of them white, it would be a daunting challenge to make anything out of that lead.

A very small needle in a very large haystack indeed!

When she knocked at Ashok's house again, Jenifer opened the door and invited Sophie in then asked, "How was your visit with Mrs. Chawla?"

"Fine," Sophie said and, looking around, asked, "Where is your husband?"

"Oh, he seems to be quite upset and has gone out for a walk. Did you want him to be here this evening?"

"Actually," said Sophie, deliberating on the opportunity presented to her, "I'd like to talk to you first and then speak with you two together."

Jenifer sank into a sofa with her shoulders drooping and her face showing fatigue.

"How is your marriage?" Sophie asked abruptly and point blank. She did not believe in wasting time, especially when a week had passed since the disappearance and she was afraid that the trail by now might have gone cold.

Her shocked expression made it obvious that Jenifer was taken aback by the bluntness, as well as by the nature of the question.

"What do you mean? And what does my marriage have to do with Amy being kidnapped? Ashok would never do anything to hurt her or take her away from me," she shot back.

Although Jenifer looked displeased, Sophie knew that now she had her full attention.

"Like I've said before, we must eliminate the most obvious possibilities to focus on what could be really relevant. Now it may sound odd but I have to ask you this. Do you have any inkling that Ashok could have something to do with the kidnapping? Have you two being quarrelling or talking about separation or divorce? I must know the truth to proceed further," Sophie insisted with a stern voice.

"You are being ridiculous. We may have had our differences but there has never been talk of separation or divorce. We're no different than any other couple trying to make things work. We love each other and we both very much love Amy," she affirmed steadfastly.

Sophie paid more attention to those pained blue eyes than the resolve in Jenifer's voice and wondered how deeply she had been hurt by her marriage. She allowed a few moments of silence to linger between them to cause Jenifer to reflect on the gravity of situation. She needed to categorize and compartmentalize her issues in order to assign the priority to Amy's disappearance that it deserved. Sophie decided to help her.

Twenty-Three

The battle of wills continued and Jenifer assumed silence, perhaps hoping to draw attention away from her and focus it on Amy.

"You still haven't answered my question." Sophie was unmoved.

"Because your question is ludicrous. Why would Ashok do anything to hurt Amy?" She answered her question with a question.

"Not to hurt but to protect her, to keep her here in case you were thinking of taking her away. That is my question and I'd like you to answer it." Sophie was beginning to realize that Jenifer was strong and could stand up to her grueling interrogation.

Jenifer again kept silent and this time Sophie's question went unanswered. Sophie had enough ammunition to make Jenifer talk. This time she decided to try the soft approach.

"Jenifer," Sophie said affably, and lowering her voice, she continued. "Let me explain something to you. Time is a luxury that we cannot afford. We must act now. Every day lost is diminishing our chances of finding Amy. Missing children is a nasty business. It is reported that an estimated 800,000 children go missing each year, and that is more than 2,000 children every day."

"I know and that is why I wanted Ashok to leave this wretched country and return to the US. Monstrosities lurk behind the facade of the placid face of India," she said with downcast eyes.

Sophie considered Jenifer's sad face and, shaking her head from side to side, said, "I was giving you the statistics of the US that you consider so safe for children. And I guess it is worse in India. So do you see the urgency of us having an open discussion on every piece of background information on Amy?"

Jenifer could not hold her tears back anymore. "Is that what you think? Just one of the statistics, my Amy; just another number for you, one of the thousands that go missing every year?" She sounded hysterical. Her face was red with anger and her fists clenched.

Sophie was ready for her emotional outburst. In fact, she was counting on it, because she knew that when people are overwhelmed with anxieties and emotional turmoil, it is best to break them down before the building process can begin.

"Jenifer, the pain in your face tell me how much you love and care for Amy. I'm sorry that I had to lean on Ashok a bit but it is all for the benefit of Amy. All I want you to do is to be honest with me. I'm on your side." Sophie paused for moment to let Jenifer reflect on her offer and then continued, "No, Amy is not just one of the thousands missing or a merely a number, because if she was then I wouldn't be here. I'm not going to quit till I find Amy and that is a promise."

A show of confusion passed over Jenifer's face as she looked at Sophie with imploring eyes. Sophie leaned forward to stress her argument, "Look, I can't rule out the involvement of Ashok or his family for the sake of Amy's recovery but what I've learned in a very short time is that this appears to be the work of a professional. With no clues and meticulous planning, this is the hallmark of organized crime and we have to proceed with care."

Jenifer sat abstracted, remote, her spirit far from the sad present. A powerful hold seemed to envelop her into another reality. And the hold seemed to grow stronger by the minute. She wanted to break free. She needed a trusting friend.

Sophie paused for a moment, and watching the changing expressions on Jenifer's face, realized that the time had come for her to play her trump card. The moment she walked through the door the first time and talked with Jenifer, she had realized that Jenifer was pleased not because the FBI was involved, but rather she seemed comfortable that a female FBI agent was involved. In a foreign land, Jenifer was lost without her friends and could not trust the local law enforcement agencies. That was the impression Sophie had deduced. Sophie held both of Jenifer's hands in hers and, looking straight into her eyes, said, "Not as an FBI agent but as a woman, I understand the torment you must be going through. You must feel quite alone in this distressful situation and if you could find it in your heart to trust me then I can assure you that we will find a way to get Amy home, back to you."

"I want to trust you but I don't believe that you can even begin to understand what I am going through, this is just another case to you," said Jenifer in a tone that was devoid of anger but expressive of her doubts.

A brief glimpse of sadness floated across Sophie's face and after a momentary pause, she said in a low voice, "I know exactly what you are going through. I once had a baby brother whom I loved very much but lost him due to the cruelty that surrounded us. I had hoped that someday love would blot out all the sorrow, but whenever I listen to my heart, I end up crying alone. And you know why? When I shut my lips, sealed them in protest, the world wanted me to speak out against the wrongs, but did not care when I was screaming for justice. So, I am out there now, getting justice for others, to find peace instead of pain in my soul."

The softest tone can deliver the most severe blow. Jenifer was struck by this confession, and her facial muscles began to relax with Sophie's assurance. As she looked back at Sophie, with the gentle, protective care in her blue eyes, and at the same time, the quiet realization of destiny, her cognizance fluttered into sudden coherence. She only wanted to help to save Amy, even to save her from the wretched marriage. Maybe she could help her to change the flow of history. A precipitous realization played in her head that it was perhaps providence that she should meet a woman of such resolve, such strong will. With her friendship, her help, it might be possible for her to even reverse the bad history of her life.

"You need to be truthful and trust me to help you," said Sophie, her words breaking Jenifer's trance.

Jenifer blinked several times involuntarily and then in a small voice responded, "Ashok and I don't talk much these days and if we do, somehow we end up arguing." Jenifer hesitated for a moment and then yielded, "Ash, he was such a romantic person but my problem was that I could get very impatient. I'm a little confused at times and can't sort out my priorities between family, career and parents. My stepfather didn't approve of my marriage and my so easily giving up my career, and he definitely did not approve of my moving to India. But then he didn't try very hard to persuade me otherwise either. Ashok's parents don't say much and when they do, they are sarcastic in their remarks. Amy is all I have and now she is gone." Jenifer's shoulders shook slightly first and then as her sobbing became apparent, her body started to tremble.

Sophie let her have a cry, thinking it might help her release her tension, anger and perhaps, to some extent, her resentment.

Twenty-Four

Sophie could feel that Jenifer's resentment went deeper, much deeper than she was showing. There was a deep-seated anger in her that she had not managed to reconcile with her present condition. Sophie had seen too many such situations in her patients when she worked as a physician.

Sophie waited, continuing to watch Jenifer, and after several moments when her crying subsided and she wiped her tears, she continued, "I don't know why, but I feel guilty of things that I'm not responsible for bringing about. I don't even know who my real father is. After my mother passed away, my stepfather gave me away and I was adopted by a young couple. My new stepfather is a nice enough man but he is so distant. We have no real relationship. I wish my real father was here or my mother was still alive to help me through this dreadful situation. Unfortunately, this has been causing me a lot of stress and it may have strained my relationship with Ashok. Maybe if our relationship were not so tenuous then Amy would still be here. I feel so alone without her."

Jenifer finally met Sophie's gaze and saw her intently staring at her. She stammered, "Oh, I'm sorry. You see, here I go again on the blame and guilt trip. I don't really know what to do."

"That's okay," assured Sophie, "that is why I am here. Tell me about Amy. Was she unhappy because of your strained marriage? Did she have many friends?"

"Amy is a lovely child; she might be a bit spoiled, being the first child and the first grandchild in our family. Unhappy, I don't think so. Maybe a little quiet sometimes, but then all children are moody, aren't they?"

When no response came from Sophie, Jenifer seemed a little uneasy as if she had failed to answer the question correctly so further explained, "I don't think we paid too much attention to teaching Amy how to be street smart. We were always there for her. We never allowed her to walk the few blocks from Mrs. Chawla's house to our home. It would be always either Ashok or I who would be there to pick her up. I have been encouraging Ashok to spend more time with Amy so whenever he offered to pick her up I let him. He happened to be late by a few minutes but that is nothing unusual. Amy always waited till one of us arrived."

"Do you or Ashok have any friends that may want to hurt you or Ashok by taking Amy away? I mean, Ashok may have offended someone at work who might be upset with him? You know what I mean?" Sophie asked and carefully glanced at her wristwatch and wondered if she ought to wrap up before Ashok returned.

"None that I can think of. No, I don't think our friends are like that at all. We don't have too many friends to start with and I know nothing about Ashok's workplace or the people who work for him."

"But you do realize that Ashok is the owner of a multi-million dollar business and kids of such wealthy parents get kidnapped all the time for ransom? Are you sure that Ashok or his parents have had no warnings, no phone calls from anyone asking for money?"

"Are you suggesting that Ashok and his parents might be keeping me in the dark and have been contacted by the kidnappers? It is quite possible because they don't really share any information, private or business, with me and I pay no attention to their wealth for I have no interest in it."

"It is a possibility that we will have to consider."

"Oh, Ashok could not keep such a secret from me," said Jenifer, nodding as if reassuring herself, "his parents could, but not him. Just looking in his face I would know if he is hiding something. He is a very transparent man, you know?"

Sophie decided not to push Jenifer any further and thanked her and told her not to worry and that she would be back soon. But she did advise her to probe Ashok a little deeper in case his parents might know something. Sophie gave Jenifer her card and asked her to call if she remembered anything that could be of use.

Tomorrow was Amy's birthday, Jenifer told her, sobbing again.

Happy birthday, Amy!

Twenty-Five

B y the time Sophie returned to her hotel and finished dinner in her room, she felt exhausted. Suddenly the phone in the room rang. "Hello," said Sophie, thinking that it was either room service or the front desk. "This is Ian Grunfeld, how did your investigation go today?"

Sophie was taken aback by this unexpected phone call and answered, "Mr. Ambassador, I cannot discuss anything about the case on the phone. I will make an appointment to see you tomorrow. Goodnight now." And without waiting for his answer she put the phone down.

She wanted to go through today's findings and update the case file, but gave up the idea; as soon as she laid her head on the pillow, she was fast asleep.

The next morning Sophie looked out her bedroom window and saw the pallid sunlight scattered over the tree-tops. She walked into her washroom and started brushing her teeth. She remembered her encounter with the serial killer in Nairobi and shuddered, overcome by mixed emotions of fear and excitement. She saw the reflection of her neck in the mirror and she could imagine the knife at her throat. She brushed her teeth with new vigor, tying to put distance between her memories and her present-day thoughts. On this chilly morning she could feel sweat trickling down from the back of her neck to the small of her back. The echoes in her mind had subsided but were not completely eradicated.

What kind of monster takes a little girl away from her parents? she mused. Whenever she faced danger she thought of the untimely and horrific death of her kid brother and the rage and strength that emerged through such thoughts made her capable of facing and tackling evil monsters, including serial killers and kidnappers. She promised herself that she would find this deranged person who abducted little girls and bring him to justice.

She used the coffee machine in her room to make herself a cup of strong coffee. She sat by the window overlooking the garden below and reviewed the details of Amy's case.

Not many clues, none that could give her a positive lead. A shiny white car close to the house was not much to go on, but nevertheless, Sophie thought that it deserved further investigation. She decided that later that day she would go back to Mrs. Chawla's neighborhood and talk with her neighbors. But first she wanted to contact the local law enforcement agencies and let them know of her involvement and to follow their protocol. But before that she had to pay a visit to the US embassy to see the ambassador.

She finished her coffee, showered and dressed. She came down and asked the concierge to call her driver. About thirty minutes later she was in the ambassador's office.

After a cursory greeting the ambassador inquired, "So what did you find out yesterday? Have you made any progress? I expected you to call me to keep me updated?"

Sophie crossed her legs and leaned back in her chair as if demonstrating her resolve to not be intimidated by the position of this diplomat. She responded, "Mr. Ambassador, we have to get one thing straight. I am happy to receive any help that you and your office can offer me but I am not at liberty to discuss the case with you or anyone else, for that matter, at the embassy."

"Well," growled the ambassador, "that is not acceptable. Goddamn it, I'm the one who insisted on the FBI's involvement and deserve to know what the hell is going on."

"Then you would need clearance from the FBI as I would from my superiors. There are protocols one must follow," Sophie answered calmly.

"I'll see to that and right now," he retorted, pressing the intercom button and ordering his secretary to connect him with the FBI.

Moments later Ian was addressing Andrew Hunt. After a couple of minutes he passed the phone to Sophie, saying, "He wants to talk to you."

Sophie stood up and took the phone. "Listen," said the voice on the other end, "share just enough information to keep him placated and off my back. God, it's late here, I don't want to be hounded by diplomats. Take control, okay?"

Sophie said a few words in response, indicating her compliance, and returned the receiver back to the ambassador. With a little smile on his face, he asked, "So, now that the protocol is sorted out, what did you learn yesterday?"

Sophie explained whom she had talked with without giving any details of what she had learned. She added, "It's early yet and I've missed a week of proceedings in this case. This morning I need to see the local law enforcement authorities and get whatever details they may have."

"Don't waste your time," said the ambassador, changing his tone, reflecting his genuine interest in offering help. "I could make a phone call to the highest authorities and get you to see the top ranking police officials. Better still, I'll come with you and that should open all the doors."

"That may prove to be counterproductive," countered Sophie, "just ask your office to make me an appointment and let us see how this evolves."

Reluctantly, the ambassador backed off and his secretary made an immediate appointment for Sophie to meet with the highest authority, the Commissioner of Police at the New Delhi Police Headquarters located at the Indraprastha Estate.

Twenty-Six

A t ten o'clock Sophie arrived and was received by the secretary of the Commissioner of Police, informing her that she was expected, and showing her to the Commissioner's office. On their way the secretary warned, "The CP is determined and not to be trifled with. Please be careful."

It took Sophie a couple of moments to hide her astonishment when she was introduced to the lady Commissioner of Police, Sushma Rao. Sophie was impressed to see that in modern India, women who had been oppressed for generations by the traditional shackles of Indian men had accomplished so much and in such a short period of time. Initiatives and persistent efforts catalyzed by the courage of women long enslaved by religious and social customs could accelerate the realization of changes even in a society that is plagued with age-old traditions.

"So, what's the big mystery?" asked the CP, coming around her desk and shaking hands with Sophie. "It's rather unusual to see the FBI getting involved in a missing child case, not to mention the constant pressure we are facing from the Ambassador himself to find this girl Amy. Why is he so insistent on pursuing this case? We have had cases with Americans involved in the past but his predecessors never interfered."

While Sophie took a momentary pause to respond, the CP added, "We've thousands of such cases and cannot give preferential treatment, you understand? If we did the parents of thousands of missing children would be very upset to see that foreigners have more rights in India than Indians do themselves. You know what I am saying?"

"I do and I apologize for this unnecessary interference from the embassy. I'll see what I can do about that," said Sophie, wondering herself why the Ambassador was getting so involved in what would be considered by all measures a minor case. Besides, so far, no connections were indicated for this kidnapping to be politically motivated.

"I don't get it," said the CP, shaking her head. "Is this missing girl related to some senior politician back in the States, or worse, here in India? Hell, I even got a call from the Home Minister about this missing girl. Your ambassador went to see him. I hope that the press doesn't get hold of all this or the importance of this child, otherwise finding her is going to be a daunting task. I'm trying to help you here."

"Again, I apologize," said Sophie, feeling a little frustrated with the unnecessary interference of her embassy in the case and, lowering her voice, said, "and I will do everything possible to put a stop to it now that I am here. In fact, it wasn't me but my embassy that insisted on my seeing you. I won't take too much more of your time and would like to offer my services in supporting whoever is the investigating officer on this case."

At that point there was a knock on the door and an orderly brought in two cups of tea and an assortment of biscuits, placing them on a corner coffee table between a couple of comfortable sofas. As soon as he left the CP, gesturing with her hand, invited Sophie to join her for tea.

They moved to the plush sofas and the CP spoke again, "This is going to sound very odd, and what I'm going to advise you do is against the rules. But since your ambassador and the Home Office are getting involved, I cannot take any chances. If you really want to solve this case then you'd be better off working on your own than working with us. Take my advice and don't even let the local police know that you are involved. I would keep this meeting private and confidential. If you must know what we have been doing, then all such cases, including yours, are under the control of the Special Commissioner of Police, head of the Crime Division. His name is Anil Mathur and I believe he has assigned an inspector as an investigating officer and his name is Ram Prasad."

"Excuse me, Commissioner Rao, but I'm a little confused," said Sophie. "What you just said about—"

"Listen," interrupted the CP, in an authoritative voice that seemed more out of habit than intentional. "I rose to this position because of the tremendous support I received from the leader of the Congress Party. She despises any corrupt government and has made it her crusade to first wipe out corruption from all ministries and governing bodies before her government can address corruption in the private sector. Corruption is our biggest curse and the root cause of many violent, illegal and immoral activities."

"So, you've the bigger agenda of fighting corruption, and I understand that," said Sophie, replacing her cup on the saucer, "but how does that affect the police force? Shouldn't they be an integral part of implementing the anti-corruption program?"

Sushma's facial muscles tensed as she looked up at the ceiling as if making up her mind about something and then responded, "The Delhi Police is the biggest metropolitan police in the world with 149 police stations.

It is composed of 11 Special Commissioners, 17 Joint Commissioners, 9 Additional Commissioners, 74 Deputy Commissioners, and 272 Assistant Deputy Commissioners. As the Commissioner of Police I directly control the Special Commissioners, who in turn control the rest of the organization as well as Deputy Commissioners of the North, South and East. Under this organization we manage close to sixty thousand police officers that claim to be overworked and underpaid. The Delhi Police jurisdiction covers almost one and a half million square miles of the city with close to seventeen million people."

The CP paused for a moment, wet her lips with her tongue as if trying to get rid of a bad taste in her mouth, and then in an introspective voice continued, "Delhi being the capitol of India is the center of a wide range of political, cultural, social and economic activity. There is a lot of money here and corruption in the police force is rampant. Turning a blind eye to organized crime groups, taking bribes to distort justice, and custodial deaths have created a lot of distrust and the general population does not trust our police or the justice system. It will take time, courage and a lot of organizational changes to create an honest police force. So, like I said before, all I can offer you is the advice that you work as independently as possible."

After several minutes of friendly small talk, with Sophie clarifying how the FBI operates and how she made it to where she was, and the Commissioner explaining how fortunate she was to get the support of the leader of the elected party, they parted company. The Commissioner extended her personal assistance to Sophie if and when desired, and again reminded Sophie, if possible, to keep the US embassy out of the police system.

Twenty-Seven

In the evening Sophie played various scenarios in her head of her next step over a glass of wine and then she punched up Andrew's number. "Agent Kramer, what is going on there? I've had a couple of complaints about your slow progress; you want to fill me in?"

"Those complaints couldn't be from our favorite Ambassador, could they?" laughed Sophie. "I've only been here a couple of days and he wants miracles." Sophie stretched her legs out on top of the desk and leaned back in her chair, and then continued, "Well, the police authorities that typically would be an asset are jeopardizing my investigation. I will have to fight this war on two fronts, three if you include the Ambassador."

"Care to elaborate?" said the voice on the other end.

Sophie, choosing her words carefully, said, "For example, the Delhi police cannot be trusted and its Commissioner of Police, who is the head of the entire Delhi Police Force, is advising me to stay away from them, while the Ambassador of our embassy himself is hell bent on interfering and in the process upsetting a lot of concerned parties. Jenifer is having some complicated issues in her life with her husband, her parents, and her career, that are making her lose focus on Amy, the real victim to whom we should be giving priority."

"I'll see what I can do about the embassy," said Andrew, in a reassuring voice. "I'll talk with someone here to put pressure on the ambassador to back off. We still need to stay active with the case and get behind the scene to start sowing the seeds to start dismantling the crime groups that are involved in generating funds for terrorism through prostitution. Amy should be your focus, but our scope is much bigger and has not changed."

"And I am with you on this," she responded, firm conviction in her voice. "I'm getting new information on how the crime groups in India have reorganized to evade the legal system. I'm afraid our information in the files is rather obsolete. I'll get this information over to you shortly and expect it will open some new leads for me too."

They talked only for another couple of minutes and then Sophie, after ending her conversation with Andrew, turned the TV on and watched the local news. All she could focus on was how the giant wheels of progress in their relentless pursuit of power were crushing the poor and the downtrodden.

Monday morning started with the usual cacophony of streets packed with cars and trucks belching acrid blue smoke, suffocating both humans and vegetation alike. The sun was up, but not visible, as a thick cover of clouds blocked its rays. As Sophie started through the hotel lobby, a man dressed in a businesslike black suit hurried out from behind the reception and approached Sophie, saying, "Dr. Kramer, a visitor is waiting for you. He is sitting over there in the corner. He wouldn't give his name but asked for you and said he would wait till you came down." Sophie nodded and walked over to where the man was sitting and looking at her with inquisitive eyes.

"Agent Kramer?" he asked, as he stood up and extended his hand.

"Do I know you?" asked Sophie, shaking his hand. He had large hands and the physique of a soldier. Built strong, he had square shoulders, a stiff posture and a square chin. With a neatly trimmed moustache and short hair, he could have easily been an army officer. The only mismatch was the suit he was wearing with an open collar white shirt. It looked old and ill-fitted, as if a hand-me-down from his father or a second-hand item.

There was also something odd about this man, Sophie felt. She continued to hold his hand and added, "Are you here in an official capacity or has someone asked you to see me? How did you know who I am and where I am staying?" As his hand became clammy, she let it go, but not without offering a small smile that flickered on her lips for a brief moment, which he did not notice.

He looked around cautiously and in a whisper, introduced himself. "My name is Ram Prasad and I'm the investigating officer for the kidnapping case you are following. I heard of your visit to our facility and wondered if I could be of any assistance?" He put his hand in his inside jacket pocket and pulled out a business card to give to her and said, "Not as a full time endeavor, but whenever you may have need of me."

"Do you have your police identification badge?" asked Sophie.

"Yes, of course," said he, politely, and produced his credentials.

"Have you been asked by your superiors to work with me?" she asked, wondering if he knew about yesterday's meeting with the Commissioner of Police. Having been warned, Sophie did not want to get involved with the local police, but could not pass up an opportunity to learn of the developments to date in Amy's case directly from the investigating officer.

Sophie saw a curious expression on his face as if he has been caught doing something wrong. His eyes darted left and right and he did not answer her question.

Twenty-Eight

What Sophie felt when she shook his hand now took a definitive form in her mind. She wanted more time to reaffirm her deduction so asked, "You have time for coffee?" She was keen to learn from him what he had on Amy's case and what he could tell her about the crime groups involved in prostitution.

He nodded and they walked to the coffee shop where Sophie ordered two coffee lattes.

Sophie wanted to put him at ease, so instead of directly addressing Amy's case, she asked him to shed light on the prostitution problems of India. He let out a big sigh and said, "There are more than twenty million prostitutes in India and as many as one-third of them are less than eighteen years old. People say that the prostitution business is a part of our ancient heritage from the days of the *Vedas,* but the truth of its destructive effect still lies hidden. Ever since the downfall of the Mughal Empire, the conditions of the underbelly of society have deteriorated to deplorable levels."

Sophie smiled inwardly, thinking that India truly was straddling its past and future in its current rampant corruption, and asked, "How do you know so much? Are you associated with any prevention initiatives?"

"Oh, no," he said, wringing his hands, showing his suppressed anxiety. "I'm a lowly officer of junior grade. I believe in the Gandhi philosophy, its mandate to lead a virtuous life and aspire to serve for the higher purpose."

Sophie smiled at his honesty and quizzed, "I know that globally, prostitution is an over-$100 billion business, so what Indian covers are backing it up and what do they do to entice young girls into prostitution?" Sophie wanted to test the depths of his knowledge first, and at the same time let him feel in control before directly discussing the case.

"The real problem, if you ask me," said Ram, leaning forward as if imparting a secret, "is poverty and the mores of the society we live in. Poverty is one of the main causes, which brings destitute woman to the doors of prostitution. A woman suffering economically, often ill treated by parents or seduced by a boyfriend who later turns out to be a pimp or procurer, and lastly, uneducated or with a very low education level, rarely finds any other way to feed herself other than prostitution. And then there are social factors, which degrade the status of such women. One such factor is the view of women being a commodity—which is inescapable in the popular manifestations of culture in India. The harsh reality is that women who have had sexual experiences are considered to be *used goods* or *characterless,* and are unlikely to ever marry. They become impoverished cultural outcasts."

"How is such a huge problem staring us in the face allowed to spread at such an alarming rate?" asked Sophie, in a contemplative voice, as if talking to herself, "and why aren't people fighting to uproot it?"

"Forgive me, Agent Kramer," he interrupted, looking determined to speak his mind, "but our problem of prostitution is no different than the US problem of drugs. I know we're struggling but we're working to find means to manage and contain the problem first before we can attempt to eradicate it."

"Touché," said Sophie, laughing. "Well, I didn't mean to point fingers." After a pause she asked, "Tell me, if one is to look for a particular child prostitute, you know, like a particular type of girl, how would one go about it?"

"Excuse me," he said, looking startled. "I'm not sure if I understand your question?"

"I'm trying to learn from you what you know and can share," Sophie answered.

Ram, rubbing his chin, responded, "I see. Well, child prostitution is maybe the most degrading yet the most prolific and profitable business today and no market is bigger than Mumbai, which accommodates more than 200,000 prostitutes, and claims to be Asia's largest sex industry center. Trafficking and sex tourism is controlled by both big businesses and politicians, and under their protection, it is growing unabated like a cancer."

Sophie examined Ram's face to determine if he could be trusted. She was advised not to trust the police and she remained quite aware of that warning. He looked agitated. She wanted to ask him a vital question but decided that a few moments of silence may help him find a little equanimity. After waiting, Sophie asked, "Inspector Ram, would you know how Mumbai prostitutes obtain protection? And how the girls are brought into it? I mean, who operates their procurement? Maybe, just maybe, there is a link between New Delhi and Mumbai prostitution? Businesses this big must compete through cooperation, you know what I mean?"

"I'll see what I can find out," said Ram, nodding his head, making notes in his file. Sophie, placing her coffee cup back on the table, studied him intently and asked, "You haven't told me why you are here. And how do you know what case I am working on?"

"Well, it is very difficult to keep secrets in our police force. It is not often we get a visit from a FBI Special Agent. I heard here and there about your visit to the Commissioner of Police, and we currently have only one case involving an American, so I put two and two together."

Sophie realized there was more to Ram being there than he had said so far, because for one thing, he hadn't said anything about Amy. Sophie decided to go for the jugular, "Ram, I have been advised not to work with you, not just you but anybody from the police force, and do whatever I need to do on my own."

"I would have given you exactly the same advice," said Ram, without even a moment's thought. "We're all very corrupt at the Delhi police force, but then the whole world knows that." Ram paused for a moment and when he spoke again his tone conveyed a half-envious and half-expectant feeling. "I was hoping to learn something from you about your investigating techniques if you were working on Amy's case, for there is nothing we could teach the FBI, or tell you, about this matter."

Now that the topic had finally gravitated to Amy, Sophie took the opportunity to say, "So, what do you know about the case? You're the investigating officer."

"There are only two possibilities," he said, lowering his voice, "either she was abducted for money, and demand for such will be forthcoming in a few days, or for prostitution. I hope it is the former; otherwise, we are never going to find her."

"And what have you done so far?" Sophie persisted.

"Talked with a few people in the neighborhood, checked through some of our files, and that is about it. Lack of resources at the department means we are not really equipped for such cases. We are waiting for the kidnapper's next move."

"And did your superiors ask you to work with me?" Sophie probed.

"Actually no," said Ram haltingly, "if I made a mistake in approaching you, then I am sorry, and I will leave you alone. For an Indian policeman to get an opportunity to work with the FBI, you don't understand how rare that is." Ram was wringing his hands again as if something was troubling him.

"Okay Ram," said Sophie, "I'm not sure if we can work together, but we can always talk now and then. If you get me the information that I asked for earlier then I will see how we can collaborate on some of the aspects of the case."

A momentary glint in his eyes did not escape Sophie's attention.

Twenty-Nine

R am nodded, shook hands and left, promising to return soon. After his departure, Sophie remained in the coffee shop, starting to construct a foundation in her mind with the information she'd received from Ram. She wanted to look for a relationship between the general information on trafficking and the specific case of Amy to determine if there was a link. She had this curious feeling that there could be one, but she didn't know what buttons to press that would lead her to uncover it.

Later that morning, at about eleven o'clock, Sophie arrived at the house directly opposite Mrs. Chawla's. She knocked on the door and in response heard the barking of a dog.

"I'm coming!" someone shouted from inside the house, with the sound of feet shuffling across the floor. A minute later an elderly Indian man, tall and sturdy, opened the door. He appeared to be in his late seventies.

"Yes? Are you from the church?" He gave Sophie a puzzled look.

"No. I'm not from a church. I'm a police officer. May I come in?"

"Police officer? You don't look like one. Are you sure you're not from the church or Jehovah's Witnesses? I am a Hindu, you know, and of Brahmin caste, so I don't need any church," said the man in an uninviting and unwavering tone.

Sophie took out her FBI badge and showed it to the man. He looked more puzzled now than he did before and, giving her back the badge, stared at her inquisitively. "I am not from the Delhi Police. I am from America. In your neighborhood there lives an American lady; her name is Jenifer, and her little girl Amy has been kidnapped from that house right in front of your house. Well, actually, from her doorstep. I am investigating that case and it is in this regard that I would like to ask you a few questions. I won't take much of your time."

Sophie wondered if the gentleman would still refuse for he just stood there gaping. "Do you mind if I come in?" she asked.

"Dreadful business. Did you say a little girl? Dreadful. Yes, you'd better come in," he said, stepping aside. "My name is Mr. Kapour. Actually, I am a retired judge, but that was a lifetime ago. Nobody cares here what you once did for this country. Come in, come in."

He had prominence without title, grace without motion, and presence without recognition. Sophie entered the house, closed the door behind her and walked behind the old man shuffling his way back to his drawing room. "Yes, come to think of it, I've seen pictures of the little girl on TV. A cute baby, but I don't know much about it. American, you say? Huh. All right, how can I help?" Mr. Kapour slowly lowered his tall body into a large armchair.

The way he held his head suggested a sense of stubborn resolve, as if he were used to holding on his own. His nose and mouth were straight, like a mask, and the expression was rigid with a relentless, unyielding male will. He gave her the impression of a man who never makes a mistake, who knows his surroundings, and who will not bend to another's will, will never give in.

Sophie sat by the fire and opposite him, and took in her surroundings. A small low drawing-room; white walls hung with black-and-white, framed photographs of a group of people she presumed to be his family; curtains and furniture of faded tapestry; and a window by the side of front door, through which she caught a glimpse of the street and the house of the piano teacher. Within, mahogany, upholstered armchairs were drawn up about a hearth that appeared to always have a fire smoldering; a large table piled with old novels and frayed picture-magazines; and near the table on the floor, a small basket in which sat a Lhasa Apso staring at Sophie. The man now stretched out in his armchair, his legs covered by a thick shawl, his hands occupied with a folded newspaper. He was a sturdy, handsome man with brilliant white wavy hair, a black moustache, and tender, sad eyes under the bold arch of his black brows.

The dog was quiet now with more of a friendly than an inquisitive look on its face. His basket was lined with an old blanket. Sophie wondered if she had ever seen a better vision of an old man and a dog than what was in front of her.

He lifted his shoulders and spread his hands with a gesture of finality and fatality, while his face took the blank, ageless look of misery, like a *Sadhu's*. As if there was no hope. Suddenly his face broke into a smile of profound melancholy, almost a grin, like a gargoyle. It was true Indian melancholy, very deep, static.

"He's a good dog, my old friend. Quite old now, you know. Don't worry, he won't bite. He can hardly move. He doesn't even bark much anymore." He looked at the dog and shouted, "Rover, say hello to the stranger." The dog ignored his request. He laid his head on his front paws and darted his eyes from one human to another.

"Every Friday, Amy would go to the house directly opposite yours, you know, Mrs. Chawla's house, to take piano lessons. Have you ever noticed Amy going in and out of that house?"

Mr. Kapour smiled at something as if a sweet memory of his past had surfaced in his head. After a momentary silence, wearing an abstract expression on his face, he murmured, "Sweet girl, Amy. I have a granddaughter her age but I don't see her. The wretched daughter-in-law won't allow it. Sorry, dear. You're not interested in that though, are you? Yes, Amy. She would often sit on those steps waiting for one of her parents to pick her up, and would wave to me if I were standing by the window. Nice girl."

Encouraged by this response, Sophie asked, "Did you see her on the Friday, about ten days back, the day she went missing?"

"I can't say, ten days is a long time." Mr. Kapour shook his head.

"It's important, Mr. Kapour," said Sophie, moving to the edge of her seat. "Did you see anything in the neighborhood that was out of the ordinary? Maybe some suspicious-looking person, or maybe cars that don't belong to this neighborhood? Please think back, and take your time."

"Time, yes, I have plenty of that," said Mr. Kapour, looking equally sad and serious. "Well, if it means anything, a small white car went up and down the street a couple of times in the morning and once late in the afternoon. It had been doing this routine for a few days. I watch out for these things, you know? Old, but my mind is still active. I read a lot." He pointed at the table where numerous novels and magazines were scattered about.

"That's great. Now, was that car ever stopped directly in front of Mrs. Chawla's or your house?" Sophie asked.

"Well, yes," he replied, as he leaned back and looked at the ceiling with his toothless mouth open, as if revisiting a memory. "Now I remember. It was parked right in front of my house. Always my house; and that is why it irritated me. Oh, it must have been there for about an hour or so obstructing my view. That Friday, because of it, I could not wave goodbye to the little girl."

"Did you see the driver or the license plate? Is there anything you can tell me about this car or the person driving it?" Sophie's curiosity was piqued.

"No. I'm sorry, I can't. My eyesight is very poor and I can't see all that well," Mr. Kapour said glumly. He took out his glasses from his shirt pocket, peered at them with his poor eyes. He then grabbed a corner of his scarf and tried to rub his glasses clean. After few moments he put them on his nose and blinked his eyes several times as he moved his eyebrows up and down.

Sophie noted his thick glasses and a faint smile teased her lips. "Thank you so much, you've been very helpful. I will leave you with my card and if you think of anything else, please give me a call. I'll see myself out." Sophie placed the card on a side table, got up, folded her hands together to say goodbye Indian-style and left.

Thirty

She somehow knew that doing a house-to-house search in this old neighborhood was not going to reveal much more than she already knew. Nevertheless, she decided to cover all the bases. So she wandered up and down the cobblestone street, knocking on doors. In fourteen of the eighteen houses on Mrs. Chawla's side and sixteen houses on the opposite side of the street, residents responded to her knock. They all were aware of what had happened but could not provide any useful information or clues. But quite a few confirmed seeing a small, white car that seemed to have frequented the area several times for a couple of weeks prior to Amy's disappearance and since then had vanished.

The small, white car was an important clue but how to unravel its significance? She glanced up and down and discovered that there were no CCTV cameras on this street. She walked over to the children's park and sat on a bench for a while, deciding to try a different angle in deciphering the meaning behind the presence of the white car. She had to think from a kidnapper's point of view rather than what the people in the neighborhood saw. If it indeed was the car responsible for Amy's disappearance, then what precautions would a kidnapper take?

Suddenly she slapped her thighs with the open palms of her hands and cried, "What the hell! Why didn't I think of it before?"

She'd just connected the only two clues she had managed to gather so far. She theorized that the kidnapper must be a professional, especially if he was meticulously casing the area of Mrs. Chawla's house to find a suitable time to abduct Amy. She further figured that the kidnapper, being a professional, would not use his personal car. The small white car looked shiny and new. "Of course it was shiny, it was a rental," she said aloud.

But no sooner were her spirits lifted by this revelation, than they were dashed by the thought that she was in New Delhi, one of the most densely populated cities in the world, and perhaps most rental cars here were compact, for India produced its own cars, all small in size.

But she decided not to give up and would further pursue her theory. After all, she did not have much else to go on and she knew it. She headed straight back to the hotel, and once in her room from the desk, pulled out a thick city phone book.

Seventeen different car rental agencies were listed with multiple offices in the city. Sophie realized that she could not afford to waste time by going to every office and sifting through their records, yet finding the elusive small, white rental car was the only real lead she had. She had no choice but to cover all the seventeen offices. She decided not to include Ram in her investigation just yet, at least not until she could confirm his true motive for contacting her.

The next morning she visited various car rental agencies and, showing her FBI credentials to confused office managers, was able to examine rental contracts around the date that was a week before Amy's disappearance. She smiled at her tall, slim and curvaceous reflection in a mirror at one of the rental agency offices and realized why she was being given such easy access to the rental agreement records.

One by one she visited all seventeen rental agencies and photocopied all the contracts that were taken out the week before Amy's disappearance and involved white cars; it took her the whole day to do so. In the evening, sitting in the privacy of her hotel room, she started to comb through three hundred and fifty-seven car rentals. People from all over the north and south of India had hired these cars and Sophie let out a big sigh, knowing that it would be impossible to interview all of them in a short period of time. Every minute was precious if she was to find Amy alive and unharmed. At the same time, Sophie knew she had to continue with the lead in the hopes of finding the identity of the driver who she believed might have abducted Amy.

"There has got to be a way to shorten this list!" she murmured as she ran her fingers through her hair.

Sophie pondered her question, looked at the papers placed in a thick file on the table, and thought that someone flying in from outside New Delhi, kidnapping Amy and flying out was unlikely. It was more probable that a local rented a car to kidnap Amy.

With that possibility in hand, she went through all the contracts and pulled out those that were signed by people with a local address. "There we are," she said aloud excitedly, "I have only thirty-seven people to question."

Suddenly a thought occurred to her and she revisited the thirty-seven contracts, rejecting five that involved women hiring a car. She had narrowed it down to thirty-two now.

"Thirty-two," said Sophie in a determined voice. "I might as well follow this lead to the end." She scratched her head as if trying to remember something and said in a contemplative tone, "Funny, thirty-two is the number of Jenifer's house."

Thirty-One

Sophie was about to retire for the evening when her phone rang. "Yes, Andrew, I was going to call you," she said.

"What have you got so far?" he asked.

"Well, maybe nothing. But I've a hunch that a local kidnapped Amy and used a small, white, rental car. I'm discarding the possibility that Amy could have been kidnapped by one of Ashok's office workers for revenge, as no body has been found and no demand for ransom has been made. We can also reject the idea that she could have wandered off somewhere on her own, because by now someone would have seen her and reported it to the police. Despite the fact that she is five, it has to be some professional crime group abducting her for the purposes of prostitution, or some sick person for some other sinister purpose. My only lead to date is my hunch."

"Anything you have to back up that hunch?" asked Andrew.

"Well, as I mentioned a couple of days back, Indian crime groups are reorganizing. This is how they operate here: A contractor who is hired by a procurer often kidnaps the girls. The procurer then offers the girls to a business entity and several of them here are fronts for prostitution rackets. Now we can't raid all these business entities in the hopes that one of them might have Amy, but perhaps we could determine who the contractor is that kidnapped Amy because, unlike procurer and business units that are spread all over the nation, a contractor is likely to be a local. Do you see where I am going with this?"

"Where did you get this information?" the voice on the other end sounded concerned.

"From the investigating officer of the Delhi Police, Inspector Ram Prasad. But before you say anything, I'm simply using him to squeeze information out of him without sharing any of my findings, and it is all off the record. Besides, I'm curious about the motive Ram had in approaching me."

"I've got bad news for you," said Andrew. "Ram may be disappearing from the scene shortly. I heard his name today. The ambassador apparently went down to the police station and gave the Special Commissioner of Crime Division, Mr. Anil Mathur, for whom Inspector Ram works, a warning and told them to get their act together. Apparently he made quite a scene. The Indian Home Office has lodged an official complaint against the ambassador. He is a loose cannon and I need to have him subdued."

"Andrew," said Sophie contemplatively, "there could be an opportunity in this for us. What he is doing is very unusual. Let me have one more shot at the ambassador and see what I can do."

"All right," said Andrew, "but don't piss him off. He's not a fan, remember?"

"Oh yeah," said Sophie, "I know where I stand with him. I think I am beginning to get a picture of what is troubling him. I will speak with you soon."

"Okay, let's give it a try, but if nothing turns up in the next couple of days then we'll have to come up with something else. Keep me in the loop."

She had this strange feeling that her hunch was right, but too much time was wasted in getting the results she wanted. The ambassador was being a nuisance and once and for all she was determined to put a stop to it. She turned the TV on and then turned it off. She lay in her bed, staring at the ceiling, wondering what was missing in her investigation. There had to be other ways she could expedite the discovery of the identity of the driver of the white car. Suddenly a thought came to her: one stone, multiple birds. She dialed the number Ram had given her. As soon as she was connected, she asked, "Ram, I've some names that I'd like you to run through your computer and see if any of these men have a record."

"Absolutely, I'll call you from the office after I run the search. How did you collect these names?"

"I'll tell you after you run the search. Here are the names."

After she gave him all the names, she put the receiver back on the cradle and smiled. Ram didn't mention the ambassador's visit. Her plan was beginning to take shape.

The morning was quiet in the restaurant as Sophie played with the sugar cubes, making a little tower by placing one on top of another. Her cell phone sat on the table next to her coffee mug. She looked at her watch. It was nine-thirty. *Where is Ram?* she wondered. *Why hasn't he called?* Time ticked by slowly and then at about ten she saw Ram rushing into the restaurant.

"I thought I might find you here!" he said in an excited voice.

"You're late," she said, and seeing the exuberance on his face, asked, "Have you found something?"

"Only one," he said, "only one has a record. He uses many aliases but his real name is Shamsher Singh. He is a small-time crook. Where did you get these names anyway?"

"Well done," said Sophie, signing off her breakfast bill, without offering anything to drink or eat to Ram. She snatched her phone off the table and said, "Let's go pay him a visit. If you want to help me, then let's bring him in for questioning, shall we?"

"Questioning for what? What has he done?"

"Does he have to do something for us to question him? You said he is a crook, so find something," said Sophie and Ram, looking perplexed, nodded in the affirmative as they left in his car.

Thirty-Two

Ram had the address Shamsher gave. He lived in a rundown little place on the edge of the city. No one was home. When Ram questioned neighbors he was told that they'd just missed him. Ram drove down the road from his home slowly and two blocks away they saw a large man wearing a long, black leather coat and multicolored wool hat. "Follow him for a while," instructed Sophie. Shamsher Singh turned into the back street of a local bazaar and stopped at a newspaper stand. There he bought a newspaper and continued walking.

The time was approaching noon as Shamsher Singh entered a small bar at the end of the road. "Can he recognize you in plain clothes?" asked Sophie.

"No, we've never met," answered Ram, "but let me go in and I'll arrest him and take him to the station. This kind of bar is no place for a lady."

"Good," said Sophie, getting out of the car. "I don't see any ladies around so let's go."

The bar exuded a pungent smell and had perhaps never seen daylight. Even in the middle of the day the lights inside the bar were on. A few bulbs without shades were hanging from the ceiling, their shafts of light revealing the strips of peeling paint on the walls, in a bad state of disrepair. For decoration there were wall posters of Indian movies. The scenes on all the posters had a common theme, showing bulging breasts, singing heroes and bad men being shot with blood flying everywhere. Cheap pressed-wood chairs and Formica-top tables lined the walls.

A few people were drinking beer out of large bottles. In a corner two men sat at a table playing a card game with a lot of dirty-looking rupee notes scattered around them.

These men waved to Shamsher Singh to join in and that he did after ordering them a round of drinks. Suddenly the barman came around from behind the bar and approached Ram and Sophie standing in the doorway, saying, "You're in the wrong place. Find yourself another bar, somewhere else." His voice was rough and his demeanor threatening. The bartender, a rough-looking man with greasy black hair parted in the middle and wearing yellow silk shirt and blue jeans, stood defiant and ready to act.

Quick as a flash Sophie pulled out a hundred-rupee note and said, "Just one beer and we will be out of your establishment. Don't worry; we're not journalists, just tourists."

He grasped the note and pointed to a table in the corner. After their beer arrived, Sophie said, "Let's just see if anything happens, maybe we'll get lucky and grab his employer too. So tell me," she took a long sip of her beer and continued, "what really got you into the police force?"

Ram took a couple of short sips and after a moment of silence said, "My father was a police officer and he used to tell me how honorable this profession is. Would you believe that the Delhi police date back to 1237 when the chief of police then was known as *Kotwal?* The institution of Kotwal came to an end with the crushing of the revolt of 1857, and the last Kotwal of Delhi was Gangadhar Nehru, father of Pundit Motilal Nehru and grandfather of Pundit Jawaharlal Nehru, India's first Prime Minister. Who wouldn't be proud to belong to such an institution?"

"Very impressive indeed," Sophie agreed, and then, tapping the table with her index finger, she looked at Ram and then at the barman and then back at Ram. She said, "Call the bartender over; I need to ask him a question."

Ram, with a look of uncertainty, responded, "You'll have to let me in on it. Maybe I can help you better if I know the plan."

"You're helping plenty," said Sophie, picking at some imaginary speck, and then added, "you wanted to work with and learn from the FBI. Well, we are working and all will be revealed in time. If I explain everything, then where is the detective work? You've got to watch and try to understand the plan; that way you'll be fully engaged as a partner, right?"

Sophie knew Ram didn't have a clue what she was talking about but the man's pride was at stake so she saw him nodding his head and he waved to the barman to come over. As the greasy-looking man came closer, he frowned and said, "What?"

Sophie leaned over and whispered something in Ram's ear. His brow narrowed. She nodded. As he pulled out his police badge and showed it to the barman, the man appeared startled and stepped back, saying, "You said you were tourists."

"We lied," said Sophie, "we're the police and I assure you, if we wanted, we could find many violations here, including illegal gambling, to shut you down. But instead, here is another hundred for you if you can tell me something about that man sitting over there playing cards. The one with the black leather coat. Now remember, this time we are doing you a favor, so don't play games with us."

The bartender stared at her hard and then with a sudden jerk, grabbed the back of a chair, pulled it out and sat down. He pocketed the hundred-rupee note lying on the table and in a low voice said, "Well, his name is Shamsher Singh. I don't like him. He is into drugs, burglary, and all sorts of stupid, illegal dealings. Recently he must have made some money because he's been coming in and spending a lot."

"When did this spending spree start?" asked Sophie.

"About ten days ago."

Sophie was about to ask another question when suddenly a beer bottle struck the head of the barman, sending him to the floor. Shamsher and his two friends stood with broken beer bottles in their hands, poised as if ready to attack.

Thirty-Three

Sophie stayed calm as she was trained and well-prepared for just such a situation.

"Who are you two and why have you been following me?" Shamsher roared. Then he saw Ram's police badge on the table and he took a swipe with the broken bottle at Sophie. She leaned back to miss it and simultaneously pushed the table into the three standing men. The corner of table got one man in his groin and he doubled up on the floor with a contorted face, in piercing pain.

Sophie stood and her right foot came up high and caught Shamsher right under his chin. He fell backwards and as he screamed, groaning and cursing, Sophie pulled out her Glock and repeatedly in quick succession fired three rounds in the air. The third man stepped back and dropped the bottle. Everyone froze. "Stay where you are," she shouted, "we're police officers and any further resistance will have serious consequences." She looked around and everyone started to back up slowly. Ram handcuffed Shamsher and with Sophie still holding her gun pointed at the others, they walked out of the bar and back to Ram's car.

After throwing Shamsher in the back of the car, Ram, sitting in the driver's seat, said to Sophie, "Wow, you could have killed them, where did you learn to fight like that?"

"Part of my job, and I wouldn't hesitate to use my gun, either, if the situation warranted it."

"Oh, I don't doubt it," said Ram admiringly.

At the police station Shamsher was booked for illegal gambling, assault and battery on police officer, and resisting arrest. As the desk sergeant finished booking Shamsher, he looked up and gave a smart salute. Sophie smiled at this but then, seeing fear in Ram's face, realized that the sergeant was saluting an officer behind her. It was Ram who made the introductions. "Sir, this is Dr. Sophie Kramer. And this is Mr. Yuvraj Jain, the Special Commissioner of Police of the Law and Order Division."

The Commissioner had a brownish moustache that stood out horizontally on each side of his face, and extremely small features, expressive of nothing much except a certain impudence. "Inspector," said the Commissioner in a cold voice, "what did you say your name was?"

"Inspector Ram Prasad, sir," said he in a low voice.

It seemed the man made a mental note of his name and, turning to leave, he asked Sophie in a gruff voice, "Who are you and what kind of doctor are you?"

"I'm a Special Agent from the FBI," said Sophie, in a calm and composed fashion.

Suddenly he stopped; this utterly unexpected and exceedingly simple answer perplexed him. After a momentary pause, he sputtered, "This is highly irregular. No outside law enforcement agency is to operate here without my knowledge, you understand? Now I want you, Agent Kramer, to explain what you are doing here!"

Sophie replied, "Just routine business. Trying to get acquainted with your system, it is a part of our global awareness program. I thought our embassy had informed your office? I will soon be contacting your training department, but Ram here, who brought in a felon, was kind enough to offer me a tour."

The Commissioner stared hard at Sophie for several moments. "Allow me, Agent Kramer," said the Commissioner in an irritated tone. "I'm sure the Inspector will be busy with his case. Follow me to my office and I will be happy to arrange a tour of the station for you."

Sophie followed the Commissioner. As she joined him in his office and listened to him talk, she noticed that the Commissioner was progressively getting angrier. "I know all about your ambassador but there was no specific request made by your embassy for your involvement, or I would have known. I want you to stay away from this facility and I want no interference from you. If I see you here again without proper authorization, I will be obliged to throw you in prison. Now get out and stay out!" he shouted and pressed a button. The sergeant appeared and was asked to escort Sophie out.

In the late afternoon, when Sophie returned to her hotel, she called Andrew, letting him know that she had got the man she was after and was on her way to interrogate him. When asked what she was waiting for, and why she was delaying the interrogation, she explained something about avoiding an irritated commissioner.

In the evening she asked her driver to take her to the police station. She approached the evening duty sergeant and flashed her FBI card then said, "I'm here to talk with the prisoner I brought in early this afternoon. I've already met your Commissioner and have his consent." She gave him the lie easily.

"I'll have to call my superior," the man said nervously. He had heard of but never seen anyone from the FBI.

"Don't upset anyone after hours," Sophie said with a smile. "Why don't you come in with me, as that way you will know everything about my interview. You could also check the charge sheet; my name along with Inspector Ram Prasad's should be mentioned as arresting officers."

She saw hesitation fading in the sergeant's eyes and that was the moment she decided to drive her point home. "You are a policeman and you must follow what you think is right. Would you like me to call the Commissioner at home for you to talk with him? I have his number."

The officer left his desk and asked a constable to fill in his place while he brought Shamsher from his detention cell to an interrogation room.

Sophie took the lead as the policeman observed, beginning the interrogation with, "You know; you're in deep trouble, and not just with the local police but also with the US authorities. You abducted an American girl."

Shamsher looked at the sergeant and showed his uneasiness at Sophie being there by constantly blinking involuntarily. Finally he spoke, "I don't know what you're talking about."

Thirty-Four

That was a good sign, thought Sophie, because at least Shamsher had said something. No response is also a kind of response that is tougher to break. "Of course you do," said Sophie, in a cool and composed manner. Pursing her lips, she added, "We know all about your throwing money around since that girl was kidnapped. We know about your renting a car, and waiting outside the house where the girl was kidnapped. We've eyewitnesses. You're getting sloppy, Shamsher."

Shamsher sat with downcast eyes and swallowed hard. Sophie took those gestures as a sign of weakness and knew it was the right time to strike. "You didn't know that the girl you kidnapped is an American citizen, so once we get you deported to the US, nobody is going to help you there. Kidnapping little children is a very serious offense. Now on the other hand, if you cooperate and tell us who hired you, and where the girl might be, then I'm sure I could ask the authorities not to insist on extraditing you to the US. You've got to decide now before it's too late. God help you if any harm comes to the girl. Because then you're going to spend the rest of your miserable life in a US prison and there we know how to deal with people like you."

A certain fear came into his eyes. Evidently Sophie's threat worked and it seemed that Shamsher was frightened of being in a foreign prison because perhaps he had seen too many US movies about American prison life. His eyes darted from the desk officer to Sophie and then in a whisper, said, "If I tell you, will you really help me and not send me to America?" His voice trembled and beads of precipitation appeared under his receding hairline.

"Depends on what you're going to tell us," said Sophie, with urgency in her voice, "because if you lie to us then I'll make sure that you're on a plane with me tomorrow."

He looked at the sergeant, who added, "I can't help you if you lie to us. The FBI is in charge of this case and they'll do with you whatever they want. Talk first and then we'd make deals."

Shamsher wiped his forehead with the back of his hand and said, "This man came one night to the same bar where you arrested me and asked for me. He told me if I helped him he would give me five thousand rupees."

Elated with joy that her hunch was paying off, Sophie could not suppress a faint smile. She was happy that soon Amy would be found and hopefully unhurt, and she might even be able to dismantle at least a part of the prostitution ring in New Delhi.

The officer took out a pack of cigarette from his jacket pocket and offered one to Shamsher. He took one with trembling fingers and the sergeant lit it for him.

"Don't stop now, and don't give me any horseshit either," said Sophie, in a voice laced equally with caution and threat.

Shamsher's eyes were wide with fear and alarm as he said, "Well, this man asked me to get him information on a house in Shanti Road where this girl you talk about lives. I gave him all the facts on who and how many people lived there, what time the house would be empty, if there was a guard dog and also about this girl going to another house every Friday for an hour and after that waiting on the steps for one of her parents to collect her. That is all I know, I swear."

"Now that is the biggest horseshit I've ever heard," said Sophie, leaning back in her chair and then looking at the officer as she shook her head from side to side. "I don't think we're going to make any deals with this man. I know he will talk when I take him to a prison in the US. Let's get his paperwork done."

"I will break your neck if you continue with this crap," the policeman warned in an angry voice, grabbing the cigarette out of his mouth and throwing it against the wall. He added, "This is your last chance, and if you hold anything back then I'm afraid we are done here. You'll never see India again."

Sophie had to look the other way to hide her smile. Shamsher said, as if in shock and unable to speak further, "*Hawaldar.*" The sergeant shouted for the guard posted outside the interrogation room and as he appeared, the sergeant said, "Throw him in a dark cell for the night and give him no food or water and then tomorrow he is leaving with this FBI agent."

Shamsher shivered visibly and stuttered, "It's true what I have told you."

"But you didn't tell us everything," said Sophie, gesturing with her hand for the guard to leave and on his way out, he shut the door.

"One more chance," said Sophie in a harsh voice, and coming around to where Shamsher was sitting, continued, "and it is your last chance. We know it was you who rented the white car that was parked outside the house from where Amy went missing."

"Yes, I did rent a car because I was told to do that," Shamsher admitted sheepishly.

"Okay," said Sophie, "now, were you or were you not driving up and down the Shanti Road on the tenth of October and did you park in front of the house where the girl was waiting for her parents?"

Shamsher could not decide on what to say. He looked rather confused; whispered something about 'money'—glanced at Sophie, and then seeing no way out, stared at the table.

Sophie's gaze was boring deep into the back of his skull as she sat back in her chair.

"Yes, I did," Shamsher conceded as he clinched his jaws tightly. He started to sweat heavily. He looked around as if finally being convinced of no way out. "Yes, I took the little girl from the Shanti Road. But I never hurt her. Honest to god, I never touched her. I did as I was told."

"Okay, I believe you," said Sophie, "so where is the girl now?"

"I don't know. Honest. I handed the girl over to the same man who had asked me to kidnap her. I don't even know his name or where he lives. He said he would kill me if I ever talked about this."

"Can you describe him?" asked Sophie.

"Of medium height, maybe in his forties, with long black hair, face pocked from chicken pox and a deep scar on his right cheek, maybe from an old knife injury. And he was well dressed. He did not speak very good Hindi. It was more like a mix of Hindi and Urdu, so I think he could be a Muslim. That is all I know. Honest to god."

Sophie studied him closely, saying, "Well done. See, you can be helpful if you want to be," said Sophie and then looked at the desk officer. "Could you arrange in the morning for him to look at some pictures and if he cannot identify anyone, then order an artist's impression based on his description?"

The police officer called for the constable outside and told him to get Shamsher something to eat and lock him up for the night. He turned to Sophie and said, "Perhaps your presence here tomorrow may not be wise, so let me get this done and I'll call you."

Sophie nodded and shook his hand then returned to her car to drive back to the hotel and give Andrew the good news. Or was it?

Thirty-Five

It was an uneasy night for Sophie even though Andrew had congratulated her on her quick success. Her hunch had paid out handsome dividends and she now had a real chance at finding the missing Amy and hopefully bringing a happy conclusion to the case. She still was anxious, like when, after a long journey, one gets closer to one's home and is gripped with both excitement and nervousness. She wanted to find the person responsible for, and hopefully the crime group behind, Amy's kidnapping. She knew that Shamsher was only a small cog in the big ugly machinery behind the prostitution racket.

The next morning she waited impatiently and when she received no phone call from the sergeant and it was approaching noon, she called her driver and headed to the police station. There the day desk officer received her and said he could not tell her anything but if she so wished, she could see the Commissioner again. She knew it wasn't a suggestion but an order. A constable escorted her to the Commissioner's office.

"Oh, Agent Kramer," said he in a mocking voice, "training, you had said. Huh. I'm afraid your little game has got you and your friend in deep trouble. You saved me the trouble, though, of sending my staff to bring you here for questioning."

"My friend? He is not my friend. Where is Inspector Ram?" she said, without giving attention to his threatening demeanor.

"I'm the one who'll ask the questions," said the Commissioner in a stern voice, and then, wearing a grin on his face, added, "but if you must know, Inspector Ram has been temporarily suspended from the force and is being held for questioning."

"Why, may I ask?" insisted Sophie.

"Because it seems that you two harassed and mistreated a person you arrested yesterday and then you came and pulled that stunt of interrogating him and threatening to send him to America. The poor soul was so distressed that last night he hanged himself in his cell."

"Oh, how very convenient," was what Sophie wanted to say but managed to suppress her words and sank into her chair. She now realized the gravity of the Commissioner of Police's warning about not trusting the Delhi police and its officers. Her mind was in a whirl at the thought that she was up against a bigger enemy than the crime group, the potential consequences ricocheting in her head. The defenders of justice were the real criminals and the chances of finding Amy were now fast slipping away.

"I'd like you to surrender your badge and your gun and I'm afraid we'll have to detain you till we get a chance to talk with your superiors," he said, in his peculiar rough voice that had a certain derisive clang in it, and a certain indomitable quality. He didn't seem bothered that there had been a custodial death at his station.

"I'll do better than that," said Sophie, as she took out her cell to make a phone call. Suddenly the Commissioner sprang to his feet and grabbed her phone. His demanding face now darkened to disapproval. "I'll tell you when you can make a call," said he with an air of nonchalance, "your gun and badge, please." He pressed a bell on his desk and two armed police officers appeared at the door.

Behind the armed guards was Ram accompanied by another senior officer. The senior officer approached the Commissioner and said, "I believe I am right when I say that Inspector Ram belongs to my Crime Division and it is my responsibility to take action against him and Agent Kramer." He looked at Sophie and said, "Would you follow me please?"

What happened next gave Sophie immense pleasure. First it wiped the smile off the Special Commissioner Law and Order's face and then gradually his face started to contort into an ugly mask, dripping with hatred and reprisal. He shouted, "This will not be tolerated. Get her out of my office and out of this building." Grinding his teeth, and with glowing eyes, he said, "This isn't over, and I'm warning you, stay out of my way and stop interfering with our work. Just because you know the Special Commissioner here of the Crime Division isn't going to help you in the future. A man died in his cell because of you. If you have any sense, leave India immediately, and go back to your world. You haven't got a clue what you are up against. Now get out of my office." He tossed her phone on the table.

The Commissioner of the Crime Division picked up the phone and handed it over to Sophie and asked her and Ram to follow him to his office. Once they reached the room, he offered them a seat and said, "Listen, what you two did was illegal. Ram will remain suspended indefinitely. I will have to replace him with another officer to take charge of the kidnapping case. I'm the Commissioner of the Crime

Division and, amongst other things, all kidnapping cases are my responsibility."

"So, Inspector Ram works for you?" Sophie, relaxed in the amiable environment, her eyes on the miserable-looking Ram, said to the Commissioner, "You mustn't blame him. He did what I asked him to do. He is a good officer and doing a good job. I may need his help to find the American girl."

"To be honest with you," re-joined the Commissioner in a matter-of-fact tone, "the American girl's case isn't much of a priority for us. We have thousands of more serious cases of an urgent nature where the clock is ticking against hefty ransom demands. But we cannot have the unauthorized involvement of a foreign law enforcement agency. No offence, but I would much rather that this American girl was found quickly and you left our country. You share with me what you know and I'll see what I can do to help you."

Sophie explained her interviews in Amy's neighborhood and how she came to the conclusion of a rental car having been involved. The Commissioner seemed impressed with what Sophie explained and gave a stern look to Inspector Ram that seemed to say heaps about the Inspector's incompetence. The Commissioner responded, "I will make some inquiries, but Inspector Ram will remain off the case until he has been cleared. I would also recommend that you tone down your involvement while I make my inquiries."

She parted company by shaking hands and thanking the Commissioner and saying sorry to Ram. She was disappointed at losing the most important lead she had, but hoped that it had created some ripples in the New Delhi criminal world. She decided that the time had come to smooth out some of the more difficult aspects of the case, and to start that by solving the Ambassador puzzle. She headed straight for the US Embassy.

Thirty-Six

Upon her arrival at the embassy and after a short wait, the Ambassador greeted her. "This is more like it, with you coming here to give me an update rather having me chase you and the authorities."

Rather than remind him again of his unnecessary interference, Sophie decided to go to the source of problem. She looked at him with questioning eyes and asked, "Why did you never marry? Such stature, such aura, you could have had your pick?"

A little flattery would soften the edges of the harsh and direct question she would eventually ask and it seemed to have worked as he suddenly became quiet. Then the color came back into his face and with bright eyes, he assumed his original demeanor. "What an impertinent question! Are you always this rude? Besides, what does that have to do with your investigation?"

"I've a feeling," said Sophie, "that it has a lot to do with your active involvement in this case. Tell me, am I wrong?"

"Well, not that it is any of your business, but I will tell you exactly what I have told your boss. I have had a flawless career to date in all my overseas postings and I intend to leave a legacy of an unblemished record when I leave India. I am finishing my term soon here and aim to resolve any and all cases in India involving Americans. The sooner you get this into your head the better, because I am not in the habit of repeating myself."

Sophie applauded mockingly, rolled her eyes, got up and started to leave.

"Where do you think you are going?" he snapped. "We haven't finished our conversation yet."

"Oh, I'm finished with you, though," said Sophie, opening the door. "That was quite a performance, but you can't fool me. I bet this is the same bull you dished out to the FBI and I know that none of it is true. But if you want to play games then fine, we'll play games. See you later."

"Get back in here!" said the ambassador in a rage and then suddenly in a contrite voice, he added, "It's the truth. Why do you think I have an ulterior motive? What do you think is going on here?"

Sophie shut the door with a loud thump and walked over where he was sitting and, leaning over him, said, "You want to know what I think? Let me tell you what I think. I think you are Jenifer's biological father and Amy's grand-father. But the question is why you haven't had the courage to tell Jenifer that?"

The ambassador stared hard at her as if judging how much he could trust her. He then slipped one of his hands in his trouser pocket and pulled out a pack of chewing gum and offered a piece to Sophie. She declined. He unwrapped one and slipped it in his mouth. He pushed his chair back, stood up and walked to the window, as if determining how to respond.

To put him at ease, Sophie came up behind him and said, "Look, whatever it is that is troubling you, I prom-ise it will help if you talk to me about it. You may not know this but before joining the FBI, I was a doctor. I can read people's pain and also their lies. I will keep it strictly between us if that helps."

"The missing girl's mother Jenifer," he said in a low voice, "you're right, she is my daughter. I don't know how you know this because I have never told this to anyone." His voice mellowed as he spoke in a soft tone as if whispering a secret.

"I figured that much." Sophie raised her eyebrows and questioned, "You haven't mentioned this even to Andrew, have you? This could change the complexion of this case completely. We won't be looking for a child abduction case for the purposes of prostitution anymore; there could be a terrorist connection. I don't understand why such a vital piece of information is not in the case file or disclosed to the FBI. Are you sure no one knows about this?"

"I am sure," said the ambassador. "Let's sit down, shall we?" They went back to his desk and sat facing each other. He let out a sigh and, rubbing his chin, said, "It's a long story."

"I have time," said Sophie, making herself comfortable in her chair.

"It all happened a long time back. One of those foolish things, you know? I was a young Commercial Attaché in Mexico and at a party met Jenifer's mother. Her name was Victoria. It was a one-night stand. We were both drunk and one thing led to another and we ended up sleeping together. About nine months later I got this call. It was from Victoria saying that she had given birth to a little girl and she claimed it was mine. I wanted to see her and the baby but she refused. She said that she was married now and her new husband had accepted and was willing to raise the little girl as his own. Victoria said it was best for everyone concerned, especially for the little girl, that I never show up. For little Jenifer's sake I promised never to contact Victoria again provided that she send me pictures of Jenifer. That she did and I received a photograph on Jenifer's first two birthdays. Suddenly Victoria died when Jenifer was two years old. Up until her last days, Victoria had maintained that she never disclosed to her husband who Jenifer's father was. Jenifer doesn't know it either. I never married again and Jenifer and her daughter are all the family I have. Little Amy is my granddaughter, my only grandchild."

"But something doesn't add up," said Sophie. "Jenifer claims that she was adopted."

"She was. I can explain that," said the ambassador. "Jenifer was still small when Victoria died and her step-father had decided to put Jenifer up for adoption. I wasn't aware of that at the time; otherwise, I would have adopted her. Someone did and I contracted a private investigator to keep track of Jenifer's whereabouts and now and then send me pictures. But after a while the investigator retired and I lost track of Jenifer's whereabouts."

"That would explain a lot," said Sophie, sounding relieved, "including your disappearance on a fishing trip. When Jenifer showed up here with her own family, you needed time to think things through and decide how to let Jenifer know who you are."

"Yeah, yes, yes," he said abstractedly. "I was caught by total surprise finding her right here in New Delhi. I mean, what are the chances? I needed time away from this place."

"So why haven't you contacted Jenifer and told her who you are? She might have found a lot of comfort in that. She needs her father, her real father."

"After Victoria died and Jenifer was adopted, I had no way of finding out what was happening in Jenifer's day-to-day life. And then when the private investigator retired I lost touch with Jenifer's progress. So you can imagine my surprise when one day at an embassy party I saw Jenifer with her husband right here in New Delhi. We were introduced but I kept my secret. I don't know what she would think of me for not being in her life. Then this happens. Poor Amy. I thought if I could pull every favor and get Amy back to Jenifer then perhaps that would create an opportunity for me to tell her about me. Can you now see why I am so keen to get Amy back to Jenifer?"

In a moment of silence that followed, it seemed as if vocalizing his feelings empowered him with renewed strength as he, without waiting for Sophie's response, abruptly stated, "I think I am going to tell her. I realize now that darkness in its generosity offers one its cloak as security but it never offers a promise of deliverance when the morning light comes. I must go and see her." His head was bowed and his voice was low as if he were talking to himself.

Sophie mulled over what she had learned and then in a statement that sounded like more of a command rather than a request, she said, "You could jeopardize everything by doing that. If the information gets out that the current US ambassador is the grandfather of the abducted child Amy then her life could be in real danger. And no one but you would have to take the blame for it. Just think, what would Jenifer do if she found out that you had endangered Amy's life? You must keep this secret for a little while longer. You really have no choice but to trust me and stay out of my investigation. I will keep you informed, but you are not to contact Jenifer or any authorities till I say so. Do you think you can do that?"

The ambassador stared at her as if seeing her for the first time and then responded, "Yes, yes. I understand. You can count on me; I won't do anything to harm either Jenifer or Amy." The ambassador agreed to Sophie's terms and after a short chat Sophie left his office. She was convinced that he would continue to stay away from Jenifer but was not completely certain that he would not be tempted to give the local authorities a hard time, especially if the results weren't forthcoming. She had to act fast while she had the chance to work uninterrupted.

Thirty-Seven

Sophie returned to her hotel room and called Andrew. "My only lead, the kidnapper was murdered in his prison cell last night by the police authorities, I'm convinced."

"Do you want me to make noise about it?" asked Andrew. "We could rattle a few cages and put out some political pressure?"

"No, that won't do," said Sophie. "I'll have to find a way to turn this setback into an opportunity. Maybe I now have a bigger lead. Shamsher was the kidnapper but he was nothing but contract help and not the source point. The ones calling the shots are under police protection and I am damn sure that this Commissioner of Law and Order knows who they are. I'm going after the Commissioner."

"Watch your back," cautioned Andrew, "and give me a shout if you need reinforcement."

"I'll be okay," affirmed Sophie, in a determined voice. "I'll settle this myself. By the way, the ambassador will not bother us anymore. Well, at least not for a while. He turned out to be the biological father of Jenifer."

After a brief pause Andrew responded, "Are you saying this kidnapping is politically motivated?"

"No, no," said Sophie. "No one knows this. We should keep this information off the record and under wraps for a while."

They spoke for five more minutes and after Sophie managed to convince Andrew that the ambassador's connection was not a factor in the kidnapping, they ended the call. The question now for Sophie was where to start next. The grimy bar? she wondered. Where she found and arrested Shamsher Singh? But she felt convinced that the perpetrators must have been warned by now. Perhaps she ought to up the stakes? How could she make them come after her rather than chasing them, since she didn't know whom exactly to chase. Leaning back in her chair with her feet on the desk, she stared at the ceiling as if searching for an answer there. There was a soft knock on her door. She turned her head, had she imagined it? It was late and the door had a 'Do Not Disturb' sign hanging on it. There it was again and this time more insistent.

She stood up from her chair and went to the door, saying, "Who is it? I don't want to be disturbed." She looked through the peephole and quickly opened the door. "Ram, what are you doing here? How did you know which room I was in?"

"I'm a policeman, aren't I?" he answered, as Sophie invited him in and closed the door behind him.

"I'm so sorry for what happened to you—," said Sophie but was interrupted by Ram.

"Don't be. This is the kind of job I have been dreaming of. I'm the one who should be sorry for losing Shamsher. He was our key lead. I'm sure it was no suicide. Custodial deaths are a common occurrence in our prisons."

"And the Commissioner of Law and Order?" said Sophie.

"The Commissioner certainly knows," said Ram, "but we'd have a hard time proving anything. There are too many layers of corruption in our forces and it would take a lifetime to unravel them."

"What will happen to you?" she asked with concern in her voice.

"I'm suspended indefinitely and not allowed to go active till further notice but not under arrest. I guess I've you to thank for that, you made a good impression on my boss, the Commissioner of the Crime Division. Maybe you ought to work closely with him; after all, it is his case. But don't tell him everything. There is no way of knowing who you can trust."

"So what are you going to do now that you are on suspension?" Sophie wanted to focus the discussion on Ram.

"I guess now I can do what I want without them knowing. Mind you, I've no authority, and can't go through the proper channels, as they've taken my badge away. But I can still get things done, just tell me how I can help," affirmed Ram.

Sophie contemplated this for a few seconds and then said, "Well, we need you to act in an official capacity, so get yourself a badge. I'm sure you'll know where to find one. No questions, I'll finance it. Meet with me tomorrow, but not here."

"How about at the Everest Café, it is located on a quiet lane, off the main street? I'm sure your driver will know it," Ram suggested.

"Okay," said Sophie letting out a sigh. "I'm beginning to develop a taste for your chai tea. I'll be there in the morning but a little later, say, about ten-thirty? I've got a stop to make first thing tomorrow morning."

They shook hands and agreed to meet the next morning.

Thirty-Eight

A t about nine she rang the bell at Jenifer's house and it was Ashok who opened the door. "Oh, it's you," said he glumly.

"Is your wife here? And you'd better stick around, I'm sure you'll want to hear what I've come to say," she said with authority.

When Jenifer came out of the kitchen she asked Sophie, "Is there any news?"

"Let us all sit down," said Sophie, and then once they were settled, she continued. "Amy was indeed kidnapped and I did apprehend the culprit who did it—"

"Where is she!" cried Jenifer, interrupting Sophie in mid sentence. "Why isn't she with you? So you have found her? Is she okay?"

"Jenifer," she responded, raising both her hands against the barrage of questions, "you need to calm yourself. I did arrest the man responsible but as it turned out, the man who abducted Amy was hired by someone else to carry out the kidnapping. Amy has not yet been found but we are getting close and remain very hopeful."

"My God!" exclaimed Ashok. "This is India. If you have the man in custody then you can beat the crap out of him till he tells you everything. Which police station is holding him?"

"Now listen, you've got to believe in me, and the system. We had a setback. The man I arrested cannot tell us anything because he died in prison last night. But we do have something to go on and have not given up."

Sophie could see from Jenifer's body language her disappointment.

"What? Why didn't you ask him where Amy is?" Jenifer demanded, "How could you let him die without telling you Amy's whereabouts? We'll never find Amy now." Jenifer was near hysterics as her soft sobs turned into fitful crying.

"Like I said, we have leads to follow and I'll let you know as soon as I hear something," said Sophie, knowing she was lying, as in reality she had nothing solid to go on.

"So what've you got? You said you have leads," asked Ashok, in a tone of mixed disbelief and insolence.

Sophie gave him a stern look and, getting up to leave, she stared at Ashok, instructing him, "I've hope. You just take care of Jenifer and I'll be in touch soon."

Sophie couldn't help but wonder if the loss of Shamsher had put her back where she had first started.

Later that morning, Sophie met with Ram and, after a moment of silence, as if trying to make her mind up about something, she said, "Ram, what do you know about the Commissioner of Law and Order? He was hell bent to get me off the case and out of India. I think he is dirty, do you agree?"

"I wouldn't be surprised," said Ram, putting his tea-cup back on its saucer. "He and many others like him play dirty all the time. I don't get it. They are in high-ranking positions, and they have power, wealth, so why do they get involved in illegal and immoral activities?"

"Because it is war," said Sophie, as she leaned back into her chair, "and I don't mean war of power but the war of profit. With these people it is never enough. They might think that they're invincible, but they are not." Sophie touched her lips with her index finger as if deep in thought and then, after a momentary silence, continued. "Do you think you can get me any information on the Commissioner? There must be a file on him. Do you have connections inside to get me his file?"

Ram rolled his eyes, saying, "No way. That'd be like committing suicide. There are files on every officer but one doesn't know whom to trust to ask for such a confidential matter. Without probable cause and certain influence, I'm afraid there is no way."

"I could go to the Commissioner of Police, but I don't want to put her in an awkward position. You're right, without proof we can't touch him. I think we have only one option left." She leaned forward and lowered her voice. "We're going to start tailing him and find out everything we can on his daily activities."

"But what if you're wrong in suspecting him?" asked Ram, scratching his head. "It could be someone else at the police station. It could be anybody. I mean, there are so many corrupt officers there."

"Yes, you're right, I suspect," answered Sophie. "I can't prove anything yet because I don't have any dirt on the Commissioner. But I've seen something in his eyes and that tells me he is scared and confused."

Ram nodded, agreeing with her, and said, "Okay, let's do it. Would you like me to take my car or shall we go in yours?"

"Neither," said Sophie. "You rent a car, a different one every day, to deflect any suspicion and let us begin first thing tomorrow morning before he even leaves the house for work."

Thirty-Nine

The next morning Ram picked Sophie up at 7 a.m. in a dark-blue Ambassador, a rental from a local company, and they drove to where the Commissioner of Law and Order lived. He parked the car about three houses away and on the opposite side of the street. They waited. Sophie scanned the area and said, "This looks like an expensive area, all the house are large and guards are posted at their gates."

"One of the more expensive areas in New Delhi," confirmed Ram, "and it is for the elite of the city."

"Could a Commissioner afford such a place on his salary?"

Ram laughed and then said, "I guess that is a rhetorical question. No, a Commissioner could not afford such a place on his salary unless he has other means of income or has inherited a large sum of money or won a substantial lottery."

"It just keeps getting easier," she said, smiling. "It seems that he is our man and we have to find a way to bring him down. Oh, look!" The guard outside the Commissioner's house opened the gates and a large silver Mercedes emerged from the gates, turned left and eased into the thin traffic of the residential area. Ram followed at a distance. Meandering through the traffic, the Mercedes made its way to the police station without any stops en route. Time passed as Ram and Sophie waited outside the police station. After Ram checked his watch for the third time, Sophie asked, "Need to be somewhere?"

"This waiting game is making me hungry. It is eleven," said Ram, "and this is like watching fingernails grow. Would you like me to go get us something to eat?"

"Hmm," Sophie responded. "Okay, you take a cab and get a sandwich or whatever you can find and I'll stay here and keep watch."

"Oh, I know just the place for some great takeout but it will take a little time. I'll be back as soon as I can," said Ram and slipped out of the car.

Ram had been gone only about two minutes when Sophie noticed the silver Mercedes come out of the station and head west, the way Ram had gone. She quickly moved into the driver's seat, started the ignition and began following the Mercedes. She realized that she did not know the city well and so could not afford to lose sight of the luxury vehicle. Twenty minutes later the Mercedes stopped outside a movie theater, the Commissioner stepped out, bought a ticket and went inside.

Sophie parked the car and went over to the ticket window and asked, "Excuse me, but what time does the movie start?"

"It started about forty-five minutes ago," said an old man sitting behind the window. He was wearing rather thick glasses, behind which he blinked a couple of times and said, "Would you like to buy a ticket?"

She pondered why the Commissioner would, in the middle of the day, go to a movie that had already started. "Madam, a ticket?"

"No," she responded, "no, thank you."

She went back to sit in the car and waited. Twenty minutes later the Commissioner came out of the theater and as soon as he stepped into his car, the Mercedes left. She decided not to follow the Mercedes and waited at the theater instead. About ten minutes passed and she continued to stay inside her car. She began to feel hungry and suddenly realized that Ram would be looking for her. As she started the engine she looked up and saw a good-looking and well-dressed man coming out of the movie theater. He put on his sunglasses and started walking towards a dark green BMW 7 parked only a few cars away from where Sophie's car sat. She aimed and shot several pictures of him and the car. A uniformed driver hurriedly came out of the BMW and opened the back door and the gentleman nodded at him, sliding into the car.

Sophie forgot all about her hunger and started to follow the BMW. She tailed the BMW for about thirty minutes before it stopped in front of a large two-story house. A guard rushed out and opened the gates and the car drove in. Sophie stopped fifty feet short of the entrance. She took pictures of the house. After several minutes she pulled out her phone and looked at it. "Shit," she said aloud. There was a missed call from Ram. With an early morning start, she had forgotten to switch off the silent mode. She dialed Ram. An excited voice on the other end asked, "Where are you? I'm so worried, I thought you may have been arrested or worse, hurt."

"I'm okay," she said, "so relax. I'm sorry that I had to leave you behind. Look, I'll ask directions and find my way back to my hotel. Why don't you take a cab and meet me in my room in about an hour, okay?"

Forty

An hour later Ram and Sophie were eating tandoori chicken, biryani rice and samosas and while Ram ordered some tea, Sophie asked for a cold beer. Sophie related what had happened at the movie theater.

Ram almost froze in terror. "Oh, you shouldn't have gone there," he responded, and added hurriedly, "not without me. It could be dangerous for you."

Sophie pretended not to notice his reaction and casually waved off his remarks with a smile. She downloaded pictures from her camera onto her notebook computer and copied them on a flash drive. Handing over the flash drive to Ram, she said, "Look, I am trusting you with this part of the case. Look at these pictures and have them cross-referenced because I'd like to know who that man in the dark glasses is. Maybe running a check on the BMW could give us some clue to his identity."

"You think he has something to do with Amy's disappearance?"

"Too soon to tell, but for the Commissioner to go to a movie theater in the middle of the day and halfway through the movie, and then leave after twenty minutes, tells me he did not go there to see the movie. My guess is that he went there to meet someone and this someone is likely to be this man, as he came out without waiting for the movie to end, soon after the Commissioner left."

"Maybe some others came out after this man? Perhaps the movie was boring?" Ram suggested.

"I don't know about that," said Sophie, shaking her head. "I didn't wait to see if anyone else surfaced, because I followed this man to his house."

"Hmm." Ram let out a sigh and rubbed his forehead with the palm of his hand. "I wonder what made the Commissioner go to a movie theater and stay there for only twenty minutes. Obviously, as you suggested, he was meeting someone, and you think this someone is the man in the photo, the one with the BMW?"

"Why are you repeating everything that I just told you?" asked Sophie. "Now get going and bring me back the answers to these questions, please."

Ram left and two hours later called Sophie. "The man you photographed is an important person. His name is Ali Khan. He is involved in many charity programs and the co-founder of the Gandhi Memorial Centre, which is one of his key projects for destitute children. We have no official record on the man, looks like he is clean."

"You don't say?" she responded contemplatively. "And where did he get all his wealth? Large house, in an expensive residential area, a Seven Series BMW, all from his charity projects?"

"Actually, I did check out his background. It is an interesting story. He comes from a poor family," she heard Ram say. "His father was a soldier. His money has never been questioned, but from what I've gathered, he has strong connections in the government and thus was never investigated. I've been advised by my friends to tread very carefully around him. I have been told that he is not the kind who would be involved in abducting a five-year-old girl. He is a big game player."

"What about his family?" Sophie asked, ignoring his advice.

"He has a wife and two children. A boy and a girl, both young."

"I've a feeling that he is connected not only with government officials but with the police too. You know whom I mean? I've to find a way to put Ali and the Commissioner together."

"What can I do to help?" asked Ram.

"I'll let you know. I'll be in touch," said Sophie, and switched off her cell.

Later when she called Andrew and explained to him her findings, Andrew asked, "And how do you propose to enter this Gandhi Memorial Center?"

"Through the front door, how else?" laughed Sophie, and after a few minutes of further discussion, pressed the red button on her cell.

The next morning Sophie arrived at the GMC at half-past eight. Sophie asked her driver to stay in the car as she walked towards the gates of the building where an armed guard stared inquisitively at the approaching Sophie.

"How can I help you, Madam?" a Gurkha guard dressed in a crisp uniform asked Sophie.

"I'm a journalist from the US," she said, showing him her camera, "and would like to talk with Mr. Ali."

"You need to make an appointment first," he said, shaking his head from side to side. "Call Mr. Aamir and he will give you an appointment."

"Well, you call Mr. Aamir now and tell him I'm outside," said Sophie in a rather stern voice.

"Sorry Madam, you'll have to call from outside. I've my orders."

Sophie studied him for a moment and then walked right up to the gate and at the top of her lungs shouted, "Anybody there? I'm not going away. I want to see Ali."

"Please Madam," the Gurkha urged, as he grabbed her by the arm and started to drag her away from the gate, "you're not allowed in here."

Sophie saw a man walking down the path and coming to the gates. When he arrived at the gate, he asked in a perplexed tone, "What is going on and who are you?"

"I'm a journalist," Sophie answered as she pulled out a fake identity, "I'm supposed to have an appointment to see Mr. Ali. If someone screwed up, then it's not my fault, and I've come a long way, all the way from New York. I must see Mr. Ali."

It was the insistence in her voice or perhaps the determination on her face that caused the man to relent. "My name is Aamir and I don't remember making any appointment. Never mind, come in." The gates opened and she entered the compound.

Forty-One

Once she entered the main gate she noticed that a small road constructed of interlocking bricks led to an administration office building. Everything was quiet and there was no sign of life around her.

The reception room was large with deep-cushioned, expensive-looking furniture scattered about. Fresh flowers in large multi-colored glass vases accentuated the beauty of the turmeric-colored walls, adorned with exquisite oil paintings of old Rajasthan royal life. The office and its decor were equal to that of a lobby in a five-star hotel.

"Please take a seat and I'll inform Mr. Khan," said Aamir, and he disappeared through a side door that led to the inner part of the old and large building. A few minutes later and through the same door, a well-dressed gentleman appeared, the man she saw at the movie theater.

"My name is Ali Khan. It is not often that we get a journalist from abroad. What can I do for you?" Ali said, in a business-like tone.

He was a man of about forty, in his prime with unblemished skin and not an ounce of fat on his body. His muscles were not what one would call rippling, but toned and attractive. And as he looked at her abstractly, he seemed like some high-performance engine idling between gears, with his unfathomable eyes of charcoal-black pupils trained on her.

"Mr. Khan, I have heard good things about you and what you have done at this institution. I would like to write a little piece about your facility and talk to you for a few minutes, if that is okay with you?" Sophie said tactfully with a charming, rather seductive smile. Ali's smile widened. He had quite a few inquiries about the charity houses after the BBC had broadcast their documentary on GMC. Such publicity had helped to maintain his cover and the USA could be a new and exciting frontier from which to solicit aid.

Seeing him mellow with the flattery, Sophie inquired, "A lot of organizations would be impressed with what you have accomplished here. I know you're a busy man so I'll come straight to the point. How did the idea of GMC come about and how do you raise funding for it?"

Crossing his legs and straightening the crease of already meticulously pressed trousers, Ali responded, "It all started on a very small scale when this building and land came up for sale some time back and a few charities that prefer to remain anonymous, provided funding for its acquisition. We of course refurbished and expanded the building and now it serves as a shelter to runaway and destitute kids. Today we have more than one hundred such unfortunate boys and girls here. But we also place these boys and girls in foster homes through various agencies, so the numbers go up and down and we do what we can for these children."

Ali was cool and composed and Sophie needed to push him off his perch so she dug a little deeper. "What about the parents of these children? Doesn't anybody try to reunite the families?"

"That is the job of the local police. When we receive a new child we provide whatever information we have to the police and also properly register each and every one of the children with the police." The smile on his face looked as if permanently pasted there.

Sophie realized that Ali wan not an amateur and she would need to play her cards right to crack his front. She shot another arrow, asking, "How are you and your staff compensated? I mean, it's hard work and people don't do it for free, and the operating expenses alone for over one hundred kids must be enormous?"

"Giving care and a home to destitute children is award enough," Ali responded courteously, "and like I said before, we have significant support from various charities and private donors."

Sophie decided to penetrate a little deeper, so she asked, "Would these donors include some of your local politicians?"

This question seemed to wipe off some of his smile as a corner of his mouth twitched slightly. Sophie felt a sense of satisfaction as she realized she was making progress. Ali continued, "Like I said before, our donors wish to remain anonymous." Frowning now, he further added, "Whom did you say you work for?"

Sophie knew that it was a perfect time for her to give him more rope to hang himself. She noted his uneasiness but ignored his question and said, "The whole world ought to see what you've accomplished here. Would you mind if I've a quick look around, and take some pictures?"

The smile completely vanished from his face. He sat very still in his chair, his face going hard and remote. He was evidently trying to avoid something that was stuck like a spike in his consciousness.

Ali's eyes narrowed, as if he had swallowed something unpleasant, and he answered, "I'm afraid that is not possible. GMC has its rules and policies laid down by the board of trustees and even I cannot break them. Children could be further traumatized by such intrusions and we cannot expose them to any more suffering than they have already experienced. We do not allow strangers to talk to our charges," Ali stated decisively.

Sophie blew out a little breath out, wondering if she had got him now. "You allow the Special Commissioner of Law and Order to come and visit, so I don't think it would hurt if I were to spend a few minutes with the children." Sophie said this coldly. Bull's eye, she thought; at the mention of Commissioner, a little nervousness crept across Ali's face like the shadow of a drifting cloud.

"I don't know who this Special Commissioner is and besides, I have already told you that we remain transparent with the police because the children's future is at stake. You're a stranger to these children. These children hate strangers because in most cases it was strangers who plucked these kids from their homes. These children are runaways from those strangers and have found a home here. They cannot be paraded in front of yet more strangers. I'm very sorry," Ali responded, as he looked at his watch.

"Funny you don't remember the Special Commissioner. I could swear I saw you with him yesterday at the movie theater." Suddenly Sophie closed her little notebook and stood up. "I've kept you away from your work. Thank you so much. Please give my regards to the Commissioner, my name is Sophie Kramer."

Suddenly Ali's face was as white as an unpainted canvas and his mouth contorted as if he had developed paralysis. A small bead of perspiration grew on his forehead and gradually formed into a tiny rivulet traversing down towards his brows. He agitatedly wiped it with the back of his hand. "I know who you are," said Ali, slowly grinding his teeth, "and let me give you a little friendly advice. Not that it has anything to do with me, but if I were you, I would forget about the Commissioner. This is India and our culture is very old and complex. You'll not understand our ways of working and living. Don't waste your time here. Take my advice and go home."

"Well, thank you," said Sophie, walking towards the door to leave his office, "you're the second person to give me the same advice. I'll think about it."

As Sophie came out of the gate she smiled, realizing that Ali had just made his first mistake. Sophie was experienced enough to know the difference between friendly advice and a threat, and this was a clear threat. She had touched a raw nerve and she knew it.

When later she called Andrew, he asked, "How did it go?"

"Better than I expected," replied Sophie confidently, "he took the bait. Now I'll wait for his next move."

"Bait? What bait?" asked Andrew.

"Me, of course," said Sophie, "I think we have a chance now."

A chance that could cost Sophie her life!

Forty-Two

The next day Sophie decided to visit Jenifer to gather more information on her relationship with her in-laws, in particular, her mother-in-law. In the male-dominated society of India, she had learned that the only field where women historically had a stronger role was in dissolving unsuitable marriages. But unfortunately the measures used by disgruntled mother-in-laws were often fatal for the unsuitable brides. They ended up with severe burns, maimed, and sometimes dead. Besides, Sophie wanted to keep all her options open until such time that she had a conclusive lead to follow.

Sophie's car was a half a block away from the hotel when a truck coming from the opposite side suddenly accelerated and collided head-on with Sophie's car. The impact of the collision was so severe that the truck pushed her car backward about ten yards, crumpling it in the process. Sophie's car eventually turned over sideways and the gasoline started to drip from the punctured gasoline tank.

The truck reversed for about two yards as if looking to get away from the scene of the accident, but instead rammed into Sophie's car again, forcing it to skid backward for another two to three yards. The truck driver's intentions were quite clear—he was going in for the kill. Sparks caused by the second impact started a fire by setting alight a small pool of gasoline around the car. Seeing the fire engulfing the car, the truck reversed again but this time took off in the direction from which Sophie's car had come.

Sophie did not see this coming. There was not much traffic around but a few cars and scooters stopped and its passengers watched in horror as the crumpled car caught fire. No one had enough courage to rescue her and the driver from the burning car, but found plenty of time to watch the free show.

She was in shock and it took her a few moments to realize what had happened. She looked at the surrounding flames and realized she had to hurry and get both herself and the driver out of the car. She tried but could not unbuckle her seatbelt. The car was filled with shattered glass. Sophie's face was bleeding and she was pinned down between the two seats, unable to push the front seat away from her.

The driver was not moving at all. The entire steering wheel had buried itself into Mr. Singh's collapsed chest and it seemed that several of his ribs were broken. Sophie repeatedly shouted at the driver, asking him to get out, but she did not know if he was still alive.

Sophie could smell gasoline and she saw flames gradually surrounding the car. She knew that the fire would soon engulf them completely or worse, the leaking gasoline tank might explode. This was India and she knew that there was no time to wait for a rescue crew to arrive. She had to do something and fast. She managed to move her upper body sideways and with her free leg, started kicking the door away from her. The door started to give and then it fell apart. Sophie tried one more time with all her might to pull herself out of the car by dragging her trapped leg out from between the seats. But the leg was firmly wedged between the seats.

Suddenly a young man in blue jeans and white shirt who looked like a student climbed atop the car and shouted to Sophie, "I think your driver is dead; you better come out while you can. Here, I'll push the front seat and you try to climb out."

She feared that the car might blow up at anytime. Time was running out. She shouted back, "Okay, push hard, *now*."

The stranger, disregarding the fact that his body was being scorched by intense heat, gave one mighty push to move the front seat to allow Sophie more room and free her trapped leg and it worked. Sophie tumbled out of the car. The young man quickly grabbed her and helped drag her as far away as possible from the burning car to escape from the impending explosion. As soon as he helped Sophie sit against the sidewall of a house, a mighty explosion threw him off his feet.

Her jaw clenched hard as she realized that it was too late to help the driver now engulfed in the inferno.

After a while, with still no rescue services in sight, the young man offered to take Sophie to the emergency room at the hospital and she accepted. Upon arriving there, she thanked the young man for all his assistance and he simply smiled and shook her hand. The emergency workers bandaged a gash on the side of her head and attended to her several minor cuts and bruises.

An hour later she was out of the emergency clinic. She called the US embassy and talked with the ambassador, who immediately arranged for a new car and driver and insisted on seeing her. She told him that she would come to the embassy the following day. After reflecting on the events of the day, she dialed Andrew and gave him an account of what had transpired.

"This will not be tolerated," he said in a determined voice. "A deliberate attack on an agent is an attack on the entire Bureau. I'm sending reinforcements."

"Andrew, this was a calculated risk I took. I'm the one who set up this trap and Ali is walking into it. I believe I've shaken both Ali and the Commissioner and now that their cages have been rattled they are going to make rash decisions and false moves. This is working according to my plan. Let me have a few more days and I'm sure I'll have results."

There was silence for several moments on the other end of the line. Sophie spoke again, "Andrew, I need this. You cannot take this case away from me. Give me a few more days?"

"Okay, but on one condition," said Andrew, in an uncompromising tone.

"Don't put constraints on me," said Sophie vehemently. "I can't operate like that."

""You haven't heard my conditions yet," said Andrew, unperturbed. "They might help you."

Sophie closed her eyes and said in a low voice, "What are your conditions?"

"You must have gathered enough information to build a file on this case with details on Ali and the Commissioner; send that file to Matt and ask for his opinion."

"His opinion or his advice?" questioned Sophie with a hint of irritation in her voice.

She heard Andrew laugh, and that helped to calm her anxiety. Then she heard him say, "I know you better than that. You're not about to act on someone's advice as it may interfere with your intuitive methods of action. You're a hell of an instinctive player and it works for you. No, just get his point of view on what happened, okay? He's the best profiler we have."

"Thanks, Chief. I will, and you'll see results soon."

"So, what is your next move? You're not going to just sit there and let them make another strike on you, are you? I need to know what you're planning next."

Sophie let silence give gravity to her suggestion, "I'm going to get a warrant to search the GMC. I believe Ali is dirty and he uses the GMC to do his dirty work."

"And how exactly do you intend to get this search warrant, considering Ali has full police protection and every child at the GMC is registered with the police department?"

"I'll come up with something, trust me," and with that she abruptly finished her phone call.

Forty-Three

Later that day, she updated her case file and sent it as an attachment via email to Matt, asking him a few questions and his opinion on the case. The next morning when a new car and driver arrived, she went to the embassy to meet with the ambassador.

The ambassador saw her immediately and he looked as if he hadn't slept all night, announcing at her arrival, "If you can't even take care of yourself then how you are ever going to find Amy?"

Sophie gave him a stern look. "I'm putting my life on the line for your granddaughter so I don't appreciate your using that tone with me, okay?"

The ambassador shook his head, and said, "I didn't mean it that way. I know I can help if you let me. Allow me to reach the higher authorities and I can get you some real answers. And I promise to not get in your way."

"No," she said firmly. "We've made an agreement and I am going to hold you to it. You will not make a move till I say so. Just sit tight and give me a little more time. Don't be impatient. Things are working according to my plan. Just stay put."

After a few more words of assurance she managed to calm him before she left.

On the second ring Sophie picked up her phone and punched the green button, saying, "I was expecting a call from you."

"Well, I guess I owe you one for Nairobi," said Matt, "but it seems you like to live on the edge. I hear that you almost got yourself killed."

"I'm not dead yet," laughed Sophie, and then in a serious voice, asked, "Did you see the case notes that I sent to you?"

"That is why I'm calling," said Matt, with a hint of solemnity in his voice, "but first a question. What is it that you are singularly focusing on?"

Sophie reflected on this before answering, for Matt never asked frivolous questions. After a couple of moments of silence she heard him urge, "Come on, Sophie, it is not a rhetorical question. I need an answer, what are you focused on in this case? Is it Ali or the Commissioner or the link between the two?"

"Aren't they all interrelated? It is the link that is my focus," she said in an introspective voice and after a moment added, "Ali and the Commissioner are both involved and I'm trying to find out their modus operandi. Once I know that I believe I will know what they have done with Amy."

"Wrong," said Matt instantly, "your focus actually seems to be elsewhere. Think hard."

"Okay, Matt, I know they did it. I feel it in my gut," said Sophie vehemently.

"And there you have it," Matt snapped, "your gut. You see, your focus is on yourself. One last question and then I'll answer your queries. Are you trying to prove that Ali is wrong or that you are right? Again, think hard, because it is important."

"Okay, okay," agreed Sophie, haltingly. "I get it. I am too close to the situation and I need to step back a bit. From now on I will focus on Ali and force him to show his hand."

"Now you have it," said Matt in a cheerful voice, "you have the right approach, no doubt about it. Just need to shift the focus. Make him vulnerable and then let him come to you."

Sophie nodded as if reassuring herself with the suggestion, and then asked, "What do you see in this guy? What makes Ali tick?"

"Ali is one of those men who have so much repressed anger in their hearts that he hates everything in his world. He is hell bent on getting even for something that happened a long time back in his childhood. He will not stop at anything."

"So how does one trap a monster like that?" she asked.

"Ali and guys like him live by a code of conduct and ethics. That is their survival; it is their shoreline. That is what brings them close to home. And trust me when I tell you we are all trying to get home. Learn about that and strike at him where he is most vulnerable. You are in the field now so you are the best person to figure it out."

"Thanks, Matt," she said in a tone filled with gravity. "I know exactly how to go about it. You're the best."

After Sophie said goodbye to Matt she felt invigorated. The wheels in her mind were turning. She needed to come up with ideas that would propel her plan forward and allow her to come up with results. The time had come for her to push even harder.

Forty-Four

That afternoon Sophie shared a part of her plan with Ram and asked, "Can you think of any way to secure a search warrant for the GMC?"

"Impossible," said Ram, shaking his head.

"Not necessarily. In my meeting with the Commissioner of Police, she told me that she enjoys tremendous support from the Leader of the Congress Party, who is also a woman. I don't think we could ask for a higher authority than that in influencing the right people to issue a search warrant, right? You said that in India corruption is everywhere, so why can't we use it to our advantage?"

"The leader of the Congress party?" laughed Ram, "it'd be easier to get an appointment with God."

"Well," said Sophie, winding up her discussion with Ram, "let us bring both forces to bear. You pray to your god and I will plead with the Commissioner to get me an appointment with the leader of the Congress Party."

The look of amusement vanished from his face. "You're serious? You are really going after that warrant, aren't you? Oh, you don't know this country like I do." A curious expression settled on his face, but it did not resemble admiration.

"And your country doesn't know me," said Sophie, "so I guess we are even. See you soon."

After Ram left, Sophie pulled out a business card and dialed a number on her cell phone. When a voice responded, Sophie said, "Commissioner Rao, this is Agent Kramer. I'm sorry to disturb you but I need your help. You did say I could call you if I needed your assistance?."

By this time apparently the news of Sophie's accident had reached the Commissioner and she asked Sophie about her health. Sophie responded, "I'll live." She then gave a brief progress report on key points and asked how she could obtain a search warrant for GMC.

"I cannot get involved without proper and solid evidence, not if it implicates my officers. If I were to be proven wrong then I'd lose the confidence of my entire staff. What you are suggesting is a suicidal move for me. Your suggestion of getting help from the leader of the Congress party is good but it will have to be done without getting me involved or any help from me—"

Sophie, exasperated at listening to the Commissioner, interrupted with, "I'm not going to quit. There has to be a way," she insisted, "isn't there something I could do or someone I could appeal to without getting you involved? I fully understand your position but you need to appreciate mine."

Sophie's unwavering determination worked. "I'm going to give you a name and a number. You can contact him. He is a close confidant of the leader and he might be able to arrange a quick appointment. But call him after twenty minutes, okay?"

Sophie anxiously waited by the desk, staring at the number she had jotted down in her small diary. She then looked at her wristwatch and started tapping the table with her pen. She stood up and walked to the window, looking out at the grey sky. She turned around and stared at the phone. Eight minutes had passed since the Commissioner had talked to her. She opened the mini bar, took out a chilled beer, and popped open the top. She drank out of the bottle and wiped her lips with the back of her hand. Suddenly she jumped when her hotel phone sitting on the desk rang.

She picked the receiver and said, "Kramer."

"Agent Kramer," a refined and self-confident voice at the other end said, "you don't know me and I apologize for this intrusion but I got a message and your contact details from a mutual friend of ours. And I thought it would be only polite if I were to call you rather than ask you to call a stranger."

"I don't know your name," said Sophie to the voice.

"Oh, I'm sorry," he said in an amiable tone, "my name is Jai Singh. I believe you are trying to secure a warrant to search the GMC premises?"

"Better not to talk on this phone," said Sophie, hurriedly, "is there a way we could meet?"

"Why, certainly," said Singh. "I'll arrange for a car to pick you up from your hotel. The car should be there in thirty minutes. I hope that is convenient?"

"Thank you," said Sophie, relaxing a bit, "that would be fine. How will I know your car?"

"I'll get the driver to ring your room."

About forty minutes later her desk phone rang again. She answered and it was the concierge advising her that a car was waiting in the front of the hotel to pick her up.

She came down and saw from the lobby a large, black Mercedes with a neatly dressed driver in a crisp white uniform, holding the back door open, smiling at her. She slid inside and the driver closed the door. Leaning back in the comfortable seat, she closed her eyes and for the first time felt a throbbing pain in her head. She did not move a muscle or open her eyes for about twenty-five minutes, when the driver said, "Mem Sahib, we're here."

She stepped out of the car and realized that she was at a private airport and a Lear Jet was parked inside a hanger. A man in uniform approached her. "Good afternoon," he said, courteously. "I'm your pilot and the plane is ready. We'll take a short flight to Jaipur where Mr. Singh is waiting for you. Please follow me." He turned on his heels and without waiting for an answer from Sophie, walked back into the hanger. Sophie followed.

Forty-Five

Twenty minutes later they were airborne and heading west to Jaipur. As the plane reached cruising altitude a pretty girl, smartly dressed in a sari, came out of the cockpit to announce, "I'm your co-pilot, Mem. May I offer you a drink and some refreshment?"

"Not tea," Sophie said, "perhaps a scotch?"

"Certainly," said she and poured a double Glemorangie. Sophie took a sip and leaned back in her thick-cushioned seat. "Oh, thank you. You've made my day."

Waiting on the tarmac at Jaipur was a white, Seven Series BMW with a driver in red tunic and white trousers with a large red and gold-colored fanned turban. He saluted Sophie and opened the back door for her.

The sun was setting when they arrived in Jaipur. The large amber globe with its soft golden sunrays was casting long shadows from trees with their leaves gently swaying in a cool breeze. The façade of every house and building in Jaipur was covered with pink stone that was mined from a local query. They called it the pink city, city of the color of passion. The pink dwellings in an amber glow made Jaipur look like the city of a fairy princess.

The BMW glided through the busy streets of Jaipur and about thirty minutes later pulled into the drive of the Rambagh Palace Hotel. The driver came around and opened the door for Sophie. As she walked into the reception area the manager from behind the counter came around running and said, "Madam, please follow me."

They walked to the Polo bar where a sign read, 'Closed for Private Function.' Inside there was only one person who stood up to receive Sophie. She looked at the man approaching her with an extended hand. Standing at well over six feet, he was clean-shaven and smartly dressed in a black suit with starched white open-collar shirt. He had sparkling eyes that were soft brown in color. His almond-colored complexion complemented his dark brown, long hair. His slim body moved gracefully as he came to shake Sophie's hand and said, "Welcome to Jaipur, Agent Kramer. The Police Commissioner said that you're a special friend. Allow me to introduce myself," said he with a charming smile on his face, "my name is Jai Singh. I hope your journey was comfortable?"

Before Sophie could respond, his voice changed to carry an authoritative tone as he talked to the manager still standing behind Sophie. "Some refreshments and drinks. And then make sure that we are not disturbed. We'll have dinner shortly."

"Yes, Your Highness," said the manager, as he bowed and stepped out of the bar.

Sophie first looked at the manager leaving the bar and closing its doors behind him and then at her host, asking, "Your Highness?"

There was a little hesitation in his face, Sophie noticed. He paused for a moment and then said, "I am the only son of the late Maharaja of Jaipur. When my father passed away, naturally I inherited his estate and the title of Raja and Your Highness. But in modern India it means nothing and to be honest, I don't care for these pompous titles. Why does my name have to be Raja Jai Singh? Jai Singh is better."

"So shall I address you as Your Highness—" Sophie couldn't finish her sentence as he interrupted. "Oh, please don't. Just call me Jai, that will be fine, Agent Kramer."

"Sophie," she said hurriedly, "and let's discard the formalities on both sides then. Please, just call me Sophie."

"Well then, Sophie," he said, laughing softly, "how is your head?"

"My head? Oh, yes, my head." Sophie touched the site of her injury. The memory of the burning car and the body of her driver came flooding back to her. She grimaced.

"Does it hurt?" he asked, with concern. "I've an excellent physician who could take a look?"

"Oh, it is nothing," she said, waving with her hand as if purging herself of the bad memories. "Any chance of a scotch?"

"Scotch?" he said, raising his eyebrows. "I thought it was forbidden for FBI agents to drink alcohol?"

"Well," said Sophie, in a mock whisper, "if you won't tell then it will be our secret."

He laughed as he poured scotch into two glasses, saying, "I'm not a very good host, am I?"

"Terrible," she laughed. Taking the glass of scotch from him, she asked, "So how well do you know the leader of the Congress party?"

"Since the independence of India from British rule in 1947, my family has always been very close to the Nehru family and the Congress party. But why don't we talk about it over dinner. I believe dinner is being served in a few minutes outside on the lawn."

They talked for a short while over their drinks and soon they were told that dinner was waiting. As they strolled out of the bar, Sophie pointed at the sign, noting, "You've some influence here, it must be nice?"

"This used to be a part of our residential palace but we had to give some of it up for hotel purposes, as it brings in revenue," he stated casually.

"I notice a hint of accent in your English?" said Sophie, looking at the Raja inquisitively.

"Oxford," he stated. "I was there just to study. My heart is here and I love working with the Congress party. I think it is the only political party that has promise for our democratic system."

The meal was served in a silver service on the sprawling lawns of the palace by the fountains where peacocks roamed freely. The Rajasthani dishes were delicate in flavor and subtle in taste. They were also rich with cream and saffron but tender in taste. All throughout dinner Jai explained in detail the history of his family and their commitment to the Congress party. It seemed that the Congress party needed more of his family's support to keep the opposition parties out of the very important state of Rajasthan and in return, the royal family enjoyed the diplomatic privileges that the ruling Congress party had bestowed upon them. It was a mutually beneficial arrangement that worked well.

After a sumptuous dinner and long discussion, they bid each other good night as the stars above sparkled benignly.

Forty-Six

The next morning, breakfast was served but not in the hotel. It was waiting in the adjoining building that was the residential palace of the Raja and inside a room that could have housed a dinner for two hundred people. Welcoming Sophie with a smile, Jai Singh said, "Good morning. I trust you had a good sleep?"

"I'd sleep better," said Sophie, half warily and half expectantly, "if you could arrange a meeting with the leader of the Congress Party."

"I admire your commitment," said Jai, pulling a chair out for Sophie, "and knew that you'd ask me this in the morning. Well, last night I managed to get through to the leader of the party and have scheduled your meeting this afternoon."

"Really?" she responded excitedly, "that's great. Thank you. Shouldn't we be going then? We don't want to be late, do we?"

"I've the jet ready. We'll have breakfast and then be on our way. We've plenty of time."

Sophie ate her breakfast quickly as she did not want to miss this chance. She had heard and read a lot about the Congress party leader. She was a widow from the Gandhi family and the only non-Indian who had ever led a political party in the history of free India. Even when her party won the last election she, out of respect for the feelings of Indians, refused to accept perhaps the most coveted position of Prime Minister and instead appointed one of her ministers, an Indian, to take that role. The leader of the Congress party was one of the most respected women in India and she paid for that respect by committing herself to fight corruption in the Indian government.

Upon landing at a private airport and on their way to the office of the party leader, Sophie picked up Jenifer to accompany her. She introduced her to Jai Singh without giving too much information on his royal background.

Jai Singh asked Sophie before they made the stop at Jenifer's house, "Why Jenifer?"

"The party leader is a mother too," Sophie said, winking at Jai.

Sophie, with a small dressing on the side of her head to cover a surgically glued cut, and visible bruises on her face, along with Jai Singh, Jenifer and the secretary of the Congress party sat in a big room waiting to be seen by the party leader. The three large framed pictures of Mahatma Gandhi, Jawaher Lal Nehru and his daughter Indira Gandhi hung on the main wall behind a big desk. Garlands of marigold flowers were draped around the photographs.

Sophie was breathing slowly for she knew that deep intake of breaths would hurt her bruised ribs. She was thankful though that none of her ribs was broken.

After about twenty minutes, the Congress party leader entered the room and all four stood to show their respect. She shook hands with the visitors and sat on a large sofa chair close to them and away from the desk.

"Mrs. Kumar," the party leader first spoke to Jenifer in a soft but determined voice, "I can't imagine the agony you must be going through over your missing daughter, and that, too, in a country that must feel strange to you. As a foreigner and mother myself, I can appreciate your concern. The party secretary has told me that this meeting may help your case. Let me assure you that my office will help in any way it can provided it is all within its legal powers." She then turned to Sophie and said with a convincing voice, "The Commissioner Rao speaks very highly of you. We appreciate your support." She was charismatic and possessed a certain charm about her. She may have been a foreigner at one time but now she was a Gandhi. The whole of India admired her and praised her for her *Gandhian* attributes. Sophie could see why even as a foreigner, she was in control of the ruling party.

"Madam," Sophie said politely. She did not know how else to address a political party leader. "Time is not on our side. We've got to act fast if we are going to save Amy. Since the Commissioner has spoken to you then you know we cannot rely upon the Delhi Police to save Amy. I'm hoping that with your support we will be able to rescue her and in the process, might even create a crack in a large organized crime group that is involved in child trafficking right here in New Delhi."

Sophie regrouped. She was about to say something else when the Party leader interrupted. "I'm not sure how my office could be of help?" She said this in a pleasantly modulated but firm voice.

"I've not yet made a concrete case but have some evidence of the involvement of the Gandhi Memorial Centre in Amy's kidnapping as well as some of the senior police officers—" said Sophie, and as she was about to add more, the Party Leader raised her hand, as if asking for a pause. She turned to the Party Secretary and asked something in a whispered tone. The Secretary spoke in a similar tone for a couple of minutes while the Party Leader nodded.

"What exactly is it that you want?" asked the leader.

"What I need is access to the confidential files on the senior police officer involved and your office's influence in securing a search warrant for the GMC. I would also like to see the police records of the children residing at the GMC," said Sophie directly, knowing time was precious.

The party leader stared at Sophie as if weighing her judgment and the practicality of her request. Then she smiled and shook her head from side to side. She was known by her peers to be bold and pragmatic. She was used to taking risks. In a flash she made up her mind and said, "If you are wrong, Dr. Kramer, then you will embarrass the party and we stand to lose the trust of our people. But for the sake of the little girl's safety, I'm going to trust your judgment and will help you. Mr. Secretary will work with you to allow you to talk to one of the superior officers of the Criminal Investigation Department Special Bureau and you can ask him your questions. As regards to the search warrant, I'm afraid that is too premature and hence not practical at this stage. You know as well as I do that valid grounds are needed for a search warrant. That is the best we can offer you at this time. Keep me informed." Her voice indicated that this was her final decision and she was not open to any argument. Everyone in the room understood and kept their mouth shut.

The meeting was adjourned. There was no time to waste.

Forty-Seven

Sophie asked the driver to take Jenifer back to her house and promised to visit her soon. She and Jai Singh then followed the party secretary to his office where he made some calls. The driver would return for them.

About forty-five minutes later a plain-clothed Criminal Investigation Department Special Bureau officer entered the office. He introduced himself as Rakesh Sharma. He had long Beatle-era hair and bulgy frog-like eyes.

"Mr. Sharma," Sophie announced, as she stood up and walked over to the wall where the three iconic pictures were hanging, and then turned to face the officer. "I am determined to get a warrant to search the GMC premises. The Leader of the ruling Congress Part has promised to help. I know perhaps reaching out to the Congress Party is overkill, but it shows my level of commitment."

"I've never been summoned by the Congress Party, you must have some pull. It is good to have friends in high places. Who you know is the key to success in India, while conscience is smothered under the weight of corruption. I admire your commitment and here I am, and will do anything I can to help you." Either his tone laced with a disproportionate use of amiable words or the well-rehearsed stock answer generated a feeling of distrust and put Sophie on guard.

She nodded to show her appreciation, and said, "I can sense that something criminal is going on at the GMC and

I am determined to expose it. I believe that the GMC could be the front for a number of illegal activities and one or more of the Delhi senior police officers are involved. Can you tell me anything about that?"

A flicker of a smile appeared on his face as Rakesh responded, "We keep files on all senior officers and of course the police have records of every child resident at the GMC. The activities of GMC were never in question, for nothing has ever been reported that should give us a cause for concern. If the police officers are involved in something illegal, then it is only a matter of time before we gather enough evidence to bring them to justice. Unfortunately, that takes time."

Sophie saw something in his eyes, a hint of defiance that told her that her job was done and she said, as if concluding her discussion, "So you have nothing so far to charge any of the officers with or to connect any of the police officers with GMC?"

"Nothing so far," said Rakesh, "but we will keep working on it. Here are copies of all the files on children at the GMC. You may examine them and take notes, but I'm afraid I will need to take them back with me."

He handed over a bundle of files and Sophie excused herself to sit in a quiet corner to look through them as Rakesh and Jai chatted over a cup of tea. After a quick glance, Sophie noted that there were no files on Amy. Instead of reading all the files she took pictures of the photographs with her iPhone of all the children. Returning to join Ramesh and Jai, she said, "Did you ever wonder why all these destitute children at the GMC look so sad and traumatized?"

Rakesh remained silent as he neatly put away all the files in a large bag and then, looking up at Sophie, said, as if he were tired of this inconvenience, "Do they? I did not notice. As I said earlier, the case is in its infancy and we are still working on completing our files. Will there be anything else?"

Sophie looked at him with contempt and said, "No, my work is done here. Thank you for your help." Rakesh raised his eyebrows at Jai as if implying something was wrong with Sophie and then he left without another word.

Jai addressed Sophie, who was deep in thought, "Can I take you out for lunch?"

Sophie nodded and they headed off for a local restaurant. During lunch Jai was unusually quiet. Finally Sophie broke the silence, asking, "Okay, what's on your mind? You weren't so quiet in Jaipur and now it seems that you are a million miles away. Do you find what I'm doing disturbing?"

Jai, putting his knife and fork down, pushed his plate away. Wiping his mouth with a napkin, he answered, "On the contrary. I admire your courage, your dedication. I feel ashamed that you as a foreigner would risk everything to help us and our own law enforcement agencies are turning a blind eye to the corruption you are exposing. I wish I could work with you. I'd do anything to feel the way you do about your work. No, no. Not work, passion. You truly are passionate about what you do. That is so rare in our country. We all seem to be chasing the American dream in India."

What Jai really wanted to say but could not find the courage to admit was that he had never known anyone like her, and could hardly imagine someone more unlike himself; yet, from their very first meeting, a deep sense of understanding had established itself between them, or so it seemed.

Sophie first looked at him with a frown on her face and then laughed, saying, "Perhaps I liked it better when you were quiet." She added, "No, I'm joking. Don't look so sad. I like you. I like you a lot. You have such honest and warm eyes. But the job I do is not only dangerous, it also, how should I say, makes one cringe sometimes. I don't want to burden you with that"

"Try me," he appealed, "I can be very resourceful."

Sophie realized what she was about to do was not in the rulebook. But then she wasn't one who played by the rules. She said, "Okay, as you know I'm here to find the little American girl but at the same time to set the ball rolling to bring about the end of prostitution, as it is a major source of terrorist funding. But this is going to be a lengthy process and I may start it but won't be able to take it to the end. You could play a key role here. And, I'm sorry to say, India has one of the worst track records."

His eyes mirrored the smile on his face.

Forty-Eight

Jai, putting up both his hands as if in surrender, said, "You don't have to apologize; I know how bad things are here. That is why I would love an opportunity to make a difference. Tell me, how can I help?"

"Well," said Sophie lowering her voice, "I have been informed that Mumbai alone has over 100,000 prostitutes. New Delhi is not far behind that number. I don't know if you have heard that in Mumbai a woman called Shantabai is the most powerful madam, and she controls as many as 10,000 pimps and prostitutes. What she really controls is the votes of these pimps and prostitutes to influence the local elections."

Jai nodded, and seeing that Sophie was taking a breath, responded, "I know all about the politicians of India. The criminal element is creeping into our government. Only recently it was reported that forty candidates in Mumbai's municipal elections, and 180 of 425 legislators in Uttar Pradesh, have a criminal record. Disgusting!"

Sophie's eyes lit up when she realized that despite all his wealth, this royal prince had a conscience and a good working knowledge of the corrupt system. Better still, she thought, he wants to do something about it. She wondered if he had the time to find enough information to use the corrupt politicians in her favor.

She switched gears. "I understand that fighting this system will involve battling against professional criminals, but how about first getting to know in detail their operating methods?"

"Ah! Now there we are just as organized as any international crime organization." Jai moved closer to the edge of his seat, and looking around the restaurant to ensure no one was either watching or listening, he said, "You see, the crime industry in India is no longer fragmented. Thanks to the Internet, they are now working in real time. The organization is well integrated and the large crime groups even share their databases. But their net security is better than that of most banks. You won't be able to hack into it. These guys can afford the best."

Sophie was surprised that such a chaotic country could be so organized when it came to crime. She was afraid that the tighter the crime organization, the harder it was going to be to find Amy. Before the criminals had a chance to take Amy down into the black depths of their operations, Sophie had to strike. She must find a lead.

Sophie then cried, "Aha!"

"What?" Jai was startled; he looked around as if he had missed something. "What's wrong?" he said.

"We have been knocking on the wrong door," said Sophie excitedly.

"What do you mean?" asked Jai, an inquisitive look on his face.

"Something you just said gave me a clue," Sophie responded. "If Amy indeed was abducted for the purposes of prostitution then she must be heading for the higher priced market. Think about it, Jai! She is half American, white with blonde hair. How many Indian girls look like her? She is a specialty in a commodity market. A rare jewel! And the specialty, high-priced market is abroad and Mumbai controls almost all of the international market while New Delhi controls the national market and is moving to overtake the international. Am I right?"

"You know," said Jai, rubbing his forehead, "when you put it like that, it sounds plausible. I think you may have something there."

"Now if I only knew the big names in the procurement of girls for the international markets, I could save some time," said Sophie, lost in her thoughts.

Jai took out his cell phone and punched in a number. She grabbed his phone and said, "Hey, don't broadcast it. Who are you calling?"

Jai smiled and, taking his phone back and dialing again, said, "I've my own connections in the police. I won't mention anything about you or your case. Just give me a minute."

He talked on the phone for about five minutes and jotted down a few notes on a paper napkin. After he switched his phone off he looked at Sophie triumphantly and said, "I've been informed that we may want to talk to a guy named Tahaseeldar Thakur. He is in Mumbai and the most powerful man in the area of procurement. He has chains of restaurants and operates from his biggest restaurant, 'Golden Gates,' on Falkland Road in the Kamatipura region in Mumbai." His triumphant face was then overcome with worry as he added, "But it is no good."

"Do tell, I'd rather know the worst than know nothing," said Sophie, her eyes focused on him intently.

"I've been warned that this area is the brothel district of Mumbai. Obviously, there will be thousands of dangerous pimps milling about in this area. One wrong move and we are history. They may not even find our bodies."

"I'm impressed," said Sophie and demanded, "but what is this 'we' part? You're not going anywhere, it would be just me."

Jai laughed. "Yeah, sure," he said and continued, "an American law enforcement agent in Kamatipura. Don't you think you would look a little out of place on your own? An American looking for an American, they would see you coming from a mile away. They would kill you just because of the color of your skin. You'd need an Indian with you. I'm your Indian counterpart, like it or not."

Sophie, understanding his point, said, "Okay, but you will only follow my lead. No heroics, okay?"

"Sure, whatever you say, boss," mocked Jai.

"Cut that out," she chided. "So who is your police contact?"

"That is for me to know and you to find out, detective," said Jai, obviously enjoying the banter. "If I told you then that would be the end of the flow of information. I will tell you when the time comes, but until then, you'll just have to trust me, or don't the brown eyes work for you anymore?"

"You're so full of..." and she let her sentence trail off, as it wasn't necessary to finish it.

Jai suddenly turned serious and said, "I'm sorry that your time was wasted at the Party Leader's meeting. I mean, you didn't get your warrant and the CID didn't give you any information."

"I wanted neither," said Sophie casually, "and that was the plan and it is working just fine. You've to trust me on that." She gestured to a passing waiter for the bill and the restaurant manager came rushing over and, bowing deeply, said, "For your excellency and his guest the lunch is on the house. It is our honor to have you here."

"So, there are at least some advantages of having you around," whispered Sophie as they left the restaurant.

Forty-Nine

Sitting in the back seat of the Mercedes heading for Sophie's hotel, Jai asked, "I don't get it. Why was it so urgent to meet the Party Leader if you wanted nothing from her?"

"You'll have to learn to stop asking questions," Sophie returned. "All I can tell you is that it took less than twenty-four hours for my private and confidential meeting with Commissioner Rao to be known to several police officers, so how long do you think it will take when I let the CID know of my intent to bring the highest level of pressure by asking to get a warrant to search the GMC?"

Jai looked perplexed for a moment and then with sudden elation, he responded, "You mean you wanted the threat of a warrant to make it look real, but didn't really care if you got the warrant or not?"

Sophie simply smiled and he continued with vigor, "And you wanted to make sure it finds its way down to those who might be threatened by it? Oh, that was so clever, why didn't I see it that way earlier?"

"Because if you did," said Sophie, lowering her voice, "then they could too and then it wouldn't have worked. I hope this will cause enough panic for the ferret to come out of his hole."

"Well, I sure was convinced as hell that you were determined to get a warrant; you had me fooled," said Jain smiling. "So you really don't want that warrant? Just making sure."

"Far from it," said Sophie. "It would have spelled disaster for poor Amy, but if I read them right, the threat of it was totally convincing, and just what I wanted. I know that once one uses illicit means to profit from one's country, one cannot divorce himself from that country's law enforcement agencies and politicians. Now I need to build on the foundation that I have laid down, partner."

They arrived at Sophie's hotel to allow her to make a couple of phone calls in the privacy of her hotel room. After twenty minutes, while Jai waited in the lobby with an espresso, Sophie came down and they were driven to the airport where Jai's jet was waiting.

Jai's private jet, after a two-hour flight, made a smooth landing and started to taxi to a terminal building at the Chhatrapati Shivaji International Airport of Mumbai. During the flight, Sophie went over her plan with Jai several times and they agreed that Jai would do the talking, as the discussions might be in either Hindi or Marathi, and besides, it would be offensive for a woman in the presence of her male friend to talk about girls with a pimp. Sophie, putting on bright red lipstick to enhance the look of the character she would play, said, "If you are going to come with me and we are going to pretend to be tourists then none of your BMWs or Mercedes, we are going to take a taxi."

He nodded and said, "I know that much. My office doesn't even know where I am. Just the flight crew, nobody else."

"That's good," affirmed Sophie, smiling. "You learn fast."

The humidity was high and made for an uncomfortable day ahead. Sophie and Jai walked out of the airport and went straight to a taxi stand. They hired a taxi and as the taxi started to roll, Jai asked the driver to take them to the 'Golden Gates' restaurant on Falkland Road in Kamatipura.

The taxi driver slammed on the brakes and did a double take.

"*Sahib ji*, there are many better places than what you are asking for. It is not very safe for the Madam where you are wanting to go."

"It's okay, we will be just fine. We know someone there. Just drive and we'll double your fare if you wait for us. We won't be long," Jai assured the man.

The taxi driver seemed happy to get a return fare from and to the airport, and at the double rates. He ground the gears and got his old Ambassador to rumble down the road towards Kamatipura.

Finding the 'Golden Gates' restaurant proved not to be a problem. Sophie and Jai climbed out of their taxi and sauntered into the restaurant. The taxi driver parked his car along the roadside and waited, but kept the engine running.

The restaurant was dimly lit but large in size and filled with ugly and dangerous-looking men. The walls were covered with bamboo and jute decorations to create the ambiance of the South Pacific, but somehow the effect failed miserably and made the restaurant just a little more dark and miserable. There were a few prostitutes busy going about their business, chatting and drinking with customers. Sophie and Jai sat in a corner and Jai asked for two Indian Kingfisher beers while Sophie scanned the room.

"We only be selling *Lal Toofan*, it is absolutely the best in the universe. It would be meaning 'red hurricane,'" said the scrawny-looking waiter and he started to cough.

"Whatever, two *Lal Toofan* then," Jai answered.

The waiter returned and put down two Lal Toofan beer bottles and two glasses that he cleaned in front of them with his red-and-white checkered towel that had been draped over his left shoulder, the very same towel he had used earlier to wipe his mouth after coughing.

Jai pushed the glasses away with his bottle and, slipping a hundred-rupee note to the waiter, asked if they could meet Thakur.

Quick as a flash he grabbed the note and stuffed it in his trouser pocket and said, "We be calling him *Dada*, he is our savior. He comes sometime here and not sometime. I will be letting you know when he is here. Okay? You be now enjoying your beers and let me know if you be wanting some food, any kind of food." The frail man flashed a big toothless smile with a wink.

Under the glare of some menacing-looking men, they waited for about half an hour. They looked as conspicuous as prey among its predators. Jai felt uncomfortable while Sophie took sips of her beer.

A big man wearing a black sarong-like wrap around his hips, a white large-holed, fishnet covering under a vest with no shirt, with long black greasy hair combed backwards without a part, and a gold chain around his neck came over to their corner table. He looked at Sophie with hungry eyes.

Fifty

The big man inhaled deeply and let blew air out through an open mouth as if smoking a cigarette. "My name is Thakur, people call me *Dada*. You wanted to see me? Why?" he said boldly in Hindi. There was an air of arrogance and defiance about him.

"Could we buy you a beer, *Dada*? We would like to do some business with you," Jai responded politely in Hindi.

Thakur looked at Sophie intently and then laughed loudly, raised his right arm and snapped his fingers. The waiter brought a beer and a glass immediately. Thakur sat next to Jai facing Sophie.

His eyes on Sophie, he winked and said, "We don't get too many foreigners here. Well, not in our kind of business, so what brings you here? Somehow I can tell that you are not here for dinner?" He poured himself a beer and gulped it down.

"She doesn't speak Hindi," Jai said, and lowering his voice, added, "and yes, we are here for something special. We've heard a lot about this place and about the good times one can have in India, especially if one knows where to look. I've my friend here from America on a business conference. She will be in Mumbai just for a day. Do you think you could arrange something for us, money is no object, you know what I mean? My friend is rich and we like fun, all sorts of fun." Jai spoke in a casual tone and made an attempt to sound like a seasoned buyer.

"What do you have in mind?" *Dada*, in his element, was secure, confident and arrogant.

"Well, we would prefer someone young and not Indian and we want two. Maybe around six years old, because I don't want to get AIDS or anything like that, you understand?" Jai said in a businesslike tone. Sophie pretended to pay no attention to the ongoing conversation and kept her gaze on the busy restaurant. Then she did something that Jai had never seen her do. She took out a pack of cigarette, lit one and, rounding her ruby red lips, blew a ring of smoke that drifted towards the ceiling.

"Six years old is neither uncommon nor the youngest," *Dada* said as he winked at Jai. "And yes, I can arrange to supply you with foreign girls but it will cost you a little extra. All our girls are clean and we have many nationalities."

Dada looked over his shoulder at the waiter who was passing by and gestured for him to come closer. He whispered something in his ear. The waiter nodded his head vigorously in the affirmative and disappeared behind the multi-colored bead curtains covering a door that led to the kitchen area. Five minutes later the curtain parted and the two most beautiful girls that barely looked six appeared. One of them had a Chinese face and eyes with a light complexion, while other with Indian features, had long brown hair and almond-shaped, sad eyes. Both wore ridiculous, excessive make-up.

As they approached the table where *Dada* was sitting, Sophie, who started to play with her iPhone, nervously dropped it on the carpeted floor.

As an automatic reaction, Jai tried to pick it up but Sophie was quicker. "Is it okay?" asked Jai. "It's not broken, is it?"

Sophie looked at her phone, pressed a few buttons to make sure it worked, and said, "Thank god, it's fine. Had me worried for a minute."

"Well," said *Dada* in a rather cackling tone, as if amused by Sophie's nervousness, "what do you think? Aren't they beautiful?"

"This won't do," said Jai, trying to show his dissatisfaction.

"We've more," boasted *Dada*, "would you like Sri Lankan, Nepalese or Chinese?"

Jai's heart sank at the choices but he persisted. "No, no, my friend here is from America." He added hurriedly, "What we had in mind was a girl from her land, America. We thought you were the largest operation in India, in the world, and you are telling us that you cannot supply two girls from America?" Jai threw out the challenge and it seemed that *Dada* was offended by his remarks.

"I can't promise you anything, but if you want American, then we'll give you American, we can supply anything," Dada boomed.

"I need a few days. Convince your friend to stay a while. She will have such a good time that she won't forget it for the rest of her life. Come back in a week, such special girls take time," Dada suggested.

Jai spoke to Sophie in English and in a whispered tone, and Sophie pondered the decision for a few seconds and then advised Jai on what to say.

"No, my friend, it won't work," said Jai in tone that held a hint of disappointment. "She cannot stay, well, not for a week. But I'll tell you what we will do. We will take one Chinese, but the other must be an American."

"It will be $500 for the American and $200 for the Chinese," said Dada.

Sophie understood the money talk and once again whispered something in Jai's ear.

Jai turned towards Dada and said, "Like I said before, money is not the problem. My friend is going to give you a $200 deposit, but you have to convince us that you can get the merchandise." Sophie opened her handbag and took out two crisp hundred-dollar notes and put them on the table.

Dada picked up the money and said, "Give me a minute." He then took out his cell phone and dialed a number. Sophie, pretending to be busy drinking beer, watched him from the corner of her eye. After three rings there was someone on the other side and Dada this time spoke in Marathi, and after a short conversation, turned towards Jai and said, "I tried to get you two American girls but right now I've one available. Five years old. She will be here soon and I will save her for you. You will be her first customer. Because she is a virgin and an American, it will cost you $100 more. So, $600 for the American girl, okay?" he asked ardently.

"Okay," said Jai. He then turned and told Sophie about his conversation but it was cut short as Sophie expressed an urgent desire to leave. He wanted to stay longer to extract more out of Dada, but Sophie insisted, and looked as if she was in a panic. She pointed to her stomach as if having cramps.

They stood up and Dada insisted that the drinks were on the house. They agreed to meet again soon and shook hands.

Fifty-One

They slipped back into their waiting taxi and headed to the airport. "Why were you in such a hurry to leave?" asked Jai, anxiously, "he was talking like a parrot. We could have learned a lot more if we stayed. Are you okay?"

Sophie was waving her hands in the air desperately, trying to shut him up, and blurted out, "A piece of paper, a goddamn piece of paper and pen, please. Now."

Jai took out a little notebook and his Mont Blanc and handed them over to her and she, with tightly pursed lips and furrowed brow, wrote something intently, glared at her writing, tapped the notebook with the pen, covered the writing with her left hand and wrote something again and then, removing her hand, compared the two writings and said, "Yes. I think I got him. I think this is it."

"What on earth are you talking about?" said Jai.

"What is the code for New Delhi?" she asked.

"The city code is 11, what is the panic?" asked Jai, looking perplexed.

"He called New Delhi to ask about the American girl. This is the number he dialed. Call this number and see what you can find out?"

Jai, mesmerized monetarily, stared at her and then, nodding his head, took his cell phone out and dialed the number.

He heard the phone ring four times. He said, "No one is answering."

"Let it ring," said Sophie, with an expectant look on her face.

Suddenly Jai put his hand up as if asking for quiet and listened as a male voice asked on the other end, "This is Gandhi Memorial Centre, how can I help you?"

He said, "Sorry, wrong number." He shut his phone abruptly and sat there for a moment, almost paralyzed. With his eyes wide open, in a very low voice, uttered, "GMC."

Sophie punched the front seat with a balled-up fist and shouted, "Got you, you bastard, you're mine now."

"But we can't prove anything," said Jai. "I mean, none of this would stand up as credible evidence in a court of law."

"There is something else," said Sophie as she played with her iPhone, "that girl, not the Chinese-looking one but the Indian girl. I've seen her before."

"Where?" asked Jai, continuing to be surprised. "How can you be so sure?"

"I've seen her, I'm sure," said Sophie, with her head bowed, searching absorbedly through her phone listings, and then suddenly she stared at a photo on her phone and showed it to Jai. "Here, this is the picture of the same girl that I took with my phone from the police file and she looks exactly like the girl we saw in the restaurant just now."

Jai studied the picture by holding the phone close to his face and then, moving it away, said hesitantly, "Well, I can't be sure. It was rather dark in the restaurant and I didn't get to see the girls clearly."

"No problem," said Sophie, with a grin on her face and, taking back her phone, she shuffled through the photos and showed him another picture, "here, this is the picture I took of the two girls inside the restaurant. Look at it yourself and compare. The two pictures of the Indian girls are almost identical. I am telling you, it is the same girl. And you know what that means? That Indian girl in the restaurant we have just seen came from GMC. Another nail in GMC's coffin."

Jai looked at Sophie with wide eyes. "You're a wonder, you know that? When did you take this picture in the restaurant?"

Sophie laughed and answered, "Do you think I'm a clumsy person who is in the habit of dropping her phone in restaurants?"

Sophie chuckled loudly at Jai's perplexed look and her sudden burst of laughter startled the taxi driver. The taxi driver almost skidded off the road and turned back to Jai, who calmed him, assuring him there was nothing to worry about.

"This would have to be one hell of a coincidence, Sophie," said Jai. "I mean, what are the chances?"

"This is no coincidence, it's just the results of what I am trained to do. I believe that we have found Amy. And the good part is that she is still in New Delhi," Sophie said, as her voice rose in excitement.

"I think you are right. I do believe that *Dada* was talking about Amy. He called GMC and then, with the right age, right type of nationality, this could not be anybody else but Amy. It has to be Amy. It better be Amy," Jai said in an equally excited voice, and seemed pleased that he was a part of this important discovery.

Then, Sophie's excitement turned to despair.

"Jai, you realize that now we have no time to waste. If we were to wait till *Dada* gets his hands on Amy, then I've a feeling it is going to be too late to save her. A lot could happen in a few days. I know *Dada's* type. She won't be delivered a virgin, as he had said, because they train young girls by repeatedly having sex with them. We'll have to find Amy in New Delhi, because if we fail, then poor Amy would be better off dead than alive. These bastards will turn her into the living dead."

Sophie was silent and then asked, "How senior is your police contact in the organization? Can we trust him?"

Jai hesitated before answering, perhaps thinking that there was a lot to risk. "Okay, that answers my question," said Sophie, "if you've got to think about it then there is no way I'd trust him."

On their flight back to New Delhi Sophie's mind was in a whirl. Although she was certain of her discovery, she still had no solid proof. It was only conjecture at this point.

Fifty-Two

Almost all the children at GMC were kidnapped from streets or school or play grounds. In some cases families had sold them to the GMC. Typically it would be an abusing uncle or cousin who, for a double benefit, would sell the girl—to get money and to get rid of a potential problem in case the girl was making noises about reporting them. These children were kidnapped when they were very young and were traumatized both physically and mentally.

The girls were divided into two age groups. The first group contained girls of ages up to about ten years old and the second group, of ages older than ten. The oldest girl in the group was about sixteen. The male staff members repeatedly raped the girls in the second group in order to prepare these girls for the business and to create a ready supply. Most of the girls in the younger group were being mentally prepared for the business by making them watch the older girls being raped. Violent methods including beatings by fists and at times by iron rods were a common occurrence.

The GMC, run by Ali, was a training school and a holding area that kept an inventory before the product could be placed in the right market at the right price. There were some boys that were also used for prostitution but the big market was in girls. Girls were sold to brothels all over the nation. Ali was now planning to expand this business, to abduct both girls and boys to supply to both the national

and the Middle East markets. He was preparing to orga-
nize a clinic and doctor to remove kidneys and corneas for
export, from some of these children. Other children were
simply to be maimed to supply buyers in the Middle East
for the purpose of begging. He expected this to be a natural
extension of his existing prostitution business and hoped it
would be a profitable and fast-growing market. Such entre-
preneurial businesses had no bounds.

The rules at the GMC, with no exceptions tolerated,
were three very simple rules. Rule number one had to do
with communication, ordering that the children were not
allowed to talk amongst themselves about their families
or how they got there. Rule number two had to do with
health and behavior, in that no child was allowed to cry,
refuse food or look untidy. And the third and the last rule
concerned discipline, mandating that all children were
to obey every staff member completely. Punishments for
breaking any of these rules were prompt and harsh. The
staff was encouraged by Ali to look for every opportunity
to make an example out of a child if he or she was found
disobeying any of the rules.

And there were spies. Children, for small favors, like
a whole week without being raped, were encouraged to
report any infractions of the rules. As the business started
to grow, so did the rules. Lately Ali had established solitary confinement rooms in the basement. In these small
separated rooms were steel beds with thin mattresses and
shackles, and even in the daytime, no light would penetrate these places. Difficult children with repeat violations
of rules were shackled to the bed and kept in a pitch dark
room for days, without relent in the frequency of rapes.
Sometimes these children's bodies, but never their faces,

were burned with cigarettes until they learned how to obey all the rules of the GMC and surrendered their body, mind and soul completely to the will of the staff. Children feared the solitary confinement punishment and dubbed it the 'red dot' punishment, for it frequently came with the cigarette burns.

This was how the system, as devised by Ali, worked at the GMC. He was the undisputed boss and the most feared person at the facility. On his rounds, walking through the facility, no child was allowed to raise her eyes to him.

Ali had just finished his rounds and sat in his office when his cell phone rang.

"You're getting careless," said his silent partner in an accusatory tone and he continued, "I sent you a warning at the movie theater. You're using un-trusted and un-professional people for procurement. I had to take care of one of them when he got himself caught. He was going to talk. Thank goodness that stupid foreign policewoman brought him to the station. Anyway, no harm done for now, but I cannot tolerate this kind of slip-up anymore. There is a lot of noise in the system and you may have to lay low for a while."

"I know what I'm doing," said Ali defiantly. He added, "Whoever you took care of in the prison knew nothing about the involvement of the GMC or me and no way could he have said anything about us. We use contractors and are quite safe."

"Don't be so sure about that. When I talked with this guy, he said he knew Javed, or at least his name. Did you ask Javed to hire this person? Javed works closely with you at the GMC. This FBI person is very smart so don't underestimate her. She found the GMC and you, didn't she? I tell you, she is good and she has the backing of the FBI. If you have the missing American girl, get rid of her. Now."

"This girl won't be here for long. It is only a matter of a few days. I have already arranged something special for her. And it will make us very rich. We have to expand our business. I'm opening up our business to the international markets. We're heading for the big time and such moves come with some risks. But everything is under control. You take care of your side and I will get rid of the girl soon, perhaps this week."

"Do so now. Continue to do your paperwork, for no one should be able to trace these children, with all the false documents registered with us. Be very careful, the times are changing."

"I'm changing with the times, too, and so should you. I'm careful, as always," bragged Ali.

"You weren't when you tried to kill the FBI agent. That was stupid. Thank god she survived; otherwise we would have the wrath of the FBI upon us. Always discuss these problems with me first before you do stupid things like that. Haven't I taken care of such matters before? I literally have a license to kill, and can get rid of these bad elements. You know that, don't you?"

Ali hated being patronized but swallowed his anger and finally said goodbye to his friend and partner. Javed, sitting across the desk with a questioning look on his face, waited on Ali's next move.

Fifty-Three

Ali explained to Javed what he had just being talking about and said, "We need to get rid of that girl Amy, and slow down our operations here, just for a while."

"It is not the first time we have faced heat, Ali *Bhai*. This too will blow over," said Javed in a confident voice.

"I know, but people are nervous about the FBI involvement," said Ali, massaging his neck with his both hands to get rid of a cramp. An ache had started to creep up from the base of his neck.

To Ali all this was nothing more than a business arrangement. He found that trying to balance his life between rights and wrongs gave him a headache. And he tried not to think of his own two children when doing his dealings at the GMC. One of his associates had once reminded him that a professional learns to separate his personal life from his business. He liked that. He wished he could be that objective about the business because then he would not suffer from unnecessary headaches.

Javed was greedy because he worked on a percentage commission of everything Ali made. He leaned forward and said in a low voice, "Our contact from Mumbai called and they are in need of two American girls. I said we could let him have one for a while. This way we could double our profits, boss. Use Amy for a while for rich clients and then sell her corneas for your Arab client, and after all that perhaps use her as a beggar during the holy month. Hey, we could triple our profits."

Ali glared at Javed but Javed did not notice as he leaned back in his chair and continued nonchalantly, "Come to think of it, we are not going to find many blonde, white girls so we ought to use Amy simply for prostitution. She would make us a lot of money for years to come. I could get another girl for the cornea transplant, what do you think?"

"Have you completely taken leave of your senses?" said Ali, in a rising voice. "Since when have you started to go out on your own, making deals?"

"But Ali *Bhai*," Javed pleaded, "you're the one who is expanding business here and abroad, and I'm just trying to support you, I—"

"Listen," interrupted Ali, "all these years I've treated you like family. But if you start to make foolish moves then I will have to ask you to find someone else to employ you."

"I'm sorry, Ali *Bhai*," said Javed, in a trembling voice, for he knew Ali did not make empty threats. "I'll do as you say," he said, with a little bluff of self-conscious laughter.

"Then call Mumbai and say you made a mistake. We don't have any American girls to give to them. And from now on talk with no one about Amy, do nothing unless I authorize it. You got that?"

"Yes," responded Javed meekly.

"Now you have put me in a tight spot so I want you to find me a surgeon for a cornea transplant, and a good one, because I don't want the merchandise damaged in any way. I'm calling my client in the Middle East and going to ask him to be here in forty-eight hours. Do you think you can manage to find a surgeon in that time?"

"Consider it done, Ali *Bhai*," asserted Javed, as he started to contemplate which of his contacts he would approach.

"And I've a rather unpleasant task for you but it needs to be done," said Ali in a drifting voice as if his mind was elsewhere.

Javed looked at Ali questioningly, waiting for him to continue. "Oh, yes," said Ali finally. "Last night I was talking with my Arab partner about the number of crippled children he wanted for the coming holy month and I offered Amy as a cute little blind girl, as part of the package, but he said that blind children are okay but not one that looks like an American. You know, blonde-haired and white. It would attract too much attention from the authorities, he said. So, after the cornea transplant is done, Amy is of no use to us. Slash her throat and in the night dump her body in the *Yamuna* River."

"As you say, Ali *Bhai*," Javed nodded his head. He then added, "It is a pity, though, for she is one of a kind and would have fetched big money in the prostitution business."

"We will find more," replied Ali, as if agreeing with Javed, "but for now it is best if you dispose of her as soon as the surgery is done."

Javed nodded again and awaited further instructions. His face was blank and expressionless, in the suspense of wondering what other tasks Ali might have for him.

"Now go, I've things to do," ordered Ali, and pulled out his cell phone.

Fifty-Four

Sophie looked at the morning newspaper and on the third page something caught her eye. There was a picture of a young girl found shot in the head. The report said that she was found in New Delhi lying in a street face-down with a bullet hole in her head. The police had not yet disclosed her identity and suspected it to be a gang-related crime. Sophie immediately opened her iPhone and looked through all the pictures of the GMC girls, and to her horror, found a match. She felt convinced that the girl was shot to make an example out of her so that the other girls at the GMC would live in utter fear. This tactic was not new to the prostitution business and the incident renewed the urgency she felt to carry out her plan.

Sophie believed that for every problem there are at least two solutions. It's a matter of looking deeper and ignoring nothing. She was pleased with the validation of her hunch but she was well aware that she had to strike now for time was running out and she had but only one chance if Amy were to come out alive from her ordeal. A single slip or wrong move would cost Amy's life and Sophie was not prepared to take that gamble. Her plan, she knew, had to be meticulous.

She had fared until now on the thin diet of hope, but without losing her determination or doubting her intuition. Hope and intuition was all she had but now more than ever, she was certain that the time had come for that one last push to the summit.

Sophie called Andrew and discussed her plan. Andrew asked, "Do you see any glitches?"

"I'm pretty certain that Amy is still alive and at the GMC and once Ali knows that I am onto him he is likely to move her or get rid of her altogether," she stated.

"So, how do you force his hand?" asked Andrew, as if he were discussing business strategy.

"Jai has a trusted police contact but he is hesitant to use him so that option is out. I have no solid proof to convince any of the authorities to raid the place; besides, it may prove to have fatal consequences. I suspect that at the GMC they have weapons and there are too many children at risk there; in such a raid, their safety could be compromised. Besides, I don't want the victims to become hostages, which would present a very difficult dilemma. This guy is a cold-blooded murderer. A GMC girl was found murdered this morning. I have no option but to force Ali to move Amy out of the GMC and catch him in the act once they are outside the safety of the GMC premises."

"And I'm waiting for you to tell me how you intend to accomplish that," Andrew explained in a patient voice. "You do have a plan, I take it?"

"I'm sending someone into the GMC this time no force could stop," said Sophie in a firm voice.

"I think I know what you are planning. It has been done before in similar cases, but it hasn't always worked,"

"I'm out of options, Chief, and out of time. There is no other way, unless you want to send an assault team into a foreign jurisdiction and suffer casualties."

"Good luck then," said Andrew, "strike with full determination but know when to pull back."

That evening Sophie went to Jenifer's house and told them most of the details of how the police were protecting Ali, who had kidnapped Amy, and that they were holding her at the GMC. Sophie assured them that she was working on various options to get Amy out of there.

"Oh, my God," bawled Jenifer, putting her both hands over her mouth to smother a cry, "the police whom we reported everything to are involved in the kidnapping. What kind of screwed-up country is this? What is going to happen to my Amy now? I wish I never had come to this horrible place."

It seemed that Jenifer was not prepared for such shocking news, the revelation striking and drawing blood.

That was the reaction Sophie had expected. "You just have to keep up your faith. I've shared everything with you as I had promised and hope you will not act irrationally. Leave it to us, to the professionals," said Sophie with a demand in her words. She then looked at Ashok, his head hanging low. He looked withdrawn and remote. Sophie addressed Ashok this time, "I don't want you to do anything foolish. Listen to the police if they have questions but do not give out any information. Above all, never reveal anything of what I've just told you." Sophie wanted this to sink deep so everyone in that room understood the gravity of the situation. Ashok nodded while Jenifer simply stared at Sophie as if in total disbelief.

"What do you suggest we do?" asked Ashok finally looking quite perplexed and shocked.

"Pray. Pray to whichever god you believe in and above all keep hope. Pray to the god of temple of hope." Sophie's answer brought out the reaction she was expecting not from Ashok but from Jenifer who shouted, "Pray?"

"I know how difficult this is for you," said Sophie, as she looked at Jenifer and then she looked at her watch. "I've got to get going. Take my advice and stay safe, at home. I will be in touch soon."

Once Sophie was convinced that she had accomplished what she came to do she said goodbye and left them still in a state of shock.

Book V

Dark Despair

Fifty-Five

Jenifer sat in silence, pondering what Sophie had just told them. Jenifer was convinced that Sophie had not told them everything. Was Amy really at the GMC? she wondered.

Jenifer could not fathom the idea that Amy could be there, imprisoned and alone and among the rape victims. A silent rage that had been brewing inside her began to surface. It had been three weeks, what had they done with her? Such thoughts sent a shudder through her. How could someone take away my little girl and imprison her? Jenifer could not bear the thought of Amy being in some kind of prison. God knows how they are treating her, she thought.

Jenifer decided she could not just sit helpless, with Amy so close to her, right there in the same city. She had to go to the GMC and find the truth for herself. She looked at Ashok.

"Ash, we need to go down to GMC and check for ourselves if Amy is there." Jenifer looked imploringly at him, clasping her hands in mute entreaty, as though it all depended on him.

"No, we must not do anything like that or it could hurt Amy. You heard what Agent Kramer said, we must not interfere," Ashok shot back.

Ashok seemed convinced that going down to the GMC was not a good idea.

"How can you just sit there and do nothing?" Jenifer retorted. "Yes, I heard Sophie and she told us in an indirect way that Amy could be at the GMC, but she doesn't know how to deal with the local corrupt authorities. Just think for a minute, Ash," Jenifer's voice was now rising, "suppose Amy is being held at GMC like a prisoner, and if something happens to her, do you think will we'd be able to forgive ourselves if we knew and did nothing?" Jenifer stood up with fists clenched.

Since she received no response from Ashok, she reinforced her argument, "I'm sure that the staff at the GMC wouldn't deny a mother from coming and looking for her lost daughter."

"Are you kidding? They don't give a hoot if you are a mother or a father. I know this country better than you do. These people are criminals and they kill, sometimes just for kicks," Ashok was quick to answer.

"And I know my child better than anybody," she snapped. "Ash, if you are trying to frighten me, it won't work. I can deal with these people. Come on, support me on this? Let's give it a try. I'm going mad just sitting here," she pleaded.

"Jenifer, you are dealing with hardened criminals here." Ashok tried to convey his point in a soft and convincing tone of appeal. "They kill for small amounts of money. Killing someone is nothing for them. This is India we are talking about, life is cheap here."

"I know this is India. Remember, I grew up in New York City. I know how to survive in big ugly cities. This is nothing new to me," she argued.

"You saw what they tried to do to Sophie. They'll stop at nothing. They have already killed one man who was in custody; killed Sophie's driver, and I tell you, they won't think twice about killing you and me. Jenifer, only professionals can deal with these people. We must wait for Sophie to come back and then we can discuss it with her." He, in frustration, was now pacing the room.

"You can discuss it with her but I am not going to just sit here and do nothing. She is my baby and I will stop at nothing to save her. I wake up in the middle of the night with nightmares that Amy is screaming for help, save me, mummy, please save me. You understand; I've got to go to the GMC and see for myself what kind of place it is. I don't care if they kill me. I'm not going to let anyone hurt my baby." Jenifer grabbed her short denim jacket and looked back at Ashok, asking, "Are you coming or not?"

Ashok had no choice.

As Ashok drove away with Jenifer sitting in the front passenger seat beside him, Sophie, who was parked just a few yards away, tapped on the shoulder of her driver who switched on the ignition and followed them. She believed that once a lioness gets the scent of her lost cub, one had better not come between them. This was the point where the nature of this case would change; Sophie was changing the state of play.

Fifty-Six

The large gate of the GMC opened to let in a stretch limousine that slowly made its way to the front of the building. From the front passenger seat, Javed stepped out and opened the back door. Sheikh, with one hand pressed against his ear, was busily talking with someone on his cell and, with the other hand holding the hand of his little daughter, stepped out of the limousine. Ali came out of the office to greet them.

Sheikh snapped shut his phone and extended his hand to shake with Ali. *"Ahlan wa Sahlan,"* said Ali, welcoming the Sheikh to his place. The Arab simply smiled back and nodded. Ali stepped back into his office with the Arab and his little girl following him. Javed was the last one to enter the office.

After tea was served, the Arab asked, "I hope it is a reputable hospital we are going to? I will spend whatever it takes for my girl's safety." They were conversing in Urdu, which the Arab spoke fluently, and thankfully, his daughter could not understand a word of it.

"Your cousin Sheikh Salem is my business partner and I have given him my word that I'll take good care of you. So please, don't worry, everything has been arranged," said Ali in a reassuring voice.

"But is it a reputable hospital?" the Arab repeated his question and this time in a stern and demanding tone.

"We know this country and this business better than most,' said Ali, lowering his voice, "and hospitals are not safe in many ways. They are not clean and most of the time the drugs they use are not from reputable pharmacies, you know? It is as much for your own safety as it is for ours to stay away from hospitals."

"So, how we are going to do this?" demanded the Arab, gazing quizzically at Ali.

"We have booked a private clinic, absolutely the best in India."

The Arab sat staring at Ali, as if not fully convinced. "So, walk me through it, what you have arranged," he said, sipping his tea.

Ali gestured for Javed to explain. "Well, we have a highly experienced ophthalmologist, Dr. Shivaram, a renowned physician, and his specialty in eyes is well known here. He has looked at your daughter's medical records and suggests we do what he calls Penetrating Keratoplasty."

"Yes, I have been told the same by our eye specialist in Riyadh," the Arab nodded, "what about the procedure? Did he explain to you how he intends to carry it out?"

Javed scratched his head for a moment as if collecting his thoughts, and said, "Under general anesthetic, he would use trephine to cut the corneas out of Amy's eyes. A similar procedure would be done on your daughter's eyes and then Amy's corneas would be sewn in place with sutures into your daughter's eyes. But I am sure Dr. Shivaram will give a much better explanation when you see him."

"And he is good?" asked the Arab.

"Yes, yes," said Javed hurriedly, "he is a very professional doctor. He lives upstairs from his surgery in a very expensive locality. Victoria Road, in south Delhi. A very desirable and expensive area, this Victoria Road, where the wealthy live, you know." A quiver in Javed's voice went unnoticed by the Arab. Before he could respond, he looked at his cell phone as it chimed a musical tone. He ignored it and put it on silent. "I've got to be one hundred percent sure," he said in a dry voice, "our traditions are religion-bound and strict. Corneas must be from a healthy and living girl. Let me see the girl, is she here?"

Ali raised his chin at Javed, gesturing for him to fetch Amy. Javed smiled and disappeared through the back door and a few minutes later appeared holding Amy's hand. Amy looked at the strangers and tried to hide behind Javed. "This is not my dad," Amy said meekly, "where is my dad?"

Ali got up and kneeled in front of Amy, cupping her small face in his hands. "This gentleman is a friend of your daddy's. As I promised, you will see your daddy tonight. Come and say hello to this nice gentleman."

Amy peered out at the Arab from behind Javed and smiled. "Hello," she said, with a smile on her face and continued, "I'm going home tonight."

The Arab seemed to ponder something and that worried Ali. He asked, "Is everything to your satisfaction, Sheikh?"

"I think," said the Arab haltingly, "we may want to postpone the surgery for a couple of days. I need a little more time to be convinced of this."

"Why?" said Ali, "I mean, is something wrong with the girl? You will not get a chance like this again. It is rare to find such a perfect candidate in India."

Amy looked with a puzzled face at Ali and then moved her gaze to the frightened Arab girl and smiled, as if to comfort her amongst the arguing adults.

"No, no," said the Arab hurriedly, "the girl is perfect. But I still need a couple of days. I cannot hurry into something like this. Maybe one more day."

Ali looked disappointed. He wanted this to be over and done with. His cell phone rang. "Would you please excuse me, I need to take this," said Ali, unhappy with the delay requested by the Arab. He stepped outside the office through the front door and answered, "I'm busy right now, is it urgent?"

"I'd say," came an angry voice on the other end, the voice of his police friend. "The FBI agent has gone all the way to the Leader of the Congress Party to secure a warrant to search the GMC premises. What are you doing to piss all these authorities off? The warrant is not yet granted, but you never know, because the pressure is coming from the office of the Congress. I don't want the home office getting involved. You know what would happen if they found out what goes on at the GMC? You and I and several others would be all finished. And it all started with that stupid girl you've got there. She is not worth all this trouble. She could jeopardize our entire organization. Get rid of her today, and I mean now. I will not ask you again."

Ali was about to say something when raised voices penetrated the compound.

Fifty-Seven

It seemed that someone was fighting and shouting with the guard at the gate. Through the gate bars Ali could see a young couple arguing and struggling with the guard. He quickly promised his friend that he would take care of Amy today, switched off his phone, and strode back into the office. "What is going on?" asked the client as his little girl clung to him with fright.

"The guard will take care of it, it is nothing serious. Just some crazy people off the street," said Ali, confident of the skills of his security guard.

Suddenly the noises from outside sounded louder and nearer. Ali asked Javed to take Amy and his guests inside the facility into a waiting room while he tended to the disruption. He assured the Arab, "It is nothing, I am sure, but just to be on the safe side, please wait inside while I resolve it. It should take only take a minute. It may be some belligerent reporters."

No sooner had the displeased Arab and the two little girls left the room with Javed and the door shut behind them, than Ali's main office's front door burst open and Ashok and Jenifer rushed in with the guard in tow.

Ali asked angrily, "What is the meaning of this? Who are you?"

"Mr. Khan, I apologize for this intrusion," said a frantic Jenifer. "I have one very simple request. You are Mr. Ali Khan? Yes, right, look, you must have heard of a recent case of a girl, Amy, who was kidnapped. I'm her mother and my name is Jenifer and this is my husband Ashok. I have been led to believe that Amy might have been brought here by mistake. I'd just like to check out your facility for myself. Please?" Jenifer looked breathless and her eyes were filled with fear, yet she stood there looking self-confident, intent on her mission.

Ashok had never seen this side of the normally impatient and argumentative Jenifer. She seemed to be in total control. Javed came back into the office and looked at the intruders with questioning eyes.

"This is unbelievable," said Ali in a harsh voice, "we cannot allow strangers to just walk up here and start wandering through the facility and asking questions. I've never heard of this case, or of Amy. Now please leave."

"Look, I'm a mother who is searching for her missing baby. All I want is to take a quick look around to be certain if Amy is here or not. Okay? It won't take long."

"Madam," said Ali, frowning, "I'm giving you this last warning to get out or I'll call the police and have you arrested for trespassing and causing a disturbance."

"No need to call the police, we mean no harm," said Jenifer, trying to control her rising emotions of anger and frustration. "I assure you that I'll not upset any of the children here. I just need to have a moment to look," pleaded Jenifer.

Ali turned to Javed and said, "Call the police and have these people removed from the premises." Then, turning to Jenifer, Ali said, "Now if you would please leave, because the police will be here any minute and it will not be pleasant." Ali delivered the threat with certainty, a threat full of promise.

"Why?" cried Jenifer. "Why won't you let me have a look? The children won't even know that I am here. Please." She clenched her fists, seething inside.

"Look," said Ali, now changing his tone from one of anger to one that employed diplomacy, "no matter what you say, it will upset the children, and I cannot allow it. Look, the police have been here and are fully satisfied that there is no unregistered child living at the GMC. The police know the children here and you should talk with them. There are proper ways of going about these matters. I can give you my personal guarantee that there is no one called Amy in this compound so there is no possibility that your daughter could be here."

Who can understand the power of quietly smoldering embers; when least expected, they erupt into a raging fire. Jenifer's body began to shake with fury that she felt towards Ali. Fury that she could be so close to Amy and yet not able to reach her because of this belligerent fool. "All I need is not even ten minutes to take a little walk-through and I promise I won't ask any questions." This time Jenifer spoke in a harsh voice with a stone-hard stare. She would not turn back without knowing if her Amy was here or not.

Ashok felt embarrassed and he felt angry. He thought Jenifer was being very reasonable and Ali was being rude and downright hostile to her. Ashok came to Jenifer's aid. "Why wouldn't you allow us or just my wife to see if our daughter is here? Even if our daughter is not here, it will settle the mind of my wife and I promise we'll never bother you again."

When he received no response from Ali, he tried again, this time using a different approach. "Mr. Khan, we are from the same country, the same race, even from the same city. I was born here, right here in New Delhi. How it could do any harm if my wife takes a little stroll through the facility? Why are you making this so difficult?"

"Look," Ali responded this time with a gentler tone, "don't get me wrong, I do sympathize with you and your wife. I've children of my own. But the children here have suffered enough. I will not expose them to any further distress by letting strangers come in among them. It is very hard to gain the trust of these children and I've promised them no strangers will ever bother them again." Ali said this firmly as he continued to buy time for the police to arrive and remove these trespassers.

Noting that his words had little effect, he focused on Ashok and spoke in a considerate manner. "Since you are suffering from the loss of your child, you of all people should understand that these children are suffering too, and it is for their sake that I must be strict."

He paused only momentarily and added, "Let me explain something." Ali continued with compelling argument, "Every child here at the GMC is registered with the local police. They have their full history, as much as is available, and they certainly have the date of arrival of every child at the GMC. You see, we call the police the moment any child arrives. You can check with the local police station." He smiled at both Jenifer and Ashok, indicating that he was offering them good advice.

Fifty-Eight

Ali perceived that Ashok and Jenifer were considering his offer and had not countered his advice. He decided to strike again and this time with his trump card. He put on his phony but charming smile and spoke in a soft and calm voice. "Look Ashok," Ali said in a tone that sounded affable. "Like you said, we are of the same race, so I'll do you a favor, but then I want you to promise me that you will take your wife and leave." Ali made it sound like this was his final offer. Ashok looked at Jenifer and she did not raise any objections. Ashok nodded their approval.

"What date was it that your daughter went missing?" Ali inquired.

"It was on October 10th at around 6 p.m.," Jenifer responded.

Ali went over to a steel filing cabinet. He pulled a file and from it extracted a single sheet of paper.

"The information I am going to share with you is also available at the central police department. You can verify it there if you wish. Here, it shows the entry of the most recent child that arrived at the GMC, October 1st 2012, and, as you can see, this date is about ten days before the kidnapping of your daughter. Now if I had a child registered here after the date your daughter went missing, then okay, I could understand your need to search the premises. But in the light of what I have just shared with you, you must agree that you will gain nothing by walking through the facility." Ali thought that this argument and proof should put a lid on this case.

He quickly closed the folder and placed it back in the cabinet. A stern look returned to his face. "Now, please leave. We are finished here and I've a lot of things to do."

Jenifer could not control herself any longer and started to cry. Ashok could not see Jenifer cry, especially in front of strangers. His pride was hurt. He felt helpless and he became angrier. "I don't care what your file says, Mr. Khan. My wife came here to take a walk through the facility and that is what she is going to do." Ashok stood up and the color started to rush to his face.

Ali shook his head in disbelief and said, "Now, that is not fair. You promised to leave. I tell you, there is nothing for you here. I am warning you for the very last time, Mr. Ashok. Leave now or face the consequences."

"I think you are hiding something from us, Mr. Khan. I don't believe a word you say. I am going to go inside myself and check it out. Now stand back." Ashok looked determined as he started to take steps toward the entry door.

Ali came around from behind his desk and stood in his way. Javed was standing behind Ashok.

"Don't be a fool, Mr. Ashok," Ali warned. "If you try to create trouble then we will have no choice but to physically throw you out. You know that the police are on their way; they will be here any moment. Don't make things difficult for yourself. Take your wife and go home."

Ashok was in a rage. Waves of disbelief and provoked fury were crashing over what was his otherwise calm and composed disposition. He no longer was thinking of consequences and he was beyond reasoning. It seemed that the suppressed feeling of self-degradation that he had suffered from since he returned to India was suddenly surging back to the surface, uncontrollably rushing like a tornado into his thoughts.

Ali defiantly remained standing in front of Ashok. Both stood still and gazed at one another, as though measuring their strength. Suddenly Ashok stretched both arms out, grabbed Ali's shoulders and pushed him aside against the wall. It seemed that Javed was half expecting some trouble but he didn't think Ashok would push Ali so hard. Javed took Ashok from behind while Ali regained his balance and lunged at Ashok. He threw a power punch and hit Ashok hard in his face. Ashok's feet deserted him as he collapsed in Javed's grip. Ashok started to bleed through his nose and was stunned for a moment by the strength of the blow he had received.

Jenifer had never seen Ashok fight like this. She felt a sudden surge of anger rise from the pit of her stomach. Instinctively she ran behind Javed and tried to pull him off Ashok. One of Javed's arms came loose and he swung around, letting Ashok go. His fist caught the side of Jenifer's head and she went flying into a wall. Her head hit the wall hard and she slumped to the floor.

Fury within Ashok erupted like a dormant volcano. In one fierce motion he picked himself up from the floor and squeezed Javed's throat with his hands. Javed fell to the ground and Ashok sat on top of him. With his knees digging deep in the man's ribs, Ashok's hands were choking the breath out of Javed. Ashok's stranglehold tightened around Javed's throat and his eyes started to bulge.

Right at that moment four policemen came rushing into Ali's office and wrestled with Ashok, forced him off Javed and pushed him to the ground face-down.

Ali, who was shaken by the incident, quickly regained his composure and addressed the Inspector, "There was a misunderstanding. No need to arrest them. Just take them out of here and issue them a warning not to come back. I won't be pressing charges."

Ali had quickly deduced that the last thing he wanted was further complications with authorities regarding his business. He shouted at his guard to be more vigilant and watch his post.

The police dragged Ashok and Jenifer out from the GMC and the Inspector admonished them with a stern warning, and leaving them behind, took off with his constables in his Jeep. Ashok helped an inconsolable Jenifer back to their car where she sat tired, drained and exhausted.

They drove to their home in silence. Sophie, sitting in the back seat of her car, nodded her head as if satisfied with what she saw, her determination resolute.

Fifty-Nine

Outside Sophie continued to wait patiently in her car. Minutes slipped away and she remained convinced that the deal was going down today and Amy would be leaving with the Sheikh. That would be her chance to intervene and catch the culprits in the act. Suddenly her cell phone rang. She looked at it and let out a sigh of exasperation. "Yes, Andrew," she intoned. "I'm afraid this is not a convenient time."

"Sophie," said Andrew in a stern voice. "I need to know what is going down. I just had a call from the ambassador. He is furious. Apparently Jenifer called the embassy reporting an assault on her. What is worse is that she has told them that Amy is likely to be at the GMC. The ambassador has become unstoppable now and through his political connections is putting pressure on the Delhi police authorities to raid the GMC. He is trying to get a warrant. I need to know what is going on."

"The police authority is unlikely to respond to his pressures," said Sophie, her voice controlled. "Such a raid won't happen or at least I hope it doesn't for it would compromise Amy and the other children. I need to grab Amy when she is out of that facility. Inside GMC, I have no clue what kind of and how many weapons are involved." Sophie took a momentary pause and then continued, "Look, Amy is a prize that would fetch top dollars and for that GMC needs a wealthy client and guess what? A Sheikh from Arabia is inside. I've a feeling something is about to happen and I am right outside the GMC to intervene. Give me a couple of hours. Stall the ambassador, if you can. This raid on GMC must not go through."

"I will give you one hour, no more. The situation is getting out of hand," said Andrew and rung off.

As the Arab, his girl and Javed walked back into the office, Ali assured them, "Everything is in place. And I had a call from my partner and we discussed your suggestion of postponing the surgery by one day. I'm afraid my partner did not agree. The offer of Amy's corneas for your daughter is on the table only for today. We have a much bigger offer, for girls like Amy in India are rare. Since I gave you my word, we will go with you, provided it is done now and not tomorrow." Ali's tone had an uncompromising tone and he made his offer sound like it was his last. He was seriously considering calling the whole thing off and sending Amy to Mumbai.

"If it is a matter of more money—"

Arab could not finish his sentence as Ali interrupted, "No, no, no. It is not the money. We have other pressures. Now or never, you decide."

It was a dark and stifling evening. Threatening storm clouds filled the sky about ten o'clock. With a clap of thunder, the rain came down like a waterfall. The water fell not in drops, but beat on the earth in streams. Constant flashes of lightning lasted through the count of four. Then the storm passed just as quickly as it came. The rain lessened to a sporadic sprinkle, but the air remained heavy, laden with moisture.

The GMC large doors opened and a stretch limousine with dark windows emerged. Following closely behind the limousine was Ali's car. Both vehicles stopped momentarily outside the gates and then turned left and proceeded in the direction where Sophie's car was parked. She lowered herself in the seat to avoid their view, and as soon as the cars passed she sat up, looked over her shoulder and then asked her driver to turn the car around and follow the two vehicles.

Unbeknownst to her, a green Range Rover parked some distance away started to follow Sophie's car. The Range Rover maintained some distance between them to avoid detection, but kept Sophie's car in sight.

Sophie's driver stopped about twenty yards from where the two cars stopped. Ali and Javed stepped out first, looked around, and once satisfied it was safe, signaled the Arab to step out. He did and so did the two little girls holding each other's hand. They walked through the gate of a large house with a guard posted outside. The guard made a call and a man dressed in a male nurse uniform came out and shook hands with Ali and then gestured for them to follow him. The guard gave a smart salute and Ali slipped a ten-rupee note to him.

Sophie told her driver to stay put and after a five-minute pause, walked up to the guard and showed her card that read, 'Dr. Sophie Kramer.' She said, "You keep my card. I am a doctor, you see. I'm here to surprise my old friend. Please don't call, and let me through the door." She took out a fifty-rupee note and waved it in front of the guard like a carrot to a donkey. The guard frowned and said, "Sorry, Madam, you must have an appointment, and until someone comes out from the house to receive you, I cannot open the gates. I've just been told not to allow in anyone. Sorry."

Sophie did not want to make a scene, which would forewarn the people inside, and they might disappear through the back door to safety. She needed to enter the house quietly and unannounced. "Thank you," said Sophie to the guard, putting her money away. "You're a good man. I will call for an appointment."

Sixty

She walked out of the guard's sight and along the perimeter wall of the house. The wall itself was not too high for her to scale, but the rounded finish at the top had broken glass embedded in it to prevent intruders from climbing over it. Sophie wandered towards the back of the house, away from the street. She judged the wall to be about eight feet high. She took off her leather jacket and threw it over the glass pieces. She then took several steps backwards and away from the wall and then, like an Olympic high jumper, she charged towards the wall. In a single graceful and swift motion she hoisted her body upwards, resting her hands on her jacket, her body still in the air parallel to the wall, and then she let the momentum of the jump carry her over where she landed perfectly and softly on her feet on the other side.

In a crouch, she scanned the area, finding no one around, the yard silent. She ran swiftly and stood flush against the house, and then in increments moved towards the front of the hall. Once reaching the front door, she could see the guard's back as he was facing the street. She tiptoed before the front door and tried the doorknob and the door opened silently. She entered the house and closed the door behind her.

Inside, after she passed through a large hallway, she saw an empty room. She stepped into the room and pressed herself against the wall, listening for any sounds. A few seconds later she heard muffled voices. She saw another door leading to an inner courtyard. She walked alongside the wall and stood at the door overlooking the courtyard. It was empty. Across the courtyard she saw a closed door and could hear the voices coming from behind it. She crept across the courtyard and to the door, standing there for several moments, holding her breath. She put her ear against the door and heard voices quite clearly now. She tried the doorknob and found that the door was unlocked. She silently opened the door just enough to take a peek inside. She first saw three people in scrubs around an operating table on which there was the body of a small person. While one person in scrubs stood looking intently at the person lying still on the table, the other person also in scrubs was at the head of the table operating a machine.

The third person in scrubs seemed to be a woman standing quite still. Sophie's brows raised and eyes narrowed as she tried to comprehend the scene in front of her. Is this some kind of private surgery that operates as a front for Ali's rich clientele? She looked behind her, wondering if she missed a room where Ali and his guests might have gone. She was expecting drinks, music, dim lights and a bedroom, not a doctor's surgery room. Then she turned again and peered through the slight crack of the open door. She pressed forward a little more to gain a better view and this time saw the Sheikh and Ali standing in a corner perfectly still, holding masks on their faces with their hands.

Suddenly a thought crossed her mind like a bolt of lightning lights up a dark night. She shuddered at the impact of it. Seconds ticked away as she saw the man leaning over the operating table place a scalpel just above the patient's head and was about to make a cut. The shiny, sharp scalpel glinted under the bright surgery light to make its first cut when Sophie instinctively kicked the door open and burst inside the room with the force of a hurricane, shouting, "Don't move a muscle or I will shoot you where you stand."

She pointed her gun at the man with the scalpel and ordered, "Drop your scalpel and move away from the table."

Dr. Shivaram looked at Ali and then back at Sophie, not sure what to do. "Drop it now," she growled, "you have three seconds to do it or I will drop you."

Dr. Shivaram took a couple of steps back as if in a trance and, after dropping the scalpel on the tiled floor, stood riveted with terror-filled eyes.

"Good," said Sophie. And now, training her gun at Ali, she shouted, "Everyone lie face-down on the floor, now!"

Dr. Shivaram dropped to his knees and lay prone on the floor. He half turned his face to look at Sophie and in a trembling voice said, "She is not dead, honest. She is just under the effects of anesthetic. She will be okay." He then gestured with his hand to his staff and they too dropped to the floor to lie on the tile.

Ali, standing next to a glass cabinet, was defiant. His eyes burning with odium, in an angry voice, he said, "You don't give up, do you? I should have killed you when I had the chance. You don't know who you are messing with, you shouldn't have come here."

Sophie saw a reflection in the glass cabinet next to Ali, as behind her, from a dark corner, Javed lunged at her with a knife in his left hand. Sophie swiftly turned around and with her right hand, in which she was holding her gun, blocked her attacker, in the process knocking her gun from her hand, but with her right knee coming up in a powerful upward thrust, she crushed Javed's groin. As his head automatically lowered to look down, the heel of Sophie's left hand rising upward at a tremendous speed caught Javed's chin, snapping his head backward, breaking two of his front teeth. Dropping his knife, he fell to the floor doubled-up in pain. Blood started to dribble out of his mouth and he let out a sharp cry.

Sophie quickly turned around to locate her gun and saw Ali now standing only a couple of yards away holding her gun. "Like I said," Ali, looking almost insolently at her, as if taking pleasure in his impudence, informed her, "you have no idea who you are messing with. You're not going to hurt my business anymore. I don't care if you are an FBI or a CIA agent. You are finished now. I am going to put an end to your antics once and for all."

He cocked the gun and aimed at Sophie's head.

Sixty-One

Sophie's mind was churning with ideas as she quickly formulated a plan to recover from this situation. "Holding a gun to my head is not going to solve your problems," said Sophie, her hard stare holding Ali's eyes. Then she stepped back a pace and added, "Do you really think I would come here without an insurance policy? I wanted to see you go down, for I am convinced that you are behind all the monstrosities that go on at the GMC. I made a call before I came here and have already arranged for the most powerful person in this case to visit the GMC to discover first-hand what goes on there. Your secrets are already out. Killing me is not going to solve your problems."

"Huh," retorted Ali. "I know your every move. I know all about you trying to arrange a search warrant, but there is no chance of that and you know it. I have watched your every move. The Commissioner, senior police officers, even the leader of the Congress Party, no one can touch me. I also know the most powerful person you are talking about. Amy's mother already tried but failed to get past me. You think that the gate guard is the only security I have at the GMC? Inside I have armed guards who will not let anyone pass no matter who they are. No one can gain access to the GMC without me knowing and without my approval." He was shaking with increasing anger.

Sophie smiled as if unperturbed by the gun pointed at her. Facing danger with composure was second nature to her. She let out a little chuckle and said, "You are so naïve.

Even you cannot stop the person who is about to visit the GMC. No guns are going to stop this person. Allow me to show you." She put her hands up, showing she had no hidden weapon, and then with the fingertips of her right hand took out her iPhone. She then turned it on to view recorded videos. She selected one, punched play, and then turned the screen to show the video to Ali.

Ali's eyebrows arched as in bewilderment he saw a video of his wife having tea with Sophie and his two kids playing in the background at his home. Sophie turned the video off and said, "Oh, yeah, I know all about your wife and children and she is on her way now to the GMC to investigate what you do there. I think you have some explaining to do when you get home tonight," and then with a tone of overt mystery, she added, "or perhaps not."

"You," his voice choked on his mounting anger, "you're dead now. What the hell do you mean by 'perhaps not'?"

Sophie laughed to further infuriate him. She wanted to break him down to the point where he could not function coherently and relied solely upon her advice for further direction. A confused mind was easier to disarm than a thinking mind. She glared at him with her piercing eyes and said, "You don't think your wife will still feel secure when she finds out what kind of monster you really are, do you? Her first priority is the safety of her children, she told me that. And that is why I promised her a safe house after her visit to the GMC. No one but me knows where and how to find her and your children. You need me alive if you ever want to see your family again."

Ali hesitated and that was the moment Sophie was waiting for. Her plan was working and it was time for closure. She lowered her voice to add gravity to what she was about to disclose and said, "And what about the girl that was found in the street shot point blank in her head?"

Ali turned his head sideways as if not wanting to show his disbelief. He responded with contempt, but the edge in his voice was diminishing, "I don't know what you are talking about."

"Don't you?" said Sophie, raising her voice, "the girl was from the GMC. How did she end up shot dead and lying in the street? I know you have friends in the police department and they will delete her file from the police records. But I have a photo of her police file record with her picture on it. How would the police, and you, explain that?"

"No one will give any attention to your complaints to the authorities," said Ali in an unconvinced voice.

Sophie laughed and responded, "But I'm not going to the authorities with this. My job is to do investigation and not hold trial. You are going to be put on trial by a court that will listen to not only what I have to say but also to what the world has to say. By tomorrow my picture proving that the murdered girl came from the GMC will be on every Facebook and Twitter account and you and the authorities will have to answer to them. There isn't a place in the world where you will be able to hide by the time the sun comes up tomorrow. No family, no friends, you're finished. Your only hope of any redemption is to hand yourself over to me and I will see to it that you get a fair trial and your family with new identities is moved to a safe place."

He kept on glaring at her with fiery, incensed eyes, on his face a mingled expression of anger and hate. He made no answer, but Sophie saw a twitch in the corner of his mouth, a twitch of uncertainty, appear on his colorless lips that a moment later twitched convulsively. "Safe place?" he said slowly, gasping, as if the words had been torn out of him by a supernatural power.

For an instant his will broke. Almost as if his soul were seared with the recognition of his defeat. The hand holding the gun started to go limp. "That is right," said Sophie slowly, "give me the gun and everything will be all right." He was in a trance, his consciousness seeming suspended.

Just when she thought she had overpowered Ali and reached out to grab his gun, the sudden sound of heavy footsteps made everyone look towards the door and Sophie saw Inspector Ram Prasad and the Special Commissioner of Police of the Criminal Division, Mr. Anil Mathur rushing in like a blast of wind with their handguns drawn.

Ali looked startled as if someone woke him up from a dream. He grimaced and firmed up his grip on the gun again. But instead of pointing his gun at Sophie, he turned to face the police. Looking suicidal and holding his gun straight at the two police officers, he rushed over to them and stared at the Special Commissioner, saying, "What the hell took you so long?" There seemed to be an instant recovery in Ali's confidence fueled by the presence of his police friends. He shook his head as if to cast out all the threats and warnings Sophie had been throwing at him and in a voice laced with anger and hate, he said, "Now take this stupid bitch away and get rid of her or I am going to shoot her myself right here, right now. I've had enough of her. And call one of your police cars to intercept my wife's car that is on its way to the GMC. Don't let her get anywhere near the GMC. Now move!"

While the Commissioner made a call, Ram walked up to Sophie and said, "You shouldn't have interfered in our operation. Now we will have to take you in custody and I'm afraid tomorrow morning they are going to find your body hanging from the ceiling in your cell."

Sophie stared at Ram and he laughed, saying, "Yes, the Special Commissioner runs the show and he planted me with you to keep an eye on you and report all your moves. You think you are so smart but this is India. You know nothing about us and here we control everything. Turn around and place your hands behind your back."

The devilish smile on Ram's face announced his victory.

Sixty-Two

There was a curious exultation in Sophie's spirits, mingled with danger and a touch of fear. But then she always needed an element of both danger and fear to push her to the edge of the danger zone that she craved. This was what she was trained for and this was how she lived. Sophie decided to take all three men on. They might have guns but they didn't have her agility and martial arts skills. Most of all they didn't have her spirit to invite and embrace danger. She knew that to do such a thing would be to transcend magic. And she beheld, unclouded by doubt, a magnificent vision of the invincibility that one feels when one does not fear death.

She knew that there was no chance of reasoning with three men holding guns. When reason fails, the devil helps, is what she believed, and a strange grin flickered on her lips. The chance that the three men were standing close to each other raised her spirits even further.

With a sharp gleam of resolve and determination in her eyes, as she half turned to coil up her body for strength. She again saw Amy lying on the operating table. Suddenly she realized that while she was willing to take those odds, there was a chance that a stray bullet may hit the unconscious girl. The Sheikh had moved to the dark corner Javed had emerged from and in that corner was another table on which lay his daughter. Sophie now fully understood what was happening in the surgery but there was not much she could do. She turned around and let Ram handcuff her. She needed more time.

"You are making the biggest mistake of your life," said Sophie, looking unperturbed. "I had you figured out from day one and let you walk into my trap. If you think you had me fooled then you are a bigger fool than I thought you were."

"You're lying," responded Ram, still smiling. "There is no way you could have me figured out."

"Oh, you have so much to learn," said Sophie calmly. "When I shook your hand, your hand suddenly went very cold. It is a natural response from someone who is afraid and lying because instinctively blood rushes to the legs, as if preparing them to run. I knew I could not trust you but could certainly use you to my advantage."

"Whatever," said Ram, hiding his embarrassment behind a faint smile that did not escape Sophie's attention. "I'll now show you what happens to those who cross our paths. No one is ever going to find even a trace of you."

"You don't think I came here alone, do you?" Sophie's voice was remarkably composed and that was making Ram very nervous. Sophie capitalized on her success. "If you were smart then you would surrender while you still have a chance."

The Special Commissioner, who saw Ram relenting, laughed and said to Sophie, "Well, well. I must say, you have gumption. But I am afraid the cavalry is not coming. No authority, domestic or foreign, can a make a move in this city without my knowledge or my approval. I am the law here and I am going to crush you after I have had a little fun with you."

"You might think you are in control of this city but let me assure you that you are not," said Sophie defiantly. "If something were to happen to me then don't you think that the entire FBI force would come looking for me? You are finished. The only options you have are to either surrender or flee. Hurting me is going to make your case worse."

Ali interjected and, looking at the Commissioner, said, "Would you stop chitchatting and take her away? And make absolutely sure that she disappears. No one should ever find her body and this never happened, okay? Do you understand, no body, no evidence?"

Ali turned to the Sheikh and said, "Everything is under control now. There is nothing to worry about, we will go ahead with the surgery."

The Sheikh shook his head from side to side. "Are you crazy? I want nothing to do with the FBI. Not now, not today, not ever. I have seen enough for one day. I am taking my daughter back and we are done here. You want to go ahead with your other offer then be my guest, but I am not doing any business with you. And as the lady said, you should run. Don't mess with the FBI."

"Don't be so hasty," Ali entreated, desperate to take control of the situation. "You'll never have this chance again. These kinds of hiccups are common in India but we know how to control them. Don't you see that the highest authority of the law is right here with us? What else do you want? Any hasty move on your part could cause you to lose this great opportunity, as well as your deposit with us."

"You can keep the damn deposit!" the Sheikh growled. "You think I care about the money? And I can tell you this much; you can say goodbye to any business with my cousin.

Wait till Sheikh Salem hears of this. You will not do any business in the Middle East ever."

Ali threw an angry glance towards Sophie and then glared at the Sheikh. Ali then turned to Ram and asked him to lead the way out, ordering again, "Finish her off, take her somewhere and make her disappear. Her body must never be found, make sure of that." His scarlet face filled with rage showed all his latent hatred that over time he had suppressed, deep within the dark recesses of his heart.

Breathing heavily, Ali then instructed the surgeon to keep Amy there for a few hours while Javed recovered. He wanted nothing to do with her anymore and whispered to Javed to hang back and finish her off that night. "Cut her throat and throw her body in the *Yamuna* river," he reminded Javed, who nodded affirmatively. The Sheikh picked up his daughter in his arms, ready to leave.

Ram pushed Sophie from behind and they all left the room and stepped out of the house. Ram looked at the Commissioner as if asking him to explain why Sophie was still so serene despite her impending fate. He continued to glance nervously around to ensure that she had not brought anyone else with her.

Suddenly from both directions of the road about a dozen police jeeps came rushing in and screeched to a halt right in front of them, and several policemen jumped out with their rifles drawn and aimed at the Special Commissioner, Ram and Ali. Sophie saw a green Range Rover, the one she spotted earlier shadowing her, parked a short distance away and stepping out of it were Jai and the Special Commissioner of Police-Law and Order, Mr. Yuvraj Jain.

"What took you so long?" said Sophie to Jai. "I was counting on you to show up a little earlier. Get me out of these cuffs, would you please?"

As they un-cuffed Sophie, Ali, Special Commissioner of Crime Division and the Sheikh were cuffed and taken into custody. Sophie asked for an ambulance for the girls. A few minutes later an ambulance came and took charge of Amy and the other girl. Javed was also taken away, cuffed to a stretcher.

Sixty-Three

Driving back, sitting in the back seat of the Range Rover, Sophie made a call to Andrew to give him a brief report, and following that, she made another short call to the US embassy. Switching her phone off, she let out a sigh of relief and asked Jai, "So, your secret friend is Mr. Jain? I knew you were keeping an eye on me and had a hunch that you would follow me but I never knew that you would bring the cavalry. I am glad that you did. Thank you for your help too, Commissioner."

Instead of Jai, the Special Commissioner responded, "I've always suspected Mr. Anil Mathur. I hated his permanent and pasty smile, for I knew hidden behind it was a savage man. I have been following his activities and discovered that Ram was his man. When I saw you with Ram I realized they were going to trap you. So I started to chase Ram. The other day I watched you two outside the station waiting in a car and when he left you in the car I followed him to the cinema and found him talking to Ali. Then I put surveillance on Ali and started to follow his moves. When Jai came and told me what your plan was, I decided you could use a helping hand. And here we are. It's thanks to you and your courage that we wrapped all this up so quickly."

"Oh, courage comes easy," said Sophie, brushing her hair away from her face, "if one is willing to give one's life and not just live on convictions. But explain something to me. If you were against Ram and Anil Mathur from the beginning, then why didn't you just come out and help me in my investigation?"

"You don't know Delhi cops," said the Special Commissioner in a bitter tone. "To them, money is religion. They would kill for it in a heartbeat. I tried to warn you in my own way to get you out of India and leave the investigation to me. I didn't think this place is fit for a woman, FBI or no FBI. But you proved me wrong. You have a big heart and more courage than I have seen in any of my officers. I believe my government is going to give you a medal for what you have done. You cracked the biggest prostitution ring in Delhi, perhaps in the nation, and nabbed the top man involved. It is now going to come down like a stack of dominos, I will see to that. You, dear lady, certainly deserve a medal."

"Oh, there is no time for medals for me," said Sophie, chuckling. "That was my boss in Washington on the phone and he wants me back. Another assignment somewhere in South America." Leaning back in her seat, she asked Jai if they could swing by Jenifer's house.

Jenifer was crying when she heard the news concerning Amy. Ashok was crying too, even though he continued asking Jenifer not to cry. Together they left for the hospital where Amy was recovering.

Once there, Jenifer wanted Amy to wake up and say something. Amy lay silent and motionless. A few moments later she stirred, coming out of the anesthetic.

"Mummy," she cried faintly. "Mummy, you came back. They told me you were dead. I've missed you. I don't like that horrid place. Don't leave me again, Mummy."

"No, never, my baby. Don't cry. We are together now and you will never have to go anywhere alone again. We will go home soon. We'll go to the States. Oh, my baby," Jenifer sobbed.

Ashok came around to the other side of the bed and kissed Amy. Amy hugged her dad.

"Amy," he said softly. "We will never leave you. Daddy will always be there for you, my darling." Ashok was overcome by emotion as his voice broke. Ashok hugged her tight and Amy looked safe in his arms.

The doctor came to check on Amy and told Jenifer that they could take her home as long as Amy rested. Ashok tried to pick Amy up but Jenifer stepped in front of him, picked Amy up in her arms and they all left to go home. Amy curled her arms around Jenifer's neck and buried her face in her hair. Sophie asked Jenifer if she could see them all safely home. Jenifer nodded and Jai offered to drive everyone in his car.

At home and after Jenifer put Amy to bed on the sofa in the drawing room, they all sat down while Jenifer made tea.

"So what are your plans?" Sophie asked Jenifer.

Ashok responded before Jenifer could, "I'll get a security guard to watch our house and Amy will not go anywhere unaccompanied—"

"To get the hell out of here as soon as possible," Jenifer interrupted Ashok briskly. As Ashok looked offended, Jenifer continued, "I have had enough of this place and am looking forward to getting back to the States."

"It's none of my business, but you two need to resolve your differences and consider Amy's priorities. She has gone through quite an ordeal," said Sophie.

"We're leaving, Amy and I, and that is final," declared Jenifer in a steadfast tone that made her resolve apparent to

Ashok. She continued, "If you want to be with your family then you can come with us or you can stay with your parents. You'll have to make a choice."

"You're being unfair," said Ashok abruptly. "We no longer know anyone there. Your father is not interested in us. Give me some time to make arrangements and we will all go to the States. My life is with you and Amy; I just need to make some contacts."

Jenifer looked straight into his eyes and in a firm voice said, "A misunderstanding has created a huge chasm between us, but the journey over it is largely yours to make. You decide on what are the priorities of your life and then let me know what you want to do. For me, I know exactly what I am going to do."

There was a sudden and brittle silence in the room. "You understand me?" she asked, looking at him with unyielding eyes. The room seemed to shimmer and vibrate with unspoken tension. It was as if both Jenifer and Ashok knew that a moment of reckoning was at hand, that this was the moment they had to come together or forever be banished into their own separate, silent worlds.

Ashok's jaw moved a few times. His mouth opened and shut. H emitted a loud, rasping breath that made his body shudder. His hand fluttered a few times against his chest. And then, he was gone. Without a glance back, he left the house.

It was over. Her marriage was over. Just like this, in the blink of an eye, he was gone. Ashok—victim and victimizer—was gone forever from her life.

Good, she said to herself, as she shook her head mutinously: She was not going to go on like this anymore anyway. She was no longer going to be unhappy, and persecuted, and live in fear, and from now on she'd live her life in her own way. Let the door close behind her forever; she couldn't do anything to prevent it, she mused. Her eyes welled up in hot tears of anger, as she thought, what a waste, what a waste of a life.

Sixty-Four

Jenifer was about to say something to Sophie when a commotion outside the house interrupted her. She went to the window and saw a couple of cars with tinted windows and a black Lincoln Continental flying American flags pull up in front. She looked with questioning eyes at Sophie. "That would be the US ambassador from the US embassy," said Sophie, going to the front door to open it. The ambassador walked in and looked at Jenifer, then at Amy sleeping on the sofa and then back at Jenifer. He did not speak; instead, he stood there motionless.

"It is very kind of you to visit us. It isn't a convenient time, but would you please stay for some tea anyway?" Jenifer asked, feeling slightly overwhelmed with the fast-unfolding events culminating with the Ambassador's presence.

He said nothing at all as if he did not hear her. His mouth was closed, his watchful eyes seemed moist, and there was a shadow of taciturnity around him, impermeable but warm. Rather distant and placid.

"Oh, he will stay longer than that," said Sophie, gesturing at Jai for them to leave and then, turning to the ambassador, she added, "It's time. It's going to be all right."

The ambassador asked, in a whisper, of Sophie, "I'd be grateful if you would make the introductions."

"I will," said Sophie, and staring squarely at Jenifer, she said, "Jenifer, I told you that everything was going to turn out just fine. Today is the first day of your new life.

Meet your real father. He is your biological father and has been looking after your and Amy's interests since Amy's disappearance. Actually, he has been watching out for you since you were a baby."

"How are you?" he said, looking at Jenifer with a certain worry in his face, and a hint of apprehension in his eyes. Fragments of his heart reflected in tears welled up in his eyes and he blinked them away as if he did not want her to see his broken heart.

"What?" cried Jenifer, losing her balance and holding on to the back of the sofa to steady her. "You're my father?"

"I know it is hell of a surprise, but he is your father," said Sophie. "I am going to leave you two to get acquainted. Hope to see you sometime in the States. We've got to go."

Jenifer rose to her feet, looked around in wonder as though surprised at finding herself in this place, and went towards the ambassador. She was pale, her eyes glowed, she was exhausted and every limb ached, but she seemed suddenly to breathe more easily. She had cast off that fearful burden that for so long had been weighing on her, and all at once there was a sense of relief and peace in her soul. "Oh my god," she muttered, "how long have I dreamt of this? You really are my father?"

Jenifer went to the man standing with outstretched arms. The long embrace in which they held each other melted all doubts in her mind, and she took from it the certitude that what she had from this embrace was real. It was stronger than an uttered vow, and the name she was to give it in afterthought was that she had been truly blessed. This is what she had hoped for. She knew she could now start a new life. Her dreams would be realized. This settled her so much, and so thoroughly, that there was nothing left for her to ask Him, to swear to or prove to her. Oaths and vows apart, now she felt that she could have a family of her own. Amy would have her grandfather.

They wanted to speak, but could not; tears filled their eyes. They were both choked with swirling emotions, but those wet faces were bright with the hope of a future, of a full resurrection into a new life. They were renewed by their mutual warmth and affection; the heart of each held love for the other.

Driving back to Sophie's hotel, Jai said "That was quite a show. You're full of surprises. What are your plans now?"

"First flight out, back to the States," Sophie confirmed.

"Really?" said Jai, in a tone tainted with disappointment. "Can you spare a day or so? I would like you to come back to Jaipur. Last time you were in such a hurry that I could not show you all the wonderful sites. Allow me to be your host. Just for a couple of days?"

"I'm flattered but afraid not," said Sophie, laughing at Jai's pout, "maybe sometime in the future. For now, duty calls. There is a flight tomorrow at 5 p.m. and I am going to try to get on it. I am too tired to even have dinner with you tonight. But I will make a deal with you. If you are ever in Washington, I will treat you to a fabulous dinner at my favorite restaurant."

"Dinner in Washington," said Jai contemplatively. "I'll hold you to that deal."

Epilogue

The morning was cold and the air was filled with visible pollution. The horizon was murky with a thick blue-brown layer of clouds suffocating the birth of the morning sun. The pale-yellow orb struggled to rise through the acid clouds of the severely polluted New Delhi, capitol of India, and its inhabitants' lifespan went down yet another notch as the hundreds of diesel busses and thousands of two-stroke auto-rickshaws continued to pour more poison into mother earth's environment.

Sophie was at the Indira Gandhi International Airport saying her goodbyes. She shook hands with the ambassador and received a hug from Jenifer and Amy, who came to see her off. She looked around one last time but did not see Jai Singh anywhere. Oh, well, a typical spoiled maharaja, she thought and shrugged her shoulders as if to say why should she care. She turned around and walked through security to the departure lounge. Sophie was late getting through the formalities and by the time she reached the gate everyone had already boarded the plane. She was shown to her preferred and pre-assigned seat 2A in the business class. An airhostess smiled and winked at her and offered her a glass of champagne and the evening newspaper. Amy had made the front page with the sensational story of her rescue. The doors closed and the plane started to taxi towards its runway. The lavatory door opened and a handsome man stepped out. He came over to the aisle seat next to Sophie and leaned over to say, "Excuse me, Miss, would you mind if I sat next to you?"

With her head rested on her chin and staring at nothing in particular outside the window, Sophie was miles away. It seemed that his voice crashed through her reverie and brought her back to reality. She looked at him confused, and almost did a double take. "Jai? What the hell are you doing here?"

"Now is that any way to greet a friend?" said Jai, with a mock frown. "How about good evening or good to see you? Oh, well, I guess I will have to settle for 'what the hell.'"

The flight attendant doing her last checks moved up to them, collected Sophie's champagne glass and asked Jai to buckle his seatbelt. They were reaching their allocated runway for takeoff. Sophie smiled and nodded at the flight attendant as she winked at her again.

The aircraft's engines roared under increased throttle and its wheels rolled down the runway gathering speed. The plane lifted off and made a steep right turn to climb into the evening skies of New Delhi. It surged effortlessly through the polluted, blue, poisonous skies and emerged triumphantly into the sunlit world above.

"What are you doing here anyway? Are you stalking me?" she asked.

"I am just following up on your invitation to have dinner with you in Washington."

"Really?"

"Yes, really. I will stay in Washington till you call me, have that dinner and then leave. Nothing complicated, you see?"

The flight attendant came around with a drink trolley and asked if they wanted a pre-dinner refreshment. Sophie said, "A double scotch, please. I could do with a stiff drink." Jai asked for the same. Preparing their drinks, the flight attendant said, "I hope you enjoy your quiet drink, a very quiet drink."

"What on earth...?" said Sophie, as she looked around the cabin, and to her surprise found that they were the only two passengers in the large business-class cabin. She turned to Jai and said, "Isn't this odd? We're the only passengers in business class. You could have been assigned any seat and they booked you right next to me. What an amazing coincidence. And why is the entire cabin empty? Very unusual." She took the drink from the flight attendant and asked, "Isn't it curious? Why are you running so empty tonight?"

The flight attendant smiled broadly and said, "Ask your friend."

Sophie stared at Jai and she saw a mischievous smile growing into an ear-to-ear grin. It all registered and she said, "This is no coincidence, is it? Tell the truth."

"If this was the only way I could get a few hours alone with you," he said innocently. "I've a few friends in the airline business, but it wasn't easy compensating all the other passengers for taking the next available flight."

"You didn't?" said Sophie, shaking her head. "Oh, you're a spoiled one, aren't you, Your Highness?"

"I hope you don't mind," said Jai, raising his glass to her.

Sophie's most mischievous smile crept down from her eyes to her lips. "Mind?" cried Sophie. "I love it!"

"Sophie," said Jai, in a sudden change of tone, now sounding serious. "I suppose there is one friend in the life of each of us who seems not a separate person but an extension of one's self, the very meaning of one's soul. Such a friend I found—"

"Don't even go there," interrupted Sophie. "There is a vast difference between companionship and commitment and I intend to keep it that way. If it is a commitment you're looking for then I am afraid you are—"

"Knocking at the wrong door," it was his turn to interrupt her as he finished her sentence. After a little sigh, he added, "No, I was simply paying you a compliment, Rajasthani style. In our tradition, we marry outside our state or religion only to buy peace and I have no fight with the FBI."

They both laughed and clinked their glasses.

"Now," said Sophie, in a pseudo-serious manner, "no more surprises. Don't buy me the Empire State building or something like that. You promise?"

"Promise," said Jai. Then, leaning close to her, he whispered, "By the way, you don't know who owns the Empire State building, do you?"

The sun had lost its brilliance as it started to sink below the horizon. New Delhi was left far behind and the plane was cruising high above the Indian Ocean.

The End.

About the Author

Narendra, published author of several books, writes mysteries, memoires and misadventure stories and has lived in England, Canada, Saudi Arabia, United Arab Emirates, India and the USA. Having traveled to more than seventy different countries has allowed him to gain an insight into diverse cultures. He finds inspiration from his travels and life experiences and through his novels invites you to join him on a journey of life, adventure, mystery and intrigue. He lives in Canada and the USA.

www.narendrasimone.com
www.facebook.com/AuthorNarendraSimone

Praise for Narendra's Books:

Desert Song – "Reading *Desert Song* is what I imagine a few evenings to be like of listening to a master story teller take us through the descent of Beowulf. Medieval in its proportions, gruesome in its verity, raw in its necessity, *Desert Song* exposes the sinister triangulations of politics, religion, and law in a world wrought with dark forces. Our hero, Matt Slater, witnesses unimaginable crimes in his desperate search for a lost child. Startling ironies erupt on each page as Simone's first thriller hurtles us through a journey both disturbing and authentic. Before you read any other book on the Taliban, read this book first."—Almeda Glenn Miller, author of *"Tiger Dreams"*

Desert Song – A Brilliant Story Masterfully Crafted – "Right from the beginning I enjoyed Narendra's style ... the picture was drawn and I stepped right into the set ... he cleverly interweaves his characters and gives his reader intrigue and interest in learning the dangerous world of Arabia ... Once I started reading it I could not wait to finish it." – Praveen Gupta, Published Author of 14 Books

The Last Goodbye – "In his riveting story, The Last Goodbye, Narendra Simone skillfully portrays the soul of a mother/son relationship in a culture that remains an enigma to so many of us." – Mike Sirota, author of *"Fire Dance"* and *"The Burning Ground"*.

Tuscan Dream – HIGHLY RECOMMENDED – "Narendra is a widely travelled author with an eloquent writing style. Artistic descriptions of the beautiful city of Florence, creates an enriched backdrop for the characters and plot of this novel of romance and intrigue. I began reading this story and could not put it down as it transported me to a culture of great beauty, architecture and art, through the eyes of captivating characters." – Elaine Fuhr, Allbooks Reviews

Other Books by Narendra

1. Desert Song
2. Tuscan Dream
3. 1001 Arabian Nightmares
4. Kismet, Karma & Kamasutra
5. Cry of the Soul
6. Pink Balcony Silver Moon
7. The Unholy Ghost

Other Books to be published soon:

8. The Last Goodbye
9. The First Dawn
10. Long Way Home
11. Unbroken Line

Made in the USA
Charleston, SC
29 December 2014